To Addison,

# THE THERIAN INITIATIVE

**FILES LOADING. . .**

Welcome to the Flayne Institute!

Katherine White

# Man of Light and Shadows

Katherine LE White

Man of Light and Shadows

katherinelewhite@katherinelewhite.com

First paperback edition July 2021

Book design by Carrie Humphrey
Book Cover by Alejandro Castillo

ISBN 978-1-956274-00-4
www.katherinelewhite.com

For Lydia, my brain twin.
Without you, this book would never have happened

# Chapter 1

Her husband would kill her when she got home, but Céline didn't care at the moment. The smile on her face made her cheeks hurt. She had passed a little boutique in The Somerset Collection on West Big Beaver Road and seen the gown she was now wearing in the window. She shouldn't have even been in the high end shopping district to begin with, those days were long over. She had stopped and stared at it, like a kid in a candy store. Put it on, she told herself, glancing at her watch. You have three hours until you have to be there.

The clerk in the store eyed her warily when she asked to try on the gown, but when she had, it was perfect. She looked at herself in the mirror for a long time, so that the store clerk kept circling around to her and patronizingly asking, "Can I help you?"

It would be so easy to buy it. All she had to do was take out the piece of plastic and swipe.

You look so beautiful, she said to her reflection.

So she bought it, having to use her credit card. It would take her three months of her part time salary as a gymnastics and yoga instructor to pay it off, but she would. That is what she'd tell Stephane when she got home to him, she'd pay it all with her own money. Of course, that argument might not work since it was 'their' money and not 'her' money. Funny thing how that happens when one gets married. Maybe telling him how fabulous the night had been would allay some of his wrath. If his wrath was particularly rough, she could always use her feminine wiles.

She laughed out loud, "My feminine wiles," she muttered.

But she wouldn't have to use her feminine anything. The tips she received from the concert paid for the dress plus some.

She was small, light, and lean, with her pale skin looking porcelain against the navy velvet of her gown. Her auburn hair looked especially dark drawn up in a bun, tendrils curling down to show off a long, elegant neck. Her expressive, dark green eyes did not tend to show off a sexiness that would be characterized as wily, but rather a wide-eyed wonder that made her an excellent songwriter and singer. And that got her booked at The Scarab Club.

The night had gone splendidly, even if she did say so herself. To be able to do a concert at The Scarab Club in Chicago was like a dream come true. The high class club had only the top names in the business industry attend as patrons. One had to have a membership to get in, and even a second membership to get into the back room. At one time, she might have gone as someone's date, but she was happy to get in as the entertainment.

They had called her, asked her, to come and perform! It was the first time she'd not booked herself somewhere, the first time that she'd been sought out. The buzz of the evening, the thrill of the tip bills that were stuffed in her little purse attached to her wrist, and maybe even the champagne, still tingled at the ends of her limbs, at the tips of her ears.

One of the patrons had approached her before she got up on stage. An older gentleman, in a business suit, obviously having come straight from work to the concert, had leaned in close to her ear. She could smell mint on his breath and the splash of musky cologne he used. "You look nervous," he had chuckled. He'd reached over as a waiter passed them, a tray of champagne fluted balanced on his splayed hand, and nabbed one of the glasses. "Here," the patron held it out to her. "For your nerves."

She'd taken it gingerly, all the warnings of taking drinks from strangers she'd been drilled with in college screaming in her brain. But downed it once it was in her hands. This old man wouldn't have made some elaborate plan to drug her with champagne. This wasn't the movies. And it had calmed her down.

As the sparkles in her navy blue velvet gown twinkled like stars in the light of the subway train, she considered she could use another drink to calm her down.

She bounced a little at the door of the car as it pulled into the station. She had two train transfers on her way back to Evanston from Chicago. Nervous energy coursed through her, and the excited tingling began to include her solar plexus as well as her limbs and ears.

Waiting on the other side of the door were two men, both very average looking, save the smart, dark suits they were wearing. If she were to describe them, she would have had a hard time finding a distinguishing characteristic to make either of them different from any other plain businessman. Both had brown hair, brown eyes, skin not dark and not light. Their faces were strangely blank, as if they were bored. It struck her as odd, but she shrugged it off. I'd have a pretty blank face, too, if I were coming home from work at this hour. She glanced at her watch, more of a bracelet with a timepiece on it, and it read 3:23 am. The poor guys are probably exhausted from a down-to-the-last-minute project.

Both of them looked up at her entrance, and one of them smiled as she sat down beside them. "You played at The Scarab Club tonight," he said, leaning forward. He was on his way to being heavyset, his brown hair, which tickled his ears, was flecked with gray. He nodded, his round chin leading his head up and down. "You were very good."

So that's what their project was. Céline smiled widely at the compliment, her cheeks reminding her that she would have to stop doing that soon or her face would hurt when it was at neutral. "Thank you," she replied. "I had a really good time."

"We did, too," the business man said, nudging his associate. "Didn't we, Mr. Anchord?"

Mr. Anchord, whose hair was lush and showed no sign of gray, also showed no signs of having had a good time that evening at The Scarab Club. His square jaw held a decidedly bored expression. At being nudged by his companion, he nodded curtly, and hummed, "Umm-hmmm."

His words, and his stare with his dark brown eyes left her feeling unsettled.

"You do an excellent job of incorporating mythology into your lyrics," the first businessman said. "I liked how you relate modern day stories with the myths."

Céline blinked in surprise. The man had been listening to what she had been singing. Apparently Mr. Anchord was also surprised. His face changed slightly, he turned to look at his companion with an unbelievable confusion that would have made Céline afraid if she had chosen to concentrate on it. "Thank you!" she repeated. "Listeners don't usually catch that."

"The music itself was rather different, too," he said.

"Otherworldly," Mr. Anchord chimed in, his voice sounding forced.

Despite the coldness coming off of Mr. Anchord, Céline would gladly ride in her wheelhouse. There were few she could rattle on about music, especially in the tiny subset she played that was her favorite. "Oh, that's from the ancient cultures of the Mediterranean and Middle East," she explained. "Ancient Greece and Egypt, and what we know of Babylonia and Mesopotamian cultures, their music was in a different scale that ours is today." She turned to Mr. Anchord, "That's the reason it sounds otherworldly. Our ears aren't accustomed to hearing it. Like listening to another language that uses sounds that aren't present in English."

"Well, that would certainly make sense," said the first businessman.

The train began to slow down as it entered another station and Céline stood up.

So did the two business men.

"Well," she said, that uncomfortable feeling coming over her again, "this is my stop."

"What a coincidence," said Mr. Anchord. "It's ours too."

~Don't get off the train~, the unbidden thought popped into her head. The excited tingling in her body began to change to a charged fear in her chest. ~Don't get off the train~, the voice-that-was-and-was-not her voice repeated. It came from the same place that told her not to go out with Greg Foreman in high school. He was convicted of date rape only six months later. It came from the place that told her that if she had the guts to put her hand in the knothole of that old tree, she'd be grateful. The antique locket she'd found there, and then returned to the police, garnered her a $4000 reward, which paid for her and Stephane's honeymoon to visit his family in Haiti. It came from the same place that the music came from, whispering in her ears secrets that only she could hear, write down in cadence, if she only chose to listen. ~Don't get off the train,~ the unbidden thought was loud, so loud, she moved away from the door and sat down once again.

"Actually," she shook her head. "I think I was mistaken."

The two men glanced at each other, then at the door. The train began to come to a halt. Her gut twisted, and she was quite sure it was not the champagne. She stood up, her legs feeling weak, and walked toward the end of the car, opened the door, and entered the next one without saying a word. A glance behind her saw that the two men had not exited the train when the doors opened at the station, but were walking toward the adjacent car. She sped up her pace, her high heels making it hard to take a normal step forward. She was forced to pump her legs like a toddler in little footfalls. She went through the next car. A woman in a worn cardigan and pants looked up at her briefly, saw nothing that caught her interest, then looked back out the window. The men in suits were still behind her. She went in the next car, empty of passengers, only to find it was the last. The remaining door was an emergency exit. She stood against it, looking out the small window. The tracks, illuminated for a moment from the tail lights of the train, sped away at an unfathomable speed.

She twirled around, the skirt of her dress swirling lightly with the movement, to see the two men come in the door. It closed automatically behind them.

"Céline Ilorsaint," Mr. Anchord said, saying her name with the proper French accent. He advanced toward her. "You will come with us." His second phrase was in perfect American English.

"If you come without incident, Mrs. Ilorsaint" said the

heavier set businessman, "then you won't get hurt."

This must be some sort of joke, she thought. But the fear in her gut didn't subside. It wasn't a joke. "What?" it came out like a manic laugh.

The men did not answer. Mr Anchord continued toward her. The first businessman placed his hand on Mr. Anchord's arm. He looked at him with a raised eyebrow. The first one reached out to her. "Please, Mrs. Ilorsaint," he implored. "We don't want to hurt you."

She knew that the look on her face said, "You must be crazy."

Céline saw that Mr. Anchord's hand was moving in slow motion, but she could not make her own body do anything fast enough to avoid it. He grabbed her arm. She jerked her arm to get away, her body finally responding. He held her fast. Then he pulled her toward him like she was weighed no more than paper.

The fear in her gut went away. All of her own thoughts vanished. ~You have to get away from this man~, the unbidden thought told her.

The first businessman grabbed her other arm. She lifted her leg in a hard kick, using all the force of her strong gymnast thighs. Her shin collided with the man's crotch. He groaned and sank down to his knees, his lips pinched in a tight o, eyes squeezed shut, face red.

"Dammit, Perelli, you're useless," Mr. Anchord growled.

His brows furrowed and lips curled. The pressure he had on her arms increased. She tried to twist away. She didn't budge. Her only thought was to get out of his grip. She jumped off of the floor, using Anchord's shoulder to launch into a twisting vault. She was hurled into the air.

I am not going in the right direction. The wall of the car came closer to her face. She hadn't vaulted out of his grip, at all. He had thrown her. The wall hit her. Her head exploded in pain. Everything went black.

# Chapter 2

**CLASSIFIED TOP SECRET**
**PROJECT SANCTUARY**

To: ████████████████
Washington DC

From: Flayne Institute Experimental Facility
Chicago, Illinois

Subject: The Therian Initiative Update Report

████████ our chief geneticist, says he has obtained a blood type that has the right factors in it to stabilize his hybridization formula. Our research found eleven individuals within the United States of America with such blood factors, one of which residing within the Chicago, IL extended-urban area. It was decided that Agents ███ and ████ would obtain this subject, since it was in such close proximity to the facility. The goal was to obtain the subject alive and healthy.

The goal was accomplished, with specimen now in custody at the Flayne Institute Experimental Facility. is a human female, mid-thirties, Caucasian descent, with gene mutation MCR1. does not know if this is a factor in the stabilization usage of the subjects blood type/factors or not. The subject's family is lower class, consisting of a husband and two blood related children, neither of which have the MCR1 gene phenotype. The subject's family of origin, however, is a wealthy connected business family in the NW United States and Canada, and may need to be dealt with should they decide to interfere. This is unlikely as they have cut ties with the subject some years ago due to her choice of husband. However, I highly recommend that we keep an eye on the family of origin.

Subject is currently being kept under heavy sedation. After obtaining enough blood to extract the stabilizing factors for the hybridization formula, is asking permission to experiment on the subject on damage/healing tests. He suspects that if the MCR1 gene mutation, which has been linked anecdotally to a higher medication tolerance and higher pain tolerance, is involved in the stabilization factors, he may be able to use the subject's DNA to improve the formula.

Signed: Agent

# Chapter 3

"Are you comfortable?" asked Dr. Montgomery.

"Am I supposed to be?" asked Ilya, his Russian accent coming through strong.

"No, not really," Dr. Montgomery admitted. "It is meant to keep you restrained."

He breathed to keep his calm. "Is it that bad?" Ilya asked, looking at the nurse that was taking a vial of blood from him. His muscled arm flexed slightly against the restraints and he centered on his breathing again. The bright light that shone down on him did nothing to warm him. He had to look to the side or close his eyes so as not to be blinded by it. The sterile feeling of stainless steel and porcelain, along with the cold, seeped through his naked body and made keeping his anxiousness at bay harder than normal. Everything was perception. His fright was perception, caused by his own mind, not by what was happening outside in his circumstances. Tchaikovsky's Nutcracker Suite played gently in the background, perhaps an attempt to keep him calm, Ilya pondered. Or, perhaps it was to keep the doctors calm.

"I told you it was bad," Dr. Montgomery said. "But it

doesn't last long," he assured him. "Then, you will be perfect."

"Perfect," Ilya repeated. His uncertainty must have been obvious. He knew what Dr. Montgomery's version of perfect was. Despite his role in this experiment, he didn't agree with it.

After Ilya had arrived in the States, come to the facility, and had the third round of qualifying tests, a large group of candidates had been eliminated from the running. The candidates then became subjects. The number of subjects was much less than the number of candidates, but once the designation of subject was given, they were allowed a great deal more privileges than they were as candidates. That made the nasty taste of the word 'subject' go down a little better.

It was at this point that Dr. Montgomery had shown Ilya his laboratory. "I want to show you my other subjects," he had said.

"One of the other men?" Ilya had asked.

Dr. Montgomery shot him an imperious look. "Hardly," the scientist, a man about ten or fifteen years older than Ilya, unlocked the door and opened it. "Not one of them is worth a thousand of these. You, however," he looked at Ilya approvingly, "may be worthy of their appreciation."

Entering the room, Ilya saw rows of cages and terraria filled with rats. All kinds of rats, of every species that must exist. Worthy of a rat's appreciation? What in the world did that mean? How could a rat appreciate anything? "These?" he asked.

Dr. Montgomery beamed a smile at the warrior. "Yes," he said. "Do you know that rats are one of the most amazing mammals on Earth?"

IIya shook his head, his black hair shaking slightly as he did. "No, I did not."

"They are," Dr. Montgomery opened a terrarium and took out a brindle colored rat. "They can swim a mile across moving water. They can fall from a five story building and remain uninjured." He kissed the rat on the head. "A rat can go longer without water than a camel." He lifted it in the air, toward Ilya, as if to show it off. "They are one of the most adaptable mammals on the planet."

"That is quite impressive," Ilya admitted, not sure why the doctor was telling him all of this.

"Adaptability is what keeps a species in existence," Dr. Montgomery wagged a finger at the warrior, then replaced the rat back in its terrarium. "It is the cornerstone of the dominance of a species within an ecosystem."

Not sure how to take the comment, Ilya had just nodded.

"Rats are one of the most perfect species on the planet. It is only a quirk of fate that they are not in the position we are now, and we are not still one of our primate ancestors," Dr. Montgomery explained.

Ah yes, perfection, indeed, Ilya thought sarcastically.

The nurse took the needle out of his arm and smiled a small, cold smile. "All done with that," she assured him.

Dr. Montgomery leaned down over Ilya. His face, square with a light brown beard, had a covetous look. "Do you know how lucky you are?" he asked in a tone that Ilya had not heard before. "Do you know how many people have taken the physical and psychological tests and failed? Do you know how many people would love to be in your place?" The man's normally smooth voice was almost a hiss.

The vehemence with which he spoke did not allay Ilya's fears. He did know that many people had failed the tests. In fact, of all his group, only seven had passed them all. He had to take a series of them when he'd arrived in the States, The Flayne Institute claimed that doing so would place him in the best position within the company.

After the third set of blood tests, he had asked, "What

does my blood have to do with putting me in the best position for me within the company?"

"Everything," Dr. Montgomery had replied.

He hadn't realized at the time the man meant it literally.

The tests he endured were some of the most intensive he'd had, even more than some of the ones from Spetsnaz. They had gotten progressively harder and harder until they culminated at the table where he was now strapped.

From where Ilya was lying, he was beginning to doubt his own agreement to being in this place. When he had been approached by Flayne Institute for an "unparalleled opportunity", he had jumped at the chance to get out of Russia. He had assumed it was for a security position, his expertise and knowledge leant themselves to that kind of occupation. What else would a research company need with his "unique skill set"?

"We can get you out of the country," the American in the tea shop where he was hiding in Ulan-Ude, Russia had said to him quietly. "Easy, no issues whatsoever."

"How do I know I can trust you?" Ilya had asked, sipping his tea. As he said it, he was ticking off the ways he could kill the man without being detected.

"Because if you couldn't, you'd already be dead."

The truth of the statement had hit the Russian warrior in the chest like a punch.

At his silence, the American said, "You can start over." He leaned in closer, his breath smelling of the strawberry jam that had settled in the bottom of his tea cup. "A whole new life, Gospodin Leschyov. All of this will be left behind you." The man gave away his lack of Russian culture by addressing him as 'gospodin', Mister. If he was going to try to recruit him, he could at least learn the language a little.

He looked into his tea cup, almost empty. The American laid a file on the table and slid it across to Ilya. The

Russian opened it and picked up a little book. "This is a visa..."

"Everything you need is there. You just have to show up at Mukhino Airport, Gospodin Leschyov."

Ilya picked up the plane ticket that lay next on the pile of papers.

How could he have said no to such an offer? Start over in the States or be hunted down in Russia?

There was no choice.

Now, he lay on a surgery table, naked, restrained, and cold.

The nurse took another needle with a tube attached to an IV fluid bag, and placed it in his arm. "Patient is fully prepared, Dr. Montgomery."

"Start the IV, please," Dr. Montgomery said.

The nurse did as he asked.

He came to the IV bag and looked down at Ilya with giddy eyes. He held up a syringe and began to flick it to remove any air bubbles. "Prepare to become perfect, Ilya Pytrovich." He placed the needle of the syringe into the injection port of the IV tube, and slowly began to push on the plunger.

At first, Ilya felt nothing abnormal. Just the liquid dripping into his arm. Relief swept through him, perhaps it wouldn't be so bad after all, and the doctor was just covering all of his bases. Then, his arm began to burn slightly, as if the sun was shining on it for too long at the beach. I can handle this, he thought.

Then agony wracked through his entire body.

A thousand tiny stabs, the size of needles, pierced out from his body causing him to writhe. He felt his back stretch, like someone had grabbed him at the base of his spine and at the base of his skull, and pulled with the might of a machine. His vertebrae separated, twisted, changed, and came together again in some different way. The end of his spine at his tailbone burst with a fireball of pain, slashing outward, and outward, and outward, until Ilya did not think it could stretch anymore without tearing him in two. He had the impression that his legs were breaking, at every bone, they were bending, cracking in agony. His hands and feet pulled apart, came back together, and pulled apart, like silly putty. The thousand tiny needles stabbing out of him continued, from every pore in his entire body. His face felt punched in, and then pulled out, his nose and mouth were crushed under a pressure that forced its way out of him like a worm from the ground. His entire being broke and contorted in ways he had never imagined a body could.

Ilya thrashed against the straps holding him and screamed, like his body, his voice contorted. It became something animalistic and primal, and echoed back to him through the sterile room offering no comfort.

Then the agony stopped. The pain didn't. He still ached and throbbed, but the torment that had wracked though him was gone. He hurt in places that he shouldn't, places his body shouldn't have body parts to hurt. His back hurt all the way down to his legs, but his legs hurt in addition to it. His ears hurt past where his head stopped. His face hurt much farther forward than his face should go.

The transformation had been successful. The pain told him it was so, before Dr. Montgomery breathed, "Perfection!"

Ilya's vision was fuzzy, he blinked rapidly to try and clear it. Just as panic was beginning to travel the same paths as the pain, his vision cleared, and he saw Dr. Montgomery smiling down at him zealously. "Can you hear me, Ilya?"

"Yes," he answered. His jaw seemed to have the center of balance off somewhere. He ran his tongue along his teeth, and noticed that several were missing, and he had a large gap between his incisors and molars.

"Ha ha!" Dr. Montgomery cried. "Can you move?"

Ilya felt the straps being released from him, and tried to sit up. Agony shot through his back, and he stopped, turning his head to the side.

"The pain should subside in a few days," Dr. Montgomery said. "How the subject reacts to the hybridization, determines the amount of recovery time."

Ilya let out a hard breath to prevent himself from groaning. Dr. Montgomery had not mentioned that part of the process to him.

"Take him to recovery," Dr. Montgomery said. "Make sure he's as comfortable as possible." He looked back down at the Russian. "You are our prize, Ilya," he said. "You are perfect!"

When his bed was rolled into the recovery room, he noticed it was empty. He knew he had been the last of the subjects to be hybridized. A feeling of dread overcame him as the nurse left him alone in a room that should have been filled with six other moreaus.

# Chapter 4

When Céline came to, she was lying on a smooth, cold surface. She had a vague recollection of being strapped to a table and of electrodes being placed on her body.

"We're not making that one a moreau," someone said in a smooth, business-like voice.

A burning fire grew at her temples.

"What are we doing with her, then?" another voice asked, the sounds of both fading away as a blinding pain tore her through her torso.

She opened her eyes slowly. She was wearing a pale green dressing gown, like the kind that are given out in hospitals to patients who stay overnight or that she'd always been forced to wear when getting a gynecological exam. She could see through the floor, it was made from some sort of clear material, down to another floor made of gray metal sheets bolted together. She closed her eyes again, her temples burned and her shoulders and hips ached. She touched the sides of her head gently and felt the soft bubble of a blister. Pushing herself up into a sitting position, she decided to open her eyes and look straight ahead instead of down.

She blinked. This can't be happening, she thought. All around her, at different levels, were floating transparent cells. No, they weren't floating, they were clear platforms on poles suspending them in the air. Each level had a catwalk running alongside the cells, so that it looked as if each cell was on a shelf. Each had a designation on it, a combination of numbers and letters on a specimen label at the base of each platform, like in a museum. Her own cell had "H-A-2377" written on it in black marker.

Behind the designation, each cage contained a thing.

That was the only way her brain would describe it. Things. Things everywhere. In the cell across from her was a giant lizard, but the lizard had arms and legs like a human being. Another looked like a cross between a man and a bird. His neck was elongated, and his nose was a grotesque imitation of a beak. His legs were skinny, with claws at the feet. Another one held what looked like a werewolf, another a conglomeration of some kind with a human mouth and one human arm and hand. She looked down again and saw people, normal people, in lab coats. A few of them were large men in some type of police-like uniforms. This can't be happening, she thought. I have fallen asleep somewhere and am having an awful nightmare. I am still at the concert, and I have had too much to drink. Someone has put a drug in my drink and I am having some sort of bad trip...the excuses faded away as one of the normal, lab-coated human beings approached her cell on the catwalk that ran parallel to her row of cylinders.

She crammed herself to the far side of the glass canister. As the scientist passed her cell, she felt a rush of relief. Maybe this was a dream, and the scientist couldn't see her. He stopped in front of the lizard man's cell. The lizard might have been an iguana, or a gila monster, something wide and powerfully muscled. It let out a high pitched roar and sails came up on the back of its head, bright red and shaking. She started back with a scream. Any relief she felt, gone.

The man in the lab coat looked down at a tablet he was holding. "This is subject R-A-1125," he said. He reached out a finger and pressed a button on the lizard man's platform. It slowly began to descend toward the ground, a group of the uniformed men gathering around where it would land. They all had automatic weapons at the ready, pointed toward the cell. Two of the uniformed men had long rods that looked like vaulting poles. The sides of the canister disappeared, lowering into the platform itself like a garage door, and all that was left was a round, glass like disk on the floor. The lizard man let out another high pitched roar as one of the guard's poles buzzed with an electric current that arced across his body.

He let out another roar, his sails set out huge around his head, and grabbed the closest man. He threw him against the wall. The uniformed men converged on the lizard, but he flung one of his great human-like arms and sent several flying. He jumped down from his disk, grabbed a man, and slammed him into some sort of console in the middle of the room.

Suddenly the disk that held Céline began to fall. Her stomach traveled into her throat, and the breath was knocked out of her when she hit the floor. The walls around her crashed and shattered, pelting her with bits of tempered glass. She closed her eyes and curled into a ball on her platform.

She heard cries of all different kinds of animals, and words, English words, coming from voices that sounded as if they shouldn't speak. A 'spew' whizzed by her head, and she snapped her eyes open. Bullets flew, hitting the ground around her with soft 'thhh's. She crawled along the floor. She kept her head down as bullets buzzed by. Her legs slipped behind her as they slid on the material of her dressing gown. She finally got a foothold on the floor, not on the dressing gown and hoisted herself up, running in a crouch to the door following all of the other creatures. They were passing her in what seemed like herds. She kept her eyes on the exit, half running, half crawling, and then tumbled over something. The platforms and shattered walls of the cylinders were scattered about the room, and she assumed she had tripped over one of those.

Looking down, she saw a group of the things beneath her. She screamed, and edged away from them, landing on her rear-end. They were small, very small, and she was suddenly aware they were all crying plaintively. She looked into the eyes of one that was a mixture of a human and a gray tabby cat. It cried, its mouth opening to show kitten milk teeth. Then it hit her--they were children!

The lizard man seemed to be in a losing battle. Céline looked to the door, then looked at the things near her. The label on their platform read, "M-Y-23".

She scrambled toward them and swept up at the cat. It jumped nimbly on her back, and when it did so, she was assailed by the others. A bear followed the cat onto her back, which caused the cat to move to her shoulders. A goat, or a sheep, began to try to climb also, but she managed to stop it, and tuck it under one of her arms. A tiny snake wound its way around her forearm, climbing over a blister and bursting it open on Céline's arm in a stab of pain. A bird was the last one. It seemed unable to stand, so she scooped it up and tucked it to her chest with the arm that the snake clung to. Then she ran for what she hoped was an exit.

The door led to a hallway--a normal looking hallway. The things were all around, crashing into the walls, breaking down doors. One of them was torn off of its hinges by the human-chimera hybrid. It disappeared inside. When Céline reached the entranceway, she saw stairs leading downward.

She flew down them. They seemed to go on forever. The conglomeration of animal-men had disappeared and several other things passed her on her way down. She wasn't sure how she didn't trip sooner, but she finally did. Her and all the little things clinging to her, rolled down the final flight, landing in the lobby of an office building.

She landed on her hip, the little bird thing underneath her. It let out an 'awww', weak and pitiful, but it only hit the periphery of her ears. She hoisted herself up, ignored the pain in her hip, the burning in her arm, at her temples, and ran out of the front entrance, broken open by some creature that had escaped ahead of her.

She burst from the confines of the structure into the darkness of night.

Her legs began to shake with her running. Her chest heaved. She made herself go onward. The farther she got from the building, the less animal sounds from the other things she heard. She was vaguely aware she was in the business district of a city. Skyscrapers with fancy logos, their windows darkened in the night sped by as she ran. Finally, her chest would not allow her to run any longer. She ducked into an alleyway between two buildings, and sank down against a wall at the end of it.

The cat began to cry again, a high pitched little sound like a kitten mewing for its mother. The others all began to join it, and Céline felt panic rising in her again.

"Shhh," she hissed. "Chut, you have to be quiet!" It didn't seem to do any good, they all kept making noises, a cacophony of sound in the silent darkness. "Shhhhh," spit flew from her mouth as she ushered them to be quiet. The cat, mewing in her ear, was loud and incessant. She let go of the lamb, and reached up to grab the cat. "Chut," she whispered, and pressed the cat's face into her chest to muffle its cries. The bird in her other arm awwked, and she desperately grabbed its beak and clamped it shut with her hand, leaving its body in her lap.

This seemed to quiet the other three, as soon as the cat

and bird stopped, so did they. "You have to be quiet," Céline whispered, "or they will find us." She let the cat up slightly, and sighed when it didn't cry. Letting go of the bird's beak, it awwked again, and she clamped her hand back closed.

The only sound in the night air now was six heavy rasps catching their breath. The cat put its arms around her torso, and the bear had done the same thing to her back. The lamb came up beside her, pushing the cat into the bird, and sat on her now free leg. The snake stayed wrapped tightly around her forearm. She lowered her head, the smell of animal overwhelming her and she closed her eyes.

The sounds of their breathing slowed, but no more cries came from the little things. Céline kept her head lowered, she wasn't sure how long, until she heard walking on the sidewalk along the front of the alley.

She snapped her head up and held her breath. A woman in a business suit, with high heels and a briefcase, clicked-clacked across the front of the alleyway, disappearing as she walked on. Céline could see her clearly, she could see the alley clearly. The sky was a gray blue, and the stars of the night were no longer visible.

It's morning. People are on their way to work. She was stuck in an alley, in a torn hospital gown, with five weird hybrid animal people clinging to her, and people were going to begin walking by at any minute. If someone saw her, they would call the authorities. If they called the authorities, one of two things would happen. They would take her to the loony bin for the story she told, or the uniformed men and scientists would find her. Neither option was acceptable.

She looked around desperately, and saw that the wall she was leaning against had a chain link gate on the far end of it. She gently placed the cat, bear, and lamb on the ground, and stood up, gasping at the pain in her hip. All three stood on two legs. She limped to the gate, the bird in her hand, the snake wound about her forearm, and saw it was locked.

"We have to go over it," she said softly. The other three hybrid animal people followed her, like a line of ducklings. She pointed to the gate, "We have to go over it," she said again.

None of them moved.

"Over," she said again, placing her free hand on the chain link and hoisting herself up.

The cat seemed to understand immediately, and sprang onto the gate, scrambled up it, and was over in a flash. The bear followed her, albeit more slowly and much more loudly. The lamb had a good deal of trouble, his feet were like foot-hooves, and his three fingers were thick. She thought at first she'd vault over the fence, but the pain in her hip reminded her she was not going to do that. She hoisted herself up with her free hand, still holding the bird, and helped the lamb up the fence with her shoulder. Both she and lamb fell onto the other side.

Céline limped along, turning and twisting and avoiding any more climbing, until she found a small alcove off the back of a building. Crates of goods were in front of it, blocking it from view from the street. She crawled into it, the others following, and she fell to the floor. No sooner had she closed her eyes, then she fell asleep.

The smell of food wafted through the air and woke the small group of escapees. The bear's stomach rumbled audibly, followed quickly by Céline. The cat mewed, bringing Céline fully awake. "Shhh," she rubbed its head. "I know you're hungry." How am I supposed to feed us? Her purse was gone, along with all of her money, her identification, her credit card. Plus, she looked like she had just come out of a fire or a car wreck.

She peeked her head around the alcove. No one was there, so she stood up, and ignoring the ache in her hip, limped out into the alley. The three animal people followed her, the snake still on her arm, and the bird still held close to her chest. Weaving their way in and out behind buildings, the smell of Italian food became stronger and stronger. Around a corner, she saw the back of an Italian eatery. Outside the back door were heaps of half-eaten sandwiches, plates of unfinished pasta, piles of salad. She stopped, the bear hit her legs. It looked up at her, about to make a sound, when she bent down and put her hand over its muzzle. "Shhhh," she said gently. "I will get us some food," she explained. "Stay here."

She went to make her way toward the door, the three little ones following her. "No," she shook her head, "you stay here." But when she moved again, so did they.

She sighed and looked at the discarded food behind the restaurant. "We have to run," she said quietly. Is this how homeless people get food? They run behind Italian eateries and grab leftovers? She began to run, then remembered her hip with a stab of pain, her running became more like hopping. She grabbed a bowlful of the discarded food and fled around the other corner of the building. Looking behind her, the three little animal children were gone.

She let out a cry and saw they were at the refuse gobbling up anything they could find. If someone saw them, they'd call the police. She put down the bird and ran to the other three. She nabbed up the cat and the lamb and ran back behind the corner. She dropped them, turned to go back for the bear, but he was already behind her. She sighed and picked up the bird again. "Come on," she walked farther down the little alley, "we'll eat."

She dropped the food and the three animal children fell on it. She felt the pressure release on her forearm, giving her pins and needles, as the snake let go of her and fell in the large Styrofoam bowl. It reached out with two slender arms, tiny hands grabbing the remnants of someone's dinner. Céline stuffed her own hand in the bowl, closed it on something slimy, and stuffed it into her mouth. It tasted like a combination of spaghetti and olives. She put her hand in again, sat down, then put the bird in her lap.

She took some small pieces and placed them in its beak, but it didn't seem to know what to do with them. It knew it was food, it opened his beak wide and let out a weak "Awwk." When she put a piece of noodle in its mouth, it just held its beak open.

She glanced up at the others, they all seemed to be stuffing their faces hand over fist. She looked back at the bird. Why won't you eat? She finished chewing the last of the food in her mouth and swallowed. "Oh!" She reached through the other four and grabbed another handful of food. She stuffed it into her own mouth and chewed it, and spit it into the bird's beak.

The bird swallowed.

As she continued with the procedure, occasionally getting up to stealthily, or as stealthily as she could in an opened backed dressing gown, barefoot with an aching hip, grab some more food before disappearing again behind the corner, it occurred to her that she might be in some sort of twisted cartoon or comic book. Taking care of five human-animal children, running away from scientists in a lab right out of a science fiction movie, digging in the garbage for food, none of this could be real. She spit some more food into the bird's mouth.

Seeing a plastic cup was nearby, she gently put down the bird, retrieved it, and filled it with water out of an outdoor spigot. She gulped it down, ignoring the awful taste. She did it again, and again, and then she was surrounded by mews, and baws, and brrws, and a pressure coiling against her leg. The other four had figured out what she was doing and come for their share.

She filled the cup and held it for each of them as they

drank. They tried to take it from her, and each other, but she had plenty of practice with that kind of behavior. Her own two children, only two years apart in age, had gone through a stage where they did this with everything. Mediating through sharing was something she was very good at, though something she hadn't been too keen on learning.

She took a cup back to the bird, picked it up again, and tried to get it to drink. Again, it did the same as it did with the food, only opened its beak and tried to swallow.

Now that she had a moment to think, she could get a good look at each of the creatures that were with her.

The bird in her arms was white, with feathers sticking out in a sickly fashion. It looked much more bird than it did human, its eyes were wide and held no expression. Its wings were thin and at the ends of them fingers protruded, without a hand. Its legs were scaly like a bird's, but the knees looked human, and the feet were malformed, with seven long toes on each of them, ending with small, white talons. Its heart was beating very fast, and it was blinking quickly with its expressionless eyes.

The snake was tiny, it couldn't have been more than a foot long. It was a dark green, with black eyes. The only real thing that reminded Céline of a human were the little neck, shoulders, and arms. They were perfectly formed, and the same dark green as the rest of it. It slithered with its head up, shoulders and arms above the ground, to what Céline might have said at its waist. She couldn't be sure, though, as under the arms it was all the same.

The bear seemed to blend beautifully with its combination of animal and human. On all fours, it looked like a bear cub. But when it stood up on two legs, its arms fell to its sides like a human being's, and it moved its front paws like a hand. Standing up on two legs also made it quite clear that it was a he.

Same with the lamb. She thought it was a sheep and not a goat at least, but she could have been wrong. It was obviously a boy, covered with white wool. His eyes were yellow, with horizontal hourglass shaped pupils. He did not look as lamb-like on all fours as the bear did a bear, but when he stood up, he stood like a human. His feet were a human foot-shaped-hoof with two toes on the end. His three fingered hands were covered in the same white wool as the rest of him.

The cat was the most human-like of all of them. One could almost trick oneself into thinking it was a child in a cat suit. Céline couldn't tell the gender of it by looking. Its body was covered in sleek gray fur, with the darker markings of a tabby. Its tummy was white. So were its paws, which had elongated digits it could use as fingers. Its eyes were green, its pupils slits in the daylight. Its tail swished back and forth in a rhythmic motion, and she could hear a faint purr coming from her.

"Can any of you talk?" she asked.

They all looked at her and said nothing.

"I am going to guess that is a no," she sighed. "Well, I can't be calling you the bird, the bear, the lamb, the snake, and the cat, so we better come with names. Unless you all have names already."

She waited for an answer, but didn't get one.

"OK, then," Céline looked at each of them. "You," she pointed to the bear, "are Ursus." She pointed to the lamb, "You are Khenum." She took a deep breath. "You other three aren't so easy." After a moment, she said, "I will assume you're girls until I know otherwise." She looked at the snake, "You are Naga." To the cat she said, "You are Ariste." She looked down at the bird, "And you are..." she searched her brain for a mythological parallel, and unable to find a girl's name, she decided on a boy's, "…you are Aquila." She pointed to herself, "I am Céline." She stood up, the movement putting on the edge of tears. "And we have to get out of here before someone sees us."

She and the little human-animal children behind her wandered around the back ways of the buildings for hours. She had no idea where she was going. Where she was supposed to be going. Naga, no larger than a garden snake, ended up on her forearm immediately. She carried the other three with her free arm at intervals, the other arm kept Aquila close to her chest. In the time walking, she had plenty of time to think. She had to contact Stephane. He must be worried sick, the kids must be terrified. She would have to find a payphone and call him collect. What am I going to do with these little people, for she was quite sure now they were, in fact, people. They looked around curiously, held her elbow like small children do to feel safe. Could I hide them in my basement forever? Or the attic? She imagined what she would say when Stephane picked up. "Allo? Stephane? C'est Céline. Je suis á Chicago et je ne peux pas aller á la maison, parsque je ne portais sauf la robe d'hospital." <Hello? Stephane? It's Céline. I am in Chicago and I can't come home because I am not wearing anything but a hospital gown.> Looking down at the pale green material, she saw it was filthy, so were her legs. Her bare feet were black and crusted with gook. The gown was torn at the hem around her knees, but tied securely at her neck and back. The blisters on her arms, legs, and temples had burst, scabbing over and leaving pus on the pale green cotton. She laughed maniacally and shook her head at the absurdity of it, tears forming in her eyes again and this time falling down her face.

She noticed as they walked that the garbage bins were less full of garbage, the ground less full of refuse. There were more needles, razors, and condoms littering the alleys, though. When she heard no human sounds for half an hour, she ventured to take a look at the actual street.

It was empty. It looked like they were in a warehouse district, abandoned for more modern facilities. The sun was low in the sky, the quiet and openness of the street discomforting, so Céline picked a warehouse to stay the night.

The first floor was obviously occasionally occupied, having a metal bin in the middle for a fire in the winter, and strewn clothes, wrappers, and decomposing human waste. The second and third floors looked occupied too, drug paraphernalia and other things she didn't even recognize littered the floor. She decided the top floor would probably be the safest, and trekked up the stairs, her little brood of half-animals following her. As the sun set over the horizon, slowly blanketing everything in black, Céline leaned up against a wall once more, and with the little ones around her, fell asleep.

# Chapter 5

**CLASSIFIED TOP SECRET**
**PROJECT SANCTUARY**

To:
Washington DC

From: Flayne Institute Experimental Facility
Chicago, Illinois

Subject: The Therian Initiative Escape

It is with great regret that I am informing you that there has been an escape at the Experimental Facility. One of the subjects discarded for experimentation overpowered the military personnel and opened the restraining cylinders of the remaining subjects in the holding room. There was a 100% live subject loss with a 42% subject recovery.

We project that of the 68% subject non-recovery, that 90% of them will not be able survive without special measures provided by the Institute. Of the remaining 10%, due to the special nature of the subjects' phenotype, it will not be difficult to locate and reacquire or eliminate them. Any evidence of the subjects' existence will be erased, and as with all phenomena of this sort, first person accounts will be discarded by the public. Should too much interest be generated, standard smear campaign tactics will be employed.

With this following the recent breakout from the Flayne Institute Training Facility, we request an increase in military presence for security purposes to prevent further incidents.

Signed: Agent ██████████

# Chapter 6

Ilya splashed water on his face, the cool liquid heavy on his fur. He shook his head, water splaying about him, then looked into his bathroom mirror. Everything in the bathroom looked the same. The shower, now almost too small for him, was still the same pale blue it had been when he arrived more than a year ago. The toilet and sink were the same shiny white porcelain. The floor was still immaculate, the grout dark gray to contrast the tile. His toothbrush in the toothbrush holder was his, the toothpaste he'd brought with him from Russia. Nothing had changed, except for what looked back at him in the mirror.

It was not his face. It would never be his face again. His slate gray eyes were the only thing that he could identify, that belonged to him. His ears were now at the top of his head, large and pointed at the far ends, moving of their own volition, independent of the rest of his head or face. His mouth was stretched out, a muzzle, black whiskers stretching from his now elongated lips, ending in a pink nose. His face belonged to the brindle rat in Dr. Montgomery's lab, the doctor's favorite.

"Why, when all of this testing is complete, do they call the candidates moreaus?" he had asked before, throwing the basketball toward the hoop lazily.

One of the other candidates who was much farther along in the testing, cocked his head to the side. "After The Island of Dr. Moreau."

The man had said it so matter-of-factly that Ilya had not asked any further questions. Apparently, The Island of Dr. Moreau was common knowledge among Americans. The candidates and scientists informed him it was a book, not very long. He found it with a quick search in the library of the living quarters. He read it in one evening, and the next morning had not gone to his testing station, but straight to Dr. Montgomery's office.

He threw the book across the doctor's desk. "What the hell is this?" he seethed.

Dr. Montgomery picked up the book. "It is The Island of Dr. Moreau by H.G. Wells," he replied, non-plussed.

"You call your candidates moreaus when they are done with their testing," Ilya began.

"We call our candidates subjects when they are done with their testing," Dr. Montgomery corrected. "We call them moreaus after they have had their procedure."

"The procedure turns them into animals," Ilya did not ask. He knew as soon as he read the book in the doctor's hands.

"No," Dr. Montgomery put the book down, and leaned forward, his hands on his desk. "The procedure turns them into a human-animal hybrid. Not an animal, at all."

"You never said anything about human-animal hybrids," Ilya's voice was quiet.

"We told you that your DNA would be combined with that of an animal to enhance certain abilities, depending upon your function in the company."

"That isn't an animal hybrid," Ilya said.

"That is exactly what an animal hybrid is," the doctor replied, quite calm. "A hybrid is a mixture—"

"I know what a hybrid is," Ilya put his hands on the desk, mimicking Dr. Montgomery's action, only his face was a scowl. "You never said anything about becoming a hybrid," he gestured to the book, "like these."

Dr. Montgomery sighed, and pushed himself off of the desk. "Ilya Pytrovich," his voice was patronizing, "how are you going to get the enhanced senses of a particular animal if you are not part of a particular animal?"

The man can't be serious, Ilya thought. The anger that had been brewing when he'd finished the novel began to drain from him, being replaced by a dreadful realization. "You are planning on changing us into animals? You were planning on this all along? Even when the company found me in Moscow…"

"Ilya," Dr. Montgomery squinted slightly, his mouth in a line, his voice still calm, "honestly, what did you think having your DNA combined with an animal meant?"

The warrior couldn't answer. It sounded so innocuous when he'd been told, after arriving in the United States and going through the initial testing. "I thought……" he could feel disgust creeping up his stomach.

"You thought you would be able to hear a little better?" Dr. Montgomery's voice was now condescending. "That you would be able to see in the dark? That you would be faster? Or stronger?"

"Da!" Ilya grasped onto the explanation, hope lacing the revulsion in his gut.

"You will, Ilya," Dr. Montgomery sounded as if he were talking to a small child, punctuated by the drop of the Russian's patronym. "You will have that and so much more." When Ilya stared at him with wide eyes, he continued, "It is truly an idea ahead of its time."

Ilya steadied his breathing, Outside circumstances do not control inside circumstances, his teacher had told him innumerable times in his life. "I have changed my mind," Ilya said steadily. He pushed himself off of the desk, standing up straight. He was an imposing man by any standard, true to the title of Warrior he'd earned.

"Are you sure?" Dr. Montgomery's voice was disappointed. "It would be such a waste."

"I don't want to be an animal person," Ilya, despite his steadying breaths, had trouble even getting the phrase out of his mouth. It seemed to stop at his throat because of the nausea the thought caused him.

Dr. Montgomery sighed and pressed an intercom button on his desk.

"Security," the voice on the other end said.

"Gospodin Leschyov has changed his mind about participating in our project," he replied.

"We will be there immediately, Doctor." There was a slight buzz on the other end of the intercom, before it went dead.

"Such a waste," the doctor turned from Ilya shaking his head.

The warrior stood still, steadying his breath, waiting for security. They would surely walk him to his room, let him gather his few personal belongings, then escort him out of the building. He would be stuck in this half dead city, with no money, no connections, no nothing. Another breath, and the thoughts drifted off.

The door opened and four security guards came into the office. Ilya could see seven more standing out in the hall. This kind of contingency was not needed to escort him to his room. Each man was tense and held a gun in their hand at their thighs.

"Not in here, gentlemen," Dr. Montgomery said.

"Of course not in here, Doctor," said the guard in front. "We'll take him to a more private area."

"What do you mean?" Ilya asked slowly.

"We can't very well have you roaming the streets, knowing what you know, now can we, Ilya Pytrovich?" The look of disappointment on the doctor's face was deep and disturbing to look at. "Some might think that what we are doing is…unethical."

Ilya calmed his body, his mind going blank, ready for the fight he knew would ensue.

"Are you sure you do not want to change your mind?" Dr. Montgomery had smiled. "Oh, Ilya. You will be perfect, don't you see?"

He did see. He saw every time he saw his reflection.

He was not prepared for what he would see in the mirror. You have to be grateful for what has been given to you, he told himself over and over again. You have two legs, two arms, fingers, toes…On each hand he now had three fingers and a thumb, the same hand as the rat he'd been blended with. His feet sported four toes, but his pinky was now a dew claw, pushed back to the side of his foot. Both were a pale pink, the color of a human's hands after being out in the cold too long.

He thought he had prepared himself. He thought he would be prepared for anything. He had been in combat, distance and hand-to-hand. He had fought in battles that would not have been believed if he told the stories of them. He had protected so many people, in so many ways. He had killed so many people, in so many ways. He had been part of the Pride of Russia, the elite of the elite, able to carry out whatever orders his superior officers gave to him.

He had endured the loss of his family, small and intimate, but still his family. He had endured the loss of teammates, more dear to him than if they had been his birth family. Since childhood, he had been trained by one of the greatest Systema masters on the planet. He should have been prepared for anything.

He wasn't prepared for having to start from the very beginning of everything, like a little child.

He was not prepared to have no knowledge of his body. His body was his life; the graceful, purposeful movement of his body is what made him who he was, a master at the Russian Martial Art. He didn't know the body he was in, didn't know how to consciously control it.

This must be what those who are decimated in combat feel like when they are in rehabilitation, he would think and it would help him to stay motivated to relearn his physical self.

Instead of fighting an enemy he could see and touch, he was forced to fight his own instincts again, just as he did when he was a boy.

He wanted shiny things, or soft things. He would pick them up in his pink hands and feel the texture of the item, watch the light shine and absorb over the surface. Like a child in a candy store, it would sometimes take all of his willpower to put the item down, to not take it back to his room with him. His room was purposely empty, a minimalist space, with only his essentials, to prove to himself that he was not a kleptomaniacal animal.

He had to be staunch in not running and hiding when loud noises echoed in the gymnasium or outside his door. His heart would race, his breathing quicken. Flashes of incidents that had never happened to him would dart before his mind's eye—a large predatory animal coming after him, the feeling of sharp teeth sinking into his flesh.

He wanted to bite whenever anyone questioned him or told him to do something. Sometimes it was for the silly things, "Ilya Pytrovich, please take the monitor off now."

An anger would swell in him, starting at his collar bone and working its way up to his head and down to his heart. "Take your own damn monitor off," he wanted to spit, wanted to lean into the scientist speaking to him at the time and chomp his nose off. But he would take a deep breath, and pull the electrodes off of his body gently, as asked.

He had to relearn how to monitor his breathing. His breathing was supposed to be relaxed, natural, how could he do that when he didn't know what natural was! He would work himself up into a frenzy trying to get his body to do things that it could do as a human, that he'd been promised it could do as a moreau, and then realize his breath had gone haywire. He was holding it or breathing erratically. He would begin his breathing, the very basic tenet of his life as a Systema practitioner, what he thought would be natural, a pendulum swing of in through the nose and out through the mouth with a brief pause in between each one.

He adjusted the pants in the back, getting his long tail settled in a comfortable position around the fabric, and turned out of the bathroom. The long claws on his feet clicked on the tile as he walked, like his face in the mirror, something he had yet to get used to. When he didn't look down at his feet, he could almost pretend that it was the click of boots.

# Chapter 7

Céline awoke feeling a cold, hard thing against her chest. She opened her eyes, knowing what it was before she saw it. Aquila's fluttering heartbeat had become intimately familiar to her in the past two days, now it had stopped.

The bird's eyes were still open, its body rigid, its white, sparsely feathered head beginning to crane back with rigor mortis. "Oh," she cooed, her voice waking the others up. They each sniffed Aquila's body, as if in a goodbye, and then ignored it.

She got up and laid the bird down. She wished she had some other way to dispose of him, but she had to find a payphone, she had to do it stealthily, and she couldn't waste time here. Leading the other four down the stairs, they began their trek through the empty streets in search of a phone.

They found one on a corner not far from the warehouse. ~Don't call,~ came the unbidden thought. ~Don't call.~ She picked up the receiver, and heard nothing from the earpiece. It was dead. The second one they found, however, wasn't. ~Don't call,~ said the unbidden thought, ~you ought not to call. You shouldn't call, don't call.~ She pressed 0 for the operator, all four animal children clinging to her legs. She fervently hoped not to be seen.

"Hello," came a nasally, female voice onto the phone, "how may I help you?"

"I would like to make a collect call, please," Céline told her.

"What number, please?"

Céline gave it to her and the phone on the other end rang. "Oh, please be home, Stephane, please be home."

She heard a click, expecting the answering machine to come on, she looked frantically around the phone looking for a phone number for Stephane to call her back.

"We appreciate you calling," said a voice that Céline didn't recognize, "but the Ilorsaint family is not making any comments at this time. This has been a harrowing time for this family, the loss of this beloved wife and mother has devastated not only one community, but two. The memorial is taking place in Mr. Ilorsaint's homeland in Haiti in an undisclosed location. Donations can be made to the Missing Person's Fund in lieu of flowers. All calls will be screened, and those that are deemed relevant will be passed along to the Ilorsaint family. They ask that their privacy be respected at this time as they mourn this loss."

As Céline listened to the message coming from her own answering machine, her mind raced. Harrowing time? How long have I been gone? Memorial? She couldn't have been gone for more than three days. There was the night on the train, the day of her escape, and yesterday. They're having a memorial for me after three days? Haiti? He's going back to Haiti!? With the kids? With my kids?!

She looked down at the creatures hanging on her legs, and saw four pairs of pleading, frightened eyes looking up at her. They were different colors, and different shapes, with different shaped pupils, but they were eyes, and they were full of expression. They were full of consciousness. ~In Haiti,~ the unbidden thought said, ~in Haiti.~

She had to get to Haiti. She looked around in a panic, her breath coming in quick gasps. How am I going to get to Haiti? Dread crept into her body, starting at her chest and spreading through her torso and down her arms and legs. She had no way to get to Haiti. She had no money. She had no identification. She had no way to get anywhere, except to walk. She couldn't walk to Haiti. She couldn't get to Haiti.

She could walk home, surely. But what good would that do? There was no one there. If Stephane was no longer in the US, if the kids were no longer in the US, she had no one. None of the people at home were her people. They were all Stephane's.

Not a soul.

She thought for a moment, looking at the payphone. I could call Haiti collect. There wasn't a phone number to call, though, none of his family had a phone. I could call the American Consulate in Haiti. The dread finally reached her toes and the tips of her fingers. The Consulate would not accept a collect call, and she had no money, not even enough for a payphone.

She took the phone away from her ear and heard the beep of the machine. She hung up.

It was like something had fallen away from her, a crust from her eyes that made the world look different. As if she'd been looking at it all of her life with glasses and now they were off, she could see the colors were not the same shades she thought they were. The lack of sound made her feel removed from her body, the warmth of the creatures on her legs felt faraway. She began walking, shaking them off gently, except for Naga, who wound around her leg and clung tightly.

She returned to the alleys behind the buildings until she found a restaurant, and repeated yesterday's episode, her mind blank. She saw a newspaper on the ground and picked it up. She read the date. If this was today's newspaper, it meant that Céline had been gone for 18 months. How could that be? I've only been gone a few days, at most. Why would they have a memorial after only 18 months? People are missing for years and years before having a memorial. Can you even have a grave if you had no body? What do you bury? She remembered, then, reading a newspaper article once that after three days the probability of finding a missing person dropped 75%. How much did it drop after 18 months? Was it almost nothing, enough to have a memorial?

How did this happen? Her eyes went back to the creatures eating out of a dumpster, the same dumpster she had just eaten out of. I was kidnapped and missing for 18 months, she thought. Why was I kidnapped? What did those people do to me? She felt for the blisters on her temples, the ones on her arms and thighs stinging at the thought. Were they going to turn her into one of these? A…what did they call it…a moreau. She gasped, the little animal people stuffing their faces with half-consumed food. The Island of Doctor Moreau, the name of the book rang in her head. These little things must have been people…they were children. She felt the food she'd just eaten try to make its way back up her throat.

The kitten came over to her and crawled in her lap, obviously finished eating. She pushed against her with her head, and Céline began to stroke it absently with her hand. Ariste's hair was soft, it reminded Céline of her daughter, Lisabetta, when she was small, and her hair was still the silky curls of a tiny baby. This thing was a child, like her own child, whether it looked like a monstrosity or not.

If those people had kidnapped her, would they go after her own children if she tried to contact them? Would they turn her little boy and girl into one of these things, freakish animals with bits of human being thrown in?

In Haiti, Stephane and the kids had their grandmother, their many aunts, uncles, and cousins of all types within a five mile radius of each other. Stephane could live like a king in Haiti with his education. Her children would be well loved, Stephane would be well loved. A memorial would give them closure. They could move on without her. They would be safe, because she would be dead.

The four beings clinging to her had no one. You, the unbidden thought said from the place that the poetry came.

After eating, they walked back to the warehouse and climbed once more to the top floor. Aquila was still there, flies now crawling on his open eyes and open beak. She shooed them away and picked up the little bird.

That morning, she had noticed a fenced-in vacant lot next to the building. It was small, perhaps 8 feet by 10 feet, but it was overgrown with weeds. She carried the little body down the stairs, and out of the door, she squeezed through the gate, which was rusted into position, barely open. The lot had been covered with concrete at one time, but the plants were slowly taking it back. Chunks of it were cracking up, and she saw in the back left corner, a large, green weed was growing. She carried Aquila over to it and put him down.

She pulled the weed up. It was resistant, but she was determined. It left a bare space of earth and the concrete loose. She began prying the concrete chunks, the four little ones following suit. Naga looked especially silly, with her tiny arms and hands being able to only pick up a pebble and move it to the side. Once there was a space wide enough, Céline found a broken glass bottle and started to dig with it.

The four moreaus watched her for a while, as if they were examining her, waiting for something to happen. Then Ursus began to dig with his hands, his claws removing great clods of dirt as the cub dug. Soon they had a shallow hole large enough to place Aquila's body. She laid him in the hole, and began to move the dirt over his body with her hands. All of the others joined to help her. "I'm sorry, little fellow," she said. "I wish I could have done better."

With those words, the world snapped back into place and her thoughts returned. She had to figure out what she was going to do, how she was going to do it, and what she was going to do it with. She was not going to lose another one of these little ones, and she hadn't the foggiest idea of how to take care of them. Or herself. She looked up at the warehouse and saw a window on the top floor slightly ajar overlooking the lot.  She had to start somewhere, so she'd start with the top floor of the warehouse, and with this vacant lot, now a graveyard.

# Chapter 8

He walked slowly to the private dining room, a place where he was welcome to eat each and every night, but rarely did. It was always lavishly decorated, with candles and velvet. He usually took his meals by himself, or with his students. He had no desire to be watched like a lab rat when he ate his dinner. Tonight, however, was a business dinner, a schmoozing with the people with the funding. The Flayne Institute had to show off their research, after all.

Entering the room, Dr. Montgomery and five men in navy business suits were waiting for him to arrive. He hid a smug smile. The looks of those who had never seen him before were always priceless, an attempt to hide awe and horror.

Everyone stood up at his entrance, Dr. Montgomery coming up to him and placing his hand on his arm. The doctor was the only one who touched him on a regular basis, in a way that wasn't fighting or teaching. The feeling Ilya always received was as if he were something in between his favorite pet and favorite son.

"Gentlemen," said Dr. Montgomery, "this is Ilya Pytrovich Leschyov."

There was a moment of silence as the men in business suits took him in.

"Ilya Pytrovich," Dr. Montgomery went on slowly, "these are....some of our...stakeholders."

Ilya knew exactly who they were. "Politicians," he said, his Russian accent thick.

"You are an impressive man, Mr. Leschyov," an older business man, his brown hair speckled with gray, stuck his hand out to shake Ilya's. He smiled at the rat, "I'm Agent Saunders Perelli. I'm not a politician" he corrected. "But I work for them."

Ilya wrapped his four fingered hand around Perelli's in a firm grip, shook it twice, and dropped it. His face was as nondescript as his hair, brown eyes, light tan skin, eyes not too far apart and not too close together, lips not too thick and not too thin. He saw the man sweat slightly, an indication that he was uncomfortable being there, in a room with human scientists and a man in the body of a rat.

"You are doing well, I am told," he smiled broadly and put his hand on his pants, as if he was trying to keep from wiping it. "Your training going well?"

"I am already trained, sir," Ilya said. A little lie, as training is never truly done for the true martial artist, but it was true as far as these men were concerned. Ilya imagined the man didn't care one iota about one's emotional, psychological, or spiritual development. There was more to any war art than merely fighting.

Perelli cleared his throat, and Ilya got a perverse satisfaction from the sound. The three scientists and the other businessmen in the room shifted uncomfortably, as if expecting the moreau to do something unexpected. He looked down on him without bowing his head, his own demeanor calm, without worry.

"Yes, yes of course you are," Perelli said. "What exactly are you doing?" he asked, and then quickly added, "You know the details better than anyone else, after all."

"Da," Ilya answered.

Perelli waited for Ilya to say something else. The warrior remained silent. "What exactly is it you do?" Perelli prompted.

"Why don't we start our supper first?" Dr. Montgomery led Ilya to his seat next to him at the round table, and a porter immediately appeared to fill his wine glass. But instead of pouring wine into it, he replaced it with a Russian shot glass and poured in vodka.

"Of course, of course," Perelli took his own seat, looking from Ilya to Dr. Montgomery. "We have heard so much about you, Mr. Leschyov, but no one can seem to give us any details." A bead of sweat formed at the man's temple

Ilya moved his tail out of the way behind him so he didn't sit on it, "Details of what?" he asked.

"Of…" he looked at his fellow businessman, "…of your training," he held out his hands, and looked at Dr. Montgomery beseechingly.

"Ilya is training our moreaus," Dr. Montgomery said, "in the ancient art of Systema."

Another businessman cleared his throat. "Dr. Montgomery, Mr. Leschyov," he looked each in the eye in turn, "I do not mean to be rude, but our superiors, the politicians, are asking for more detailed information about what's happening within the facility. Surely the two of you understand?"

"Of course, Agent Anchord, of course," Dr. Montgomery bobbed his head.

Ilya picked up a glass of water, sitting next to shot glass, and took a long draught. It had taken him a while to figure out how to drink out of a glass. If he tried to drink it like a human, his nose would end up in the liquid, that was if he could fit his muzzle into the opening of the glass. He had learned that instead of tilting his head down to meet the glass, he tilted his head up. He brought the glass to his bottom lip, with his muzzle above the glass. He then had to tilt the glass carefully and let the liquid fall into his mouth, hitting his jaw without him spilling it.

So these were government agents. The government was funding them. He'd suspected it, but had not had confirmation. "You mean you want to know how the training of your soldiers is coming along?"

Agent Anchord looked surprised by the forthright statement. "Yes," he said finally.

"It is coming along nicely," the rat moreau said.

"Um…" Agent Perelli leaned forward and then leaned back, his eyes wide. "What exactly are you working on?""

"I believe," Dr. Montegomery put his hand on Ilya's upper arm, "he is trying to ask what 'nicely' means."

"We work on breathing," said Ilya, his voice clipped.

Dr. Montgomery let out a frustrated breath of his own.

The rat turned only his head on his long neck to the doctor and glared with his gray eyes. "You want me to train men and women how to fight," with his ire rising, his accent became thicker, "when they do not know their own bodies. The very thing they operate from, it is foreign to them. They can barely work their bodies. How are they to learn to fight?"

There was a moment of silence in the room as Dr. Montgomery and Ilya looked at each other. The look on the doctor's face was perturbed, like when a teenager tries to argue their curfew.

"You seem in perfect control of your body," Agent Anchord said in a calm voice.

Ilya turned from the doctor to the government agent, his eyes still stern. "I am the teacher," he replied. "I have had more practice."

He saw each of the men in business suits start, as if his statement had triggered something in them. Two of them reached for where Ilya thought they would have holsters, and the other three sat with their arms tense, about to go for their waists.

"How can someone not know their body?" asked Agent Perelli, more to himself than to anyone else.

Ilya stood up, pushing his chair back as he did. His tail lashed behind him in agitation. Dr. Montgomery stood up suddenly also, his eyes wide, his smooth manner momentarily jerky.

Agent Anchord and the other agents rose just as quickly as the doctor, two of them taking out their guns and pointing them at Ilya. Just as he had expected. "We are pouring a lot of money into you, Mr. Leschyov," said Agent Anchord, pointing a finger at Ilya, his voice no longer cordial. "My superiors are demanding an accounting of what our money is being used for, and so far we have nothing to show for our investment. We aren't paying you to teach people to breathe, Mr. Leschyov."

"The bodies these men are given, they are the bodies of animals," Ilya hissed, as if he hadn't heard the agent. "They are the bodies of something that does not belong with the mind of a man. And the mind of the man has to learn to control it, like a baby learns to control their body. Only you want the baby to be a killing machine."

"Ilya, he meant no harm," Dr. Montgomery said quickly.

"Then he should not speak," the Russian pushed the chair from behind him, and began to walk toward the door, as if daring one of them to try and shoot him in the back. Not one of these agents was a trained warrior, not a one had any sense in their heads on how to fight. Once he reached the door, he turned back toward the table. "I will give you your killing machines," he said, his voice deadly, "but I will train them. You will not tell me how to train them." He faced the door, and pushed it open hard. It banged against the wall, bouncing back at him. He knocked it again with his arm before it was out of reach, banging shut.

Agent Anchord turned Dr. Montgomery, his eyes ablaze. "This is your prize?" he gestured to the door. "You told me you had gotten me the best of the best." He pointed harshly, "He is completely uncooperative!"

"He is the best of the best!" Dr. Montgomery answered the agent in kind. "He is taking animals and making them into soldiers, just as he says!"

"We need more than someone turning them into soldiers," Agent Anchord said. "You said he would be controllable. You said he would be compliant. We have had too many moreaus--"

"You think I don't know what we've had?" Dr. Montgomery took a step forward, so he was pressed against the table. "I am the one who makes them. You don't think I see every one that doesn't make it through the procedure? Do you think the psychiatric team made a psychological examination for the fun of it? Do you think all of the genetic testing we've done is for the fun of it?"

"If he can't be controlled, he needs to be terminated from the program," Agent Anchord motioned the two agents with their guns drawn toward the door.

Dr. Montgomery backed up to the doorway and shook his head. "We will never find someone else like him. We will never find someone as trained or as talented as he is, and who is so desperate to do this." It was Dr. Montgomery's turn to gesture toward the door, "Who do you know would change themselves into one of these? Will any of you?" He looked each of the agents in the eye, his smooth voice laced with anger.

No one answered his question.

"He is our prize," he turned back to Agent Anchord.

"He is a blessing that we can never recreate. If he is terminated from the program," his voice went back to his smooth, calm self, almost hypnotic, "then there is no program."

"Everyone is replaceable, Elias," Agent Anchord said quietly. "Both you and your prize."

Dr. Montgomery had to take a deep breath to keep his anger in check. "Neither one of us is replaceable," he said, his voice still smooth. "And you know that."

"I can find another university grad student who wants to dabble in human genetics," Agent Anchord gave a smug smile. "They're a dime a dozen. And they wouldn't have to start at ground zero, like you did. They would have all of your material for reference." He put his hand on the table and leaned forward. "Face it, Elias. You would be nothing without me."

Dr. Montgomery leaned forward in a matching stance, his face passive. "There were seven men who underwent the exact same testing and procedure as Ilya. We chose martial artists for a reason." He stood back up, "It doesn't matter what kind of martial art, kung fu, karate, krav maga, systema." He waved his hand in the air dismissively, "But each of them was a master at their art. Each of them had supreme control over their bodies and their instincts."

Agent Anchord glared at the scientist.

"You will never find anyone else to replace Ilya," Dr. Montgomery continued. "You've used up all of your people and he's the only one who made it through, out of seven. You can replace me with some other grad student who is willing to do what I do," he shook his head, "but you will never get another prize."

Agent Anchord glared at him. "What am I supposed to tell my superiors?" he asked tightly.

Dr. Montgomery wracked his brain, looking from agent to agent. "I will arrange something," he said. "But you need more specific questions than 'What are you doing?'"

"How are we supposed to ask more specific questions when we have no idea what he's doing?" Agent Perelli asked.

"I will arrange something," Dr. Montgomery said. "But you need to read a book, so you can at least know what questions to ask."

"What book?" Agent Anchord said.

Dr. Montgomery gave him a withering look. "I can lend you one," his smooth voice was condescending.

# Chapter 9

Elias Montgomery was used to problems presenting themselves, they'd been doing so his entire career. From his graduate days, when the scandal of his genetic testing was blazing on the university scene, to today with Agent Anchord. In fact, Agent Anchord seemed to be attached to each and every problem his career had.

"Mr. Montgomery," the man, wearing a dark navy suit, had approached him on the university campus many years before. His hair had no gray in it then, it was all the nondescript brown of an ordinary, average man. He'd been in his teaching assistant office, sitting at a desk much like this one. The other two T.A.s that he shared the office with were not there, he couldn't remember why now. The man flashed a badge at him. "May I speak with you?"

Great, he'd thought. Now the government is after me, too? "Sure," he'd gestured to a chair for the man to sit down.

The man hadn't sat down, though. He'd stepped into the office, closed the door, and remained standing. "You are a young man of extraordinary promise," he began.

That was not what a young Elias had been expecting to hear. "Excuse me?"

"Your research," said the suited man, "shows extreme promise. You are a forward thinker, it is a shame that the university cannot see that."

"I'm sorry," Elias had stood up, the desk between him and the suited man. Was this some kind of trap? A set up to get him arrested for something? Or worse, thrown out of university to never finish his doctorate? "Where did you say you were from?"

"I'm here to offer you a life preserver, Mr. Montgomery," he said. "You know that your career is over before it even begins."

Elias had just looked at the man who had spoken his deepest fears.

"Your work with combining the 25% of DNA that humans and rats do not share is ingenious. It is even more impressive that you were successful."

Elias blinked. "Only in single cells," he said quietly, shaking his head. "Not in the entire organism. I'm not doing that research any longer."

"I would like to help you continue your research, Mr. Montgomery," said the suited man.

"What?" Elias cocked his head to the side and looked at the man as if he'd been crazy.

"My agency," the man had walked around the desk, so he was now standing in front of the young Elias, "has been watching your work with great interest, Mr. Montgomery. I am offering you the chance to continue your research."

"But the university—" Elias shook his head.

"I am not affiliated with the university," the man had said. "I represent an independent agency of the US government," he paused, "and I am offering you a chance to continue your research." He had leaned forward, his brown eyes very intense. "To continue your research to its natural conclusion."

Elias had withdrawn from the university that day, packed up his things, and moved to Chicago. He'd finished what little he had left of his degree on a more acceptable subject, and had continued his research to its natural conclusion.

Ilya Pytrovich Leschyov.

While he'd not yet perfected the combining of animal DNA with human, he'd come close enough to have almost perfect results. Of course, the beginning specimens had been superb human beings. He was no fool. He knew that had something to do with it.

He had scoured the globe to find the commanders that The US Sanctuary Project had wanted. Finding master martial artists was not hard, most Eastern countries incorporated their country's martial art in their special forces training. Their contacts in the Department of Defense had been valuable in that respect. It was finding a master martial artist that was alone and desperate enough to come to the United States to take the opportunity that was offered that wasn't so easy. Then, to find a master martial artist that passed the psychological and physical tests for the moreau process. Then, to find a master martial artist that survived the process.

Only one had, and Agent Anchord wanted him eliminated from the program.

The Agency had wanted more than one, had expected more than one. Hell, Elias had expected more than one. But so far, they only had one. Elias was willing to fight to have this one, it would take them years to find another one like him.

The Agency removed specimens from the project much too easily in Elias' opinion. So many had been eliminated because of personality flaws, because of physical flaws, because of mental flaws. Flaws that he claimed were well within the bell curve, that would have done no harm. They made soldiers out of humans with more defects than these moreaus had shown, but still they'd been thrown out of the program. How did they think an animal was going to act? An animal was not a human being, was not a drone. A moreau was an animal, instincts intact. There was only the thin veneer of civilization that kept humans from acting like animals, and that veneer was even thinner on a human turned half animal. Like any military animal, they had to be trained.

He had to convince Agent Anchord that they were being trained.

Despite the way that Ilya Pytrovich had presented it, the Russian was right. Anchord wanted soldiers made out of babies. The locomotive process had not been highly considered when ramping up the project. Each of the test subjects before had seemed to be able to move in the appropriate ways for their body type. That they would be at odds with the human thought process in their brains about how their bodies should move was a surprise to the scientist. It was like trying to teach a dog how to hold a pencil. It could be done, but it took creativity and work.

The Agency did not want creativity in its subjects, save what would become the commanding officers. So far, that was only a handful of moreaus.

Elias wanted to pull his hair out. He opened and closed his fists in an attempt to make the urge to grab something go away.

The Agency, or more specifically, Agent Anchord, did not understand the delicate nature of the entire Therian Initiative. Elias had warned him there would be a high loss rate at the beginning of the project, and indeed, there had been. As the project had progressed, and he'd refined the process, the loss rate lowered exponentially.

The physical deformities were almost eliminated, although Elias could not predict how the physical makeup of the subject would turn out after the process. There were still those who came through the process as mismatched things, not able to do anything other than breathe. Some were not able to do that. Some of their bodies were too much an animal to be useful as soldiers. All of those were sent off for further experimentation.

Some were too volatile to be entered into the program, despite being physically acceptable. Those, too, were sent for experimentation.

He wondered what kind of experiments they were doing on them nowadays. He saw no need to get further information from the subjects, other than a genome to try and determine why they might have ended up the way they did after their transformation. Now, he no longer had connections to that part of the project, at all. He had all of the information he needed.

He was much more interested in his rat research. He was forced to do other animals, or at least oversee the study of other animals, and he understood why. While a rat might excel in the Army, it would do the Navy little good. So, he continued with the research on the other animal moreaus, trying to perfect the process while at the same time fighting off the ignorant demands of the Agency.

Damned simpletons. If they would just leave the people with the brains alone, they would have had what they wanted already. But bureaucracy can't help itself, can it?

# Chapter 10

Ilya had noticed the box seating above the gymnasium when he'd first entered the room over a year ago as a human, to practice, to train, to be studied. It was almost never occupied, except by Dr. Montgomery, and his understanding from those around him, it was only Ilya whom he watched. That knowledge left him edgy, so that he had to shake the desire to bite at the glass wall up above his head.

Today, however, the average looking men, all with brown hair, brown eyes, tan skin, wearing navy suits were in the box, looking down on his class with uninterested looks on their faces. Government agents. He didn't have to look at them directly to notice it, though he did. He wanted them to know he noticed it.

As the other moreaus entered the room for his male class, the sound in the gymnasium began to fill up, each talking to each other in little groups. They tended to congregate by types, sticking to their own team. He found it hard not to be jealous of that. He was alone, no other rats had been created. None had survived the turning process.

He wondered briefly if the agents were making a

statement by watching his male class, as opposed to his female one. His very first class had been both male and female moreaus of all kinds, but he had immediately dismissed them.

"No mixed gender classes," he had told Dr. Montgomery.

"Why in the world not?" the doctor had asked.

"It is too complicated," Ilya replied.

"Why is it too complicated to explain?" Dr. Montgomery asked.

Ilya had taken a deep breath to calm himself. "It is too complicated in class."

"You aren't teaching the women something different than the men, are you?" Dr. Montgomery looked surprised.

"No," Ilya had to work hard to not be annoyed. Did these people know nothing? "I will teach them the same thing. Having men and women in the same class means that neither gets a good education."

Dr. Montgomery looked at him like he was crazy.

"The women try to outdo the men, or the men try to outperform the women. Or, the men try to be nice, and the women learn that their opponents are soft, and the men learn to be soft on their female opponents."

Dr. Montgomery opened his eyes a little wider and let out a slow, "Ahhhh." He then shrugged, "You can conduct your classes however you like," he told Ilya. "You are the teacher." He had put his hand on the rat's arm congenially and smiled up at him.

He did not allow the teammates to practice against each other in class. They were supposed to be practicing with each other during the afternoons. Morning practice was for teaching, afternoons for practicing, evenings for communion. He tried very hard to instill that in each of his students. Whether he did or not, he didn't know. He rarely saw any of them outside of the gymnasium.

He hid a chuckle as he clapped, signaling the beginning of class. The moreaus came over to him, gathering in a circle, and sitting down. Let the agents see what it is that he was teaching. He started each class as he always did, with breathing exercises. Yes, he wanted to hiss at the glass above them, we breathe.

"We have visitors today?" asked a lizard moreau, motioning with his head, perched on his long neck, toward the glass box above them.

"It would appear so," said Ilya.

Class went as it always did, breathing exercises, warm up, combat training, closing circle. He had only one rule in his classes, the moreau must keep moving during the entire session. The student could not stop moving, he must constantly be in motion. This was a rule for his students when they had been human, and it was even more important now. These beings must learn to use their bodies, bodies they did not instinctively know how to use, and they had to learn how to use them with enough proficiency so they could fight.

When class was over, one of his students, a sea otter, came over to him to speak with him privately. It was not an out of the ordinary event. The leaders of each of the teams had made it a habit to come and speak with him after class on the night they were to have dinner with him, to make sure their date was still on. Some stayed to discuss techniques they were having trouble with. He would stay as long as the student wanted in order to understand what he or she needed. Mostly questions involved basic principles, principles which were the basis for Systema itself, such as the breathing. He had never realized that breathing was such a difficult concept for people to understand.

Some stayed simply to connect with him on a personal level. Sometimes it was only to have small talk, sometimes it was to discuss items of a much more intimate nature. He was always surprised at what the moreaus told him. They were personal things, things he would have been hard pressed to share with his teammates, much less have told his commanding officer. It made him uncomfortable to know so much of what they thought about things, but it helped him to hone the classes to suit each type of moreau better.

The sea otter who came to talk with him, Dyson, was one of the students that had trouble with the relaxation exercises. He had trouble with relaxing all together. Dyson had been a gang member before his turning. Again, not an uncommon thing. Apparently, Dr. Montgomery was not above using the prison population to draw his test subjects. Dyson suffered from Post Traumatic Stress Syndrome, Ilya was sure, and not just from the changing of his body. He brought with him a great deal of heavy baggage from his gang days.

"I can't get the relaxation right," he said.

"I noticed you had trouble with it today," Ilya said. "Did you have a poor morning before coming?"

Dyson shook his head. "I had a nightmare, though, but it wasn't a bad nightmare. It shouldn't be jacking me up like this," he drew his eyebrow whiskers together in worry. "But whenever I concentrate on my breathing, I feel like I'm having a panic attack. When I try to relax, my body does the opposite."

Ilya nodded, "I see," he said, looking Dyson in the eye. He noticed in his peripheral vision Agent Anchord and the other men from the viewing box approaching.

"Very impressive, Mr. Leschyov," said Agent Perelli.

Ilya did not turn away from Dyson. "We will have dinner together tonight," he said, "and discuss this a little more."

Dyson nodded, gave the agents a sidelong glance, and walked away.

"You have said before," Ilya turned to the agent, "that I am an impressive man."

Agent Perelli chuckled, nodding slightly. "I have," he admitted. "I see you have a firm grip on your students."

"I told you I was training your soldiers," Ilya replied. "I do not lie."

"I never said you did," answered Agent Perelli. "I merely asked you to explain what you were doing." He looked around the gymnasium. It was now empty of any other moreaus. "But Dr. Montgomery was correct, seeing is believing."

"You are satisfied, then?" Ilya asked, rankled.

"I will be satisfied when one of them successfully completes a mission," Agent Anchord said. "But as for the progress, yes, we're satisfied with it."

The rat watched them go, remaining in the auditorium as it emptied out. Then, he began his own routine, one of the many he chose from when he was alone, needing to be in his body, to feel the world around him in a way other than his five senses could give him.

Closing his eyes, he began his breathing. Then his Systema sequence, a beginner one. Because the beginning is always an excellent place to start.

"So, you're the one everyone is chattering about," a voice pierced Ilya's consciousness.

He opened his eyes to see a moreau, shorter than he, a hawk, standing with a smirk on his beak. The front of his bill was rigid, so that only the back, where it connected to his head, curved upward in a smile. Ilya felt his body tense involuntarily, his leg muscles firing to run, his jaw wanting to open to bite. He took several breaths, in through his nose, out through his mouth. Though the hawk was a natural predator of the rat, he reminded himself that he was a man, and so was the fellow walking toward him.

His feathers lay against his rounded head in a lovely pattern of pale brown and white, falling across his naked chest and winged arms like a feathered cloak. He had seen the avians in the mess hall, but never conversed with any. His chocolate brown eyes seemed out of place in his avian face. Ilya would have expected golden, to accompany the hawk-like form.

"Am I?" Ilya replied.

The moreau strode into the gymnasium, his gait having a confidence that Ilya rarely saw. His clawed talons clicked on the wood as he stepped, reaching out an arm, the feathers falling gracefully from the muscles, to hold a feathered hand, each finger ending in a talon tip, out to him. ""You are," he repeated. "Even the business suits are talking about Ilya Pytrovich."

Ilya took his hand, the man's grip was firm as he shook it. "You are not a business suit," he said. "But I am afraid I do not know who you are."

Laughing, the hawk winked. "Because I'm in the aviary, not in the gym," he replied. "I'm Ayah, Commander of the Airborne Division."

Ilya raised his eyebrows. "Division of what?"

Ayah shrugged, his feathers moving elegantly. "The Therian Initiative." He looked around the gymnasium, his circular eyes blinking slowly. "Looks the same as it did when I was here." They landed on Ilya once more, "Only there wasn't a Commander of Ground Operations, then."

"I beg your pardon?" Ilya asked.

"You," he pointed a taloned fingertip at him.

"I am the teacher—" Ilya began.

"And once your students are able to actually do something, you'll be their commander," Ayah interrupted with a casual wave of his hand. "You know it, I know it. But I didn't drop by to discuss semantics."

"Then why, pray tell, did you drop by?" Ilya's accent

rolled the /r/ in pray and and drop.

"To meet you," Ayah said, the smile back on his short, yellow beak. "And to train."

"I beg your pardon?" Ilya asked again.

Ayah laughed. "You got wax in those big ears of yours, comrade?" He laughed again at Ilya's bristling. "I need someone who can actually fight to train with. And you need someone who can actually fight to train with." He held open his hands. "I suggest we train together."

"Train together?" Ilya raised an eyebrow again, his gray eyes looking the hawk moreau up and down.

"I was an airman before I was this," Ayah gestured elaborately to his body. "Part of Special Operations parajumper with the US Airforce."

It was Ilya's turn to smile. "Special Operations, eh?" he asked, crossing his arms in front of his broad chest. "I doubt they can stand up to the Spetsnaz, now."

"How about a good morning workout before we get to our day to find out, eh?" Ayah's beak was a wide grin.

Nodding, Ilya held his excitement in check. Many had been the man and moreau who thought they could give him a challenge, and he'd been continually disappointed. Best for him not to get his hopes too high, despite the hawk's bragging. "Tomorrow, then?"

"I've got nowhere to go," Ayah replied, turning to leave. "I'll be here bright and early."

# Chapter 11

"I am dead," Céline said out loud to the warehouse one day, her voice echoing in the largely empty space. The four children looked at her, as if she might be addressing them, but when they realized she wasn't, went back to playing with each other.

It occurred to Céline, very early on in her new life, that being dead was a miraculous thing. It meant one could start over completely, with none of the restrictions placed upon them by their previous life. There were restrictions, obviously, she considered in the weeks as she thought about it. She was homeless, had no identification, could not work because she had four animal-human hybrid children that needed to be cared for. She had absolutely no idea what she was going to do about any of that.

When she thought about it, she would panic. She didn't know how to get food, she didn't know how to get water, she didn't know what to do with their waste, she didn't know how to do anything! She was shocked at how well she had been provided for in her life, even after her marriage, that she had never had to worry about where a meal would come from, if she would be rained on that night, or if the clothes they had on their backs would keep them warm in the winter. The shock would deteriorate into fear, so that she had to close her eyes and breathe the way her yoga instructor had taught her in her youth in order to not hyperventilate.

"You have got to get a hold of yourself," she said. "Other people do this. You can do this." What did they need? She could at least make a mental list: food, water, clothing, a place to sleep, a place to poop.

The immediate need for food and water could not be ignored, by Céline's grumbling belly or the cries of the children around her. Even Naga, who would not unwrap from her arm, cried plaintively in a voice that Céline would not have guessed she possessed. The warehouse had toilets, workman showers, and sinks on all floors, but the water was not running. She knew from living during the frigid Chicago winters filled with main breaks from freezing, that there must be a valve at the street, and one for the building itself. She traveled down the basement, noting to herself that they would have to do some major clean up of all the floors on her way down.

The basement was dusty, cobwebby, damp, simply downright frightening. The three kids walked behind her, Naga wrapped tightly around her arm, and they walked on tiptoe, avoiding puddles of stagnant water. It stank to high heaven, Céline didn't know from what, and she had no idea how to identify any of the equipment she found. She was afraid she was going to have to simply turn on all the valves she found and hope one of them was the water, when something skittered in the corner. She screamed. All four kids screamed, and they ran back up the stairs to the ground floor.

"We'll try the street valve, instead," she said, her hands on her thighs as she caught her breath. At the street, it took her a while to find it, again, she had no idea what she was looking for. Any cover she found on the ground she opened, even the manhole covers. She turned on every valve she found until she heard the spurt of water coming from the building. She let out a whoop, smiling widely at the kids at her feet.

Ursus, his lips lax around his muzzle, smiled back at her.

She nuzzled the top of his head with her hand, "That's right," she said to him, "come on!" and ran back into the warehouse.

The basement pipes leaked. Not a lot, and it was easy to find the larger leaks in the pipes. She did what she could to fix them, even trying bubble gum at one point. She was surprised at how well the gum worked, but in the end she used a waterproof duct tape, obtained with sticky fingers from the back of an auto store. She checked the pipes on a monthly basis for failure. It had only taken one flooding to cure her of being lazy. One of the pipes on the second floor also leaked, and for a while the floor was always wet until Céline figured out how to turn the water off on that floor only.

As they ran back into the warehouse, they turned on and off faucets and water flowed from all of them. The kids crowded up on the industrial sink on the first floor and drank for minutes. Céline started to worry about the amount they were drinking. Had she almost killed them from thirst? Is that what had killed Aquila? She muscled her way in also and drank from the faucet, trying to make each of them take turns. The water tasted awful, but it was water, and it was running! Once they'd drunk their fill, and flushed all the toilets in the warehouse, which seemed to suck the water away down the drains, she decided to search for food.

She returned to the restaurants in the area, in the very early hours, all four of the kids with her. They ate their fill, and took food home in the plethora of plastic bags that littered the back streets and alleyways. The amount of edible food in the dumpsters was mind boggling. She had to actively ignore that it was in a garbage can, but once out trash and in a grocery bag, much of the produce they collected looked like it might have come from the supermarket.

Getting electricity to the warehouse was not as easy as the water. Breaking off locks and turning valves was one thing. Connecting wires was quite another. She knew it had something to do with the electric meter; she'd seen many of Stephane's friends fiddling with the boxes in between times of not being able to pay the electric bill and getting the power turned back on. What she didn't know was what to do with anything inside the meter. She scavenged a screwdriver from their dumpster diving, and was able to pry the tag off and remove the actual box of the meter. She was surprised that it just looked like a giant plug. It was obvious what was keeping it from conducting electricity—there were plastic sleeves on the plug-prongs. She had done the exact same thing when Lisabetta and Jacques had started crawling as babies in her own house with the outlets! She simply had to pull off the sleeves, plug the meter back in, and the entire warehouse had electricity running to it. She puffed up in a self-satisfied way. "That was easy!" She smiled at the moreaus. At the same time, she pushed the image of her two kids, the spitting image of their father, out of her mind.

She was frightened for a while that they would not be able to stay at the warehouse, especially at night, hearing things skittering in the walls. Who knew what they were? Did they come out and bite you while you were sleeping? None of them did. Twice in that first week, some homeless vagrants found their way into the bottom floor, and she prayed they did not come up the stairs. They didn't. She did not have a clue as to what she would do if they did. But she had to do something. She couldn't let people be here, not with the kids. If they were found out…the idea came to her in the night, when the children were moving about, and the skittering in the walls made her heart thump loudly in her chest.

She crept down the stairs, as quietly as she could, and kept in the shadows of the warehouse walls until she was as close to the homeless as she dared to get. The children were with her, they always were, and copied her motions as if they were little ducklings following their mother hen. She began to make inarticulate noises, like she'd seen in television shows about ghost hunting. The vagrants looked around, fear in their eyes. But what sent them running was when the children made the same noises, with an animal tenor. It even frightened Céline and she knew where the noises were coming from.

It soon became a game to the five of them, though Céline felt guilty about it. "Ghost", they called. When the children were old enough, they began to play it on their own. The boys would make convincing wooing and whispering noises, and the girls would run and slide in the shadows, shushing and whooshing.

"Don't let anyone see you," Céline told them.

"We won't, Mama," they promised.

However, Céline suspected they did not obey her, for it soon became semi-public knowledge that the warehouse was haunted with not only ghosts, but evil spirits from Hell. The knowledge kept people from coming to them, except on Halloween. That time of year, the brave or foolish would try their hand at ghost hunting, to be driven away by very active 'poltergeists.'

They extended their game to the neighboring warehouses, until their entire block was devoid of people and apparently full of demons. Which was perfectly alright by her, the further people stayed away from her warehouse, the better.

One year, when the children were about seven, they returned early from a shopping trip to find a drunken group of Bonecrushers, one of the local gangs whose territory butted against the warehouse district, carousing outside one of the larger buildings.

Oh, no, no, no, she thought in a rush, you will not be coming here and disturbing us. A great sense of indignation filled her chest and overflowed into her gut through her shoulders. How dare these people come to her home and put her children in danger? She put her shopping bags down and crept in the shadows as closely to the group as she dared. The four children were close behind her, clinging to the walls of the buildings. She stood for a long time in the one spot, watching them as they laughed and drank, obviously having no intention of going anywhere. She racked her brain for a way to make them go away.

"I'll take care of them, Mama," Ursus whispered, moving to pass her.

She grabbed his arm. The boy was as tall as she was now, but he was only seven. "They have guns," she whispered back, shaking her head. "Stay here."

Ursus stared her in the eye, his body tense, and she thought he would disobey her. Her heartbeat thumped not only in her chest but now in her ears, her mind going blank as to what she would do if the bear chose to move on without her permission. She knew that she would most likely not be strong enough to stop him. Then, Ursus relaxed and stood back against the wall again.

Céline looked back at the group of young men, a lull having fallen in their rowdiness. She took a deep breath in, and with her best singing voice, which was way out of practice, she belted out, "Leave!"

The group of young men jumped, looking in the direction that she and the children were hiding. They began to laugh nervously, two of them drawing handguns from the back of their pants.

"What was that?" one of them asked. He took a step in

their direction.

"Come out!" another called.

Dammit! What had Céline been thinking? Why in the world had she done that?

Ariste let out a feline growl, an otherworldly sound coming out of the dark so close to Céline's ears.

All of the young men stopped short at the sound.

"What the--?" The fear in the man's voice sent shivers down Céline's spine.

She whipped her head around to look at the kids behind her, her eyes wide in panic. Khenum was clomping into the light, while at the same time Ariste was scratching at the asphalt. Both were out of her arms reach. Her son stopped just outside of the shadows, his head down so his growing horns glinted in what little light there was. His eyes, their vertical pupils now merely slits, glared up at the men like a demon.

Céline fought the urge to run into the light between the men and Khenum and to grab Naga and Ursus and flatten them against the building. He's going to get shot. She waited for the bang of the pistols to start going off.

Ariste let out another growl in the shadows as Khenum huffed. His nostrils flared and sound from his exhale could almost be felt.

The young men broke out in a cacophony of swear words, turning and running toward more populated streets. One of them let out a string of shots in Kehnum's direction before following his comrades.

"Don't you come near me!" Céline heard one of them call. "You shot a demon, I don't want you near me!"

She paid them no more attention as their steps and voices faded. She ran toward Khenum, who still stood at the edge of the light. Upon reaching him, she hissed, "Where are you shot? Where are you shot?"

Ariste came out of the dark to stand next to him, her little body much shorter and slighter than his, her movements graceful.

"I'm not," Khenum replied. "I wasn't hit."

Céline's eyes shot to Ariste.

The cat shook her head. "I'm not hit either," she said, bringing her hands up to show her unharmed body.

Relief flooded Céline's body, relaxing her to the point that she lowered her head. Almost immediately, though, it was replaced by rage--one she hadn't felt in more years that she could remember. She snapped her head up, her green eyes intense. She raised both of her hands, and as if she was beating a drum, began to pound Khenum with one and Ariste with the other.

"Don't. You. Ever. Do. That. Again!" With each word, she whacked one of the animal children, Khenum in his shoulder and Ariste in her thigh. "Ever! Ever!" Neither child moved, though Ariste had tears forming her eyes. Céline didn't recognize her own voice, it was like someone else was speaking and she was listening from far away. Her arms buzzed with energy. The only way to dispel it seemed to be to hit something. With each punch on a child the energy seemed to disperse, almost with a soft golden glow. "Do you hear me!"

Ariste nodded.

"Yes, Mama," Khenum said, drawing the /a/ out with the bah.

Khenum's voice snapped Céline out of her thumping. She let out a small cry and raised her hands in the air to stop the rhythm she'd created with them. They felt too light and not quite attached to her body. Lowering them, she grabbed each one of their hands, and began pulling them back toward the warehouse.

She let out a sob, tears began to flow down her cheeks as she walked.

"Should I get the groccccceriesssss?" Naga asked behind her.

"Leave them," Céline managed to get out. She'd forgotten that all of them had been holding shopping bags when this started.

As time went on, they went on with it.

Slowly, the four of them pulled up the concrete in the lot adjacent to their warehouse, piling it in the corner. When the boys got older, they would heft it over the far side of the fence, until the pile dwindled to nothing. Then they tried to throw each other over. That only happened once before Céline put a stop to it with a hard tweak on their ears and a day spent in their shared bed with no entertainment. She filled the lot with plants, flowers, and vegetables. She wasn't a very good gardener, and it took her several tries to grow almost anything she tried to plant. When she saw a plant she wanted, she would take a cutting from it and carry it home.

"Isn't that stealing?" Ariste asked once. "You told us not to steal."

"Well," Céline sucked her lips in as she thought about how to explain it. "It isn't stealing because we are only taking a small piece of it."

"But we're still taking it," said Ursus, "and it isn't discarded."

"But it will grow back," Céline explained. "So we aren't really stealing, because we aren't killing the plant, and we aren't taking enough away to really notice." It was a stretch of the truth, but she brushed the occasional twinge of guilt away when she planted it.

She used English ivy along the chain link fence to block out the view from the street. In the place where she had buried Aquila, she planted a juniper bush. She thought that the berries might attract birds, and she felt that was an appropriate memorial.

Most of each night, however, was spent "shopping", diving through dumpsters and trash heaps for usable items. They went out after the sun had completely set, and it's orange afterglow had faded behind the water. With Naga wrapped around her arm, and Ariste, Ursus, and Khenum about her, they crept behind different types of stores and apartment buildings and rummaged through the garbage. They found a table, chairs, a desk, a couch (which was a doozy to get home), a television set, mattresses, beds, blankets, sheets, anything one would need to make a house a home. Granted it was dirty, and smelled, and none of it matched, but it was all unbroken. She even found a bookcase, made of solid wood. Khenum, she found out, was a strong little lamb, and with Ursus' and Ariste's help, she was able to get even the couch back to the warehouse. It took longer to clean the top floor of the warehouse than it did to find the furnishings for it, the surplus in the dumpsters was so abundant.

The best find, however, in Céline's opinion, was the dumpster behind a bookstore. It was filled with books. She couldn't believe that bookstores threw away books! Each of the covers was torn off the front, but she didn't care. She brought arm loads of them home whenever they were close by, and read through them voraciously. Books about flowers, books about robots, books about plumbing, books about motorcycles, books with love stories, books with hate stories, books with serious stories, and books with short stories.

They would watch one of the six stations that they got on the bunny ears of their little television. They watched Sesame Street, Barney, Touring Chicago with Sidney Mayer, and Painting With Bob Ross. NOVA was one of Céline's favorites.

The diamond, though, which could be found anywhere, like buried treasure on a deserted island, was a notebook with blank pages in which she could write down her thoughts. The next best thing was a notebook written in pencil, but finding erasers to empty the pages was another matter altogether. She never thought that a diary would be so important, but she understood, now, why in the past it was. The days bled into each other, time seemed surreal. Writing down her impressions or what even the mundane things that happened during the days and nights made it a real thing. It assured her she wasn't going crazy.

She taught the kids to stay in the shadows. They regularly met vagrants, gang members, and homeless people on the streets, and Céline made a point to talk to them. She was desperate sometimes to talk to someone, anyone. Most of the homeless people, she discovered, were mentally ill in some way, to the point that it took only talking to a certain individual for five or ten minutes to determine they weren't quite right in the head. The children became very good at being invisible, and they also became very good at being very frightening if they thought Céline was in danger. Naga kept her arms tucked under her as she was wound around Céline's arm, and looked like an ordinary snake, a beautiful dark green with even darker green triangles traveling up her body to crest at her head.

She had seen a homeless man with a garbage bag, standing outside of a dumpster. He was rummaging through it, and she could see that it had produce in it. "Where did you get that?" she asked, amazed.

The homeless man, dirty and disheveled, looked her up and down, looked at the snake on her arm, and said, "You get it at the grocery store. They throw food away all the time."

And he was right.

No longer did they rely on restaurant cast offs for their food, but were able to actually stock their warehouse with food like any other family. They had to obtain another bookshelf to put their goods on. She was even able to give food away to the people she met on the street, she found so much.

Céline was constantly amazed at what people threw away. Grocery stores threw food away all the time. Perfectly good food. Still in the packaging. They threw away cans, boxes, produce, breads, juice, and any number of other items.

Despite having been taken care of all of her life, she found she could take care of the five of them.

And so, days turned into weeks, turned into months, turned into years, and Céline and her children fell into an easy rhythm of life.

# Chapter 12

**CLASSIFIED TOP SECRET**
**PROJECT SANCTUARY**

To:
Washington DC

From: Flayne Institute Experimental Facility
Chicago, Illinois

Subject: Land Branch Commander Transformation

has finally brought a live subject through the moreau transformation process. The former Russian agent survived the procedure fully intact into the intended subject of a human-rat hybrid. The desired characteristics of a mostly human body, save for digitgrade feet and less than human flexible five fingered hands with the qualities wanted in the land commander thought to be helpful in the DNA of rattus norvegicus; wiliness, extreme resiliency, ability to withstand extreme food and water deprivation, strong loyalty to a group while being able to think creatively and independently. With the subject's past as a spetsnaz agent, we are fully confident that his personality traits and that of the rattus norvegicus will produce the product the Therian Initiative is looking for.

Signed: Agent

# Chapter 13

Ilya answered the knock on his door, and the sea otter, Dyson, entered his room. While the table had been set for two, the supper had not yet arrived. The only consumable on it was a bottle of Russian vodka.

"Come in," Ilya moved out of the way of the door to allow Dyson to enter.

The sea otter was taller than him, his elongated neck ended in a small head, with little semi-circle ears on either side at the top. He came into the room, bobbing his head slightly, as Ilya had noted many of the moreaus who were taller than him did. He guessed it was a sign of respect, though there had never been any spoken agreement with anyone that it was necessary.

Ilya closed the door behind him, and motioned him to the table. "Would you like a glass of vodka?"

Dyson chuckled, and nodded his head.

Ilya had a weakness for good vodka. When he was human, he spent his money on the best. Russki Standart, a wheat vodka, made from the softest water in the world and filtered through quartz, there was nothing better. It had taken a none-too-small portion of his paycheck, something that had not been that large to begin with. Here, at Flayne Institute., he was provided with all the Russki Standart he could drink. All he had to do was let the dining staff know that he was out, and a new bottle would arrive within a few minutes.

The rat poured two Russian shot glasses, taller than the tiny American things that held nothing, and much more pleasing to the eye, with a tapered body and heavy bottom. He handed Dyson his, and held up his own. "Vashe zdorovie!" To your health! he said.

"Cheers!" said Dyson, and the two of them downed the glasses. Dyson began to cough, putting his glass down so he wouldn't drop it.

Ilya laughed heartily, and reached over to pat him hard on the shoulder.

"I don't know how you can do that," Dyson coughed.

Ilya took on an offended look, his eyebrows raising and his mouth drawing back. "This is good vodka!" he exclaimed. "Smooth and sweet going down."

"I've been practicing, and I still can't…"

"Babies drink vodka in Russia," Ilya told him, with a shake of his head. "You need to practice more."

Dyson laughed, and took another sip of his drink, albeit a much smaller one this time. As he did, a knock came to the door and Ilya got up to open it. Dinner service was ready, wheeling in a cart to the rat's quarters and laying the items down on the table. Dyson looked at the spread, his eyes wide. "I…I thought…" he stuttered.

"That I got better food than all of you?" Ilya finished for him, smiling. At Dyson's slow nod, Ilya shook his head. "No," he assured him, "I get good vodka. My food is the same as everyone else's. I just get to eat it in my room." He gestured for Dyson to sit down at the table.

They ate, and chatted about everyday things. Ilya

recognized the dance now, when his students had something they wanted to talk to him about, something they found important, they would comment on all kinds of things that had nothing to do with the subject that was on their minds. They spoke about the Sea Otter Team, so Ilya knew Dyson's issue was not with any of his teammates. They spoke of Dr. Theedy, the doctor who was in charge of the sea otters. She was a weasley looking woman, with large glasses and a non-too-kind countenance. Ilya did not know much of her personally, but from what he'd heard through the grapevine, he was not upset that she was not his doctor. So, the problem was not with her. They spoke briefly of Dr. Montgomery, who did not have much to do with the moreaus after the transformation process, save for Ilya himself, and things that involved the entirety of the program. Ilya did not discuss him much, he didn't feel it was right. To him, it was like talking about a superior officer behind his back to one's subordinates. Dyson commented on how sparsely decorated Ilya's space was, and the rat knew that the conversation was coming closer to home.

Dyson had a few shots of vodka in him, and unlike the Systema warrior, did not have the tolerance for the Russian shot glasses of it. It took little time for him to come to the issue at hand. The sea otter looked down sheepishly, and Ilya was sure he would have blushed if he had still been human. "I want to steal things," he said quietly.

Ilya did not answer him.

"I want to pick things up, take them, and hide them under my bed where no one can find them." He looked up, shame on his face. Ilya felt his heart clench. "And it's dumb stuff. It's stuff like, etched glasses from the cafeteria, or aluminium foil, or shells." The man's eyes lit up at the last word. "I love shells. Whenever we eat clams, I want to take every last shell on my plate and stuff them in my pockets to take back to my room."

"Have you taken anything?" Ilya asked.

Dyson nodded, wincing.

Ilya was all too familiar with the urge to take things. Shiny things, or silky things. At one point, not long after his transformation, different shiny items began to show up in the decor in places he frequented. He wasn't sure if they'd always been there, or if he had just then paid enough attention to see they were there. At first, he would reach out and pick the item up to examine it, as if it were a new toy he'd been given, even though it wasn't his. He was entranced with the way the light played off of the material it was made of, how it felt under his fingers. He liked little things the best, he had come to realize through his self-observation, that glittered and had lots of facets. For a while, many of these types of objects were put in his path, mixed with larger ones of different sizes and textures. He had pocketed more than one before he realized what was going on.

He was being baited. Whenever a new, shiny item appeared in a room, Dr. Montgomery was also in that room, whether it be the dining room, the gymnasium, the bathroom. The doctor watched Ilya very intently as the rat examined things, trying not to be too obvious. When he had figured it out, he had been meditating on the lyrics of a hymn. The knowledge that he was being tested, that he was still, after the transformation, an experiment to be observed and manipulated, infuriated him. He had brought all the little shiny things back to Dr. Montgomery's office, and spat, "These do not belong to me. You can have them back," before scattering them on the desk. The decor was much more stable after that.

"Have you done the research I suggested you do?" asked Ilya, putting his hands under his chin.

Dyson nodded slowly. "Sea otters like to cache things in hidden places..." his voice sounded as if he had just admitted he had stolen a piece of candy from the store.

"So do sea otter moreaus, it seems," Ilya replied.

Dyson looked at him with forlorn eyes.

He was not ready to do this. When he was put in charge of training, he was thinking of human beings, and when he discovered they would not be human beings, he had not expected the animal instincts that he would encounter. Instead of just fighting his own, he had to give counsel to others in how to fight theirs. He felt so inadequate at it.

"You must decide what it is you want to do with this…desire," Ilya told him.

"I don't know what to do with it," Dyson whispered.

"I fight it," Ilya said, taking another drink of his vodka. "I do not pick an item up unless I am going to use it or take it. I do not pick anything up to examine it."

Dyson looked around Ilya's quarters, "You don't decorate much…"

Ilya shook his head. "It helps," he said gently. "That way, I am not looking for something to decorate my surroundings with, and the urge is less."

"It's like a drug," Dyson admitted, his face a mask of misery. "I want to do it all the time, and it is so hard to fight."

Ilya nodded. "Yes," he answered in the same quiet voice. "I imagine it will always be that way, somewhat." With Dyson's look of desperation, he continued, "But maybe not. Maybe, over time, this is something we will get over."

"How are we ever going to get over being animals?" Dyson said bitterly.

Ilya was quiet for a moment. "We remember our humanity," he said simply. "Remember it every moment of every day."

# Chapter 14

Céline had decided, early on in her life after the death of Céline Ilorsaint, that she would not lose another one of these little things to her ignorance. It was not one of those decisions that one comes to logically, after thinking through all of the variables and going through all of the formulas. It was one of those decisions that one comes to one simply because they come to it, and agree to keep it.

One early winter together, she had her first real scare with losing one of them. It was bitterly cold. They found construction plastic and affixed it to the broken windows to keep the cold air out. They found an old car wheel, and piled it with anything that would burn. Fallen sticks from trees became a prized commodity, and frequent visits to parks and wild areas at night became common.

Despite her attempts to keep them warm, they were always cold. In bed together, whatever part of their bodies wasn't touching someone else was cold. Awake together, the part of their bodies that wasn't facing the fire was cold. Eating together, unless the warm food was going down their stomachs, their insides were cold.

Céline had never taken much stock in the saying, "The cold and wet will make you sick." She had taken biology 101, sickness is caused by a bacteria or a virus, not the temperature. The cold does not suppress the immune system, so a bacteria or virus can't take hold any easier than it could in the summer. The cold just made you uncomfortable, not sick. But this winter, she understood why people believed it.

All three mammals caught some sort of chest cold. It started out as just a cough, things that sounded like barks and breathy, short growls. Then, the coughs became more persistent, and the barking sound turned into something that sounded rough and scrappy, coming from deep in the chests of Ariste, Ursus, and Khenum.

None of them could talk yet. Ariste could say a mew that sounded like "Mama," and when she shouted at her brothers in frustration, the shout was more like a human voice than a cat's cry. Céline had an awful time communicating with them, and was terrified they did not understand what she said.

She knew that they did, though. But that did not make the fear go away.

"Khenum," she said from corner of the large warehouse floor, the area she was making into a kitchen, slowly but surely. She had a hot plate, pots and pans, a tea kettle, bowls, plates, mugs, and flatware. She was constantly boiling water, as she had no idea whatsoever how to get the hot water heater in the building to work. She put whatever she could find in the liquid to make it taste, and sometimes, it was just hot water, sipped to keep them warm. She had found some old bouillon cubes, past their expiration date, and she placed one in each of the four mugs in front of her. She was switching them off between the broth and thyme tea. The thyme, found in a huge bag in the health food store dumpster, was supposed to help with their chests. She hadn't noticed anything yet.

He left the fire pit and came to her quickly, gingerly taking a mug by the handle in each hand, and walking slowly over to his new siblings. It was the little lamb's turn to help carry them over. All three of the walking little ones had learned early that walking too fast with the mug burned their hands. None of them had repeated the experience. Céline was glad, at least they learned from their mistakes, even if they weren't talking.

Naga was still on her arm, and Céline was scared to take her off. Being a snake, she didn't know if she was warm-blooded as a moreau or cold-blooded, and decided she would rather not find out. So she left the little thing wrapped about her arm, her head mostly tucked in Céline's shirt near her breast in an effort to keep warm. Occasionally she would feel the flick of the child's tongue against her skin, and it would send cold shivers down her body.

As Khenum and Céline came with the mugs, Ursus broke out into a great coughing fit. It seemed like he couldn't get any air in his lungs before another started. Céline spilled the liquid in the mugs she was holding in both of her hands as she hurried over to him. Putting the mugs down, placing a hand on his chest, and another on his back, she began to rub furiously. She had absolutely no idea what else to do.

Medicine was an item that she had a difficult time finding. There was almost none of it in the trash, and the ones they did find tended to be items they could not have used anyway. Painkillers were nonexistent, antibiotics could occasionally be found, but only one or two pills were left in the bottle. Occasionally they would find gas medicine, or allergy pills, but none of them needed any of that.

The bookstore frequently threw away books on herbs, and she amassed quite a collection. Luckily for her, most of the medicinal herbs that were indicated were weeds. She found them growing in vacant lots, on the side of the highway, even in sidewalks. It was easy to transplant entire plants into the garden. She used them on a regular basis when the four were little, healing cuts and bruises, and colds and headaches. They tasted atrocious, but they worked. However, with it being winter, they were in very short supply. She managed to get some in the fall, before the plants began to die off, but now she was stuck with only what she had.

And that was very little.

After rubbing Ursus to calm him, she took out one of the herbal books, in desperation to find something. As if something is going to pop up out of the page to miraculously heal them? she thought derisively. She had some strange hope that it would be so, she knew, even though it was ridiculous.

She read through the list of herbs for chest colds and coughs; coltsfoot, mullein, liquorice, marshmallow, violet, red poppy. She didn't have any of those! She couldn't get any of those this time of year! She kept reading; lobelia, flaxseed, cherry bark, hyssop…

"Cherry bark?" she said. She looked at the word again, was she reading it right, or had the cold gotten to her brain?

How many times had she read this passage before? She had sections of it memorized! But she had always read 'cherry blossoms' not cherry bark. She looked up at each of the kids, drinking their mugs, their eyes bleary, coughs coming sporadically from their mouths. She looked down at the book again.

It said cherry bark.

She could get cherry bark.

She could get so much cherry bark she wouldn't know what to do with it!

"Potty!" she said, standing up.

The three of them followed suit, all putting their mugs down and filing toward the little workman's toilet near the entrance of the floor. Getting them to go in the potty was a hit or miss action, mostly miss with Naga, mostly hit with Ariste, and somewhere in-between with the two boys. She managed to get Naga to pee in the pot this go around by lifting her tail off of her arm and holding it over the toilet. Everyone else had no issues at all.

She bundled them all up even more than they were, if someone saw them walking, they wouldn't even know they were not human children trudging behind their mother in the snow in broad daylight. All that showed on any of them were their eyes, and they were so deep within the recesses of the myriad of scarves she wrapped on them that they were only two holes out of which to look at the world.

With an old kitchen knife in her coat and plastic shopping bags stuffed in everyone's pockets, she led them all to Jackson Park, miles away. The walk warmed them as they moved, walking always did. She was loath to start it, it meant going outside, away from the fire pit, to brave the wind. But once they got moving, and blood began pumping in their veins, she was always glad of it.

The sun glinted beautifully off of the bare trees, many of them cherries in abandoned front yards, and she made a note to come to them on the way back home. Jackson Park was just as beautiful as the walk there, as if the plants were made of crystal, and a specially made light was shining down on them in their display cases to make them sparkle just so. Toward the center of the park, away from parking lots and at the end of paths, was The Garden of the Phoenix. In it, she knew from experience, was a plethora of cherry trees, more than 120 to be exact.

She started in the back of the garden, completely empty of people, and with the knife, began to peel off the outer bark of one of the lower branches. She didn't know how much she could take or from where so as not to damage the tree. "If this hurts it," she explained to the wrapped up little ones about her, "then only this branch will die. Surely branches die all the time from animals breaking them and things," she looked questioningly at Ariste, as if the kitten had an answer for her. She didn't.

She had each of the children hold open a plastic bag, which they did shakily in between coughs, as she shaved inner bark into them. They slowly filled, and they drifted from tree, to tree, to tree, until she had six bags full, each child carrying two.

The journey home was punctuated with stops to other cherry trees, which obtained the same treatment. Naga was tucked firmly inside Céline's clothes, so she could not carry anything, and it fell to Céline to make up the slack. She ended up returning home with 16 grocery bags of shaved cherry bark.

She started a large pasta pot of water, dumped as much of the bark in it as she could without stuffing it down, which ended up being about 4 bags. Then, she let it simmer.

The herbal said to let it simmer for 10 to 12 hours, but the coughing of the no-longer unidentifiable children did not abate with their return to the indoors. As soon as the water began to turn yellow, she began to ladle it out into mugs and hand it to the kids. They all drank it up, and when she tasted it, it tasted faintly sweet. "This isn't bad," she said to them with a smile. All three of them looked up at her and smiled back.

After three cups, it began to work.

After that day, their coughs had changed from awful barks to proper coughs.

On a food run a few days later, they found several bottles of garlic powder. She brought it home, made garlic margarine, smeared it on bread, and made them all eat it all day long.

Three days after that, the cough was gone.

She still met homeless people on her outings for supplies, and felt awful for many of them. They were cold, and haggard, and stuffy and coughing. To make up for her guilt at Ghost, she tried to help the homeless people she met with her herbal medicines. Her first one was dried cherry bark for cough, a cup every two hours until the symptoms are gone, then every four hours, then every five, then six, then twice a day. She became quite proficient at diagnosing people, and when she was lucky, the unbidden thought would tell her what was the matter. She would give her herbs freely to the men and women they passed, leaving her children in the shadows, and returning to them once she'd administered to them. She helped to heal infections mainly, headaches, and chest colds. The chest colds were the hardest, because she had to keep returning to the patient with a new batch of herbs and the person had to use them on a regular basis until they were well. Many simply did not. She began to understand a doctor's frustration at "patient noncompliance".

# Chapter 15

Ilya poured himself a cup of black tea from the silver teapot and opened The Chicago Tribune. It was his morning ritual before going off to practice, a time to do something normal, something…human. The rustle of the paper, the smell of ink, the black smudges that it left on his hands were all familiar sensations from his life in Russia when he read the paper every morning. While it was not the Moskovskaya Pravda, it was better than watching the news on the television.

He read it cover to cover, every day, and today a particular article caught his eye.

Husband of Renau Heiress to Return to Haiti.

It has been a year and half since Céline Renau Ilorsaint went missing after a Chicago poetry reading. The former gymnastics champion was voted one of the 'Poets To Look For' by Poets and Poetry Magazine. When she did not return home from a reading she was giving, she was reported as missing by her husband. The investigation turned cold almost immediately, having few clues to go on.

Mrs. Ilorsaint was the heiress, along with her brother

Phillip, of the Candaian based Renau Company fortune, before her marriage to Ilorsaint. After her family took her out of the company's paperwork, the Association for Civil Rights of All Colors encouraged a boycott of the company and all of their subsidiaries. The call for a boycott is still in effect.

Stephane Ilorsaint said in a written press release last Thursday, "After much debate, I have decided to return to my native country of Haiti with my two children Jacques and Lisabetta. The chances of us having our beloved wife and mother returned to us are low. With the devastation of having lost my wife, along with having the lack of support from her family and the harassment of the media, I feel returning to my family in my homeland is the safest course of action for my children."

The Renau family had no comment.

There was a family picture of the Ilorsaints, all smiling happily into the camera. A little woman, her skin pale in the photo, with auburn hair, held a baby in her lap, the color of chocolate milk. The man, whose skin was like chocolate itself, held a little girl, the same as her baby brother. They were all beautiful people, those kind of beautiful people you see in magazines. He knew that they probably weren't as beautiful in real life, where the fuzz of the newspaper printing process erased all of the imperfections in their looks, but in the picture, they were striking. He guessed, from the association that issued the boycott, that the woman's family had disowned her for marrying a black man. It happened in Russia all the time, on both sides of the marriage. Interracial couples were not looked upon favorably, and it would appear they were not here in the States, either.

He read over the press release quote again, something about it bothered him. "The chances of us having our beloved wife and mother returned to us are low." This woman was his wife. She gave up a fortune for him. After 18 months, he had stopped looking for her to return home, because of "lack of support from her family" and "harassment of the media"? Solving the harassment of the media was an easy problem, you put a boot up someone's ass. No support from her family? So what? What kind of wimp of a man needs the support of his wife's family? Did he not have friends to support him? His family could give him emotional support from over the phone, plenty of people lived that way. Several of the wives of his teammates had done it, being foreign, the large phone bill was simply another part of the woman's upkeep. You want a good woman, you let her call her mamma. Could his family not have done the same thing?

This man was giving up on his wife, after only a year and a half. He was no man. He was a coward.

He finished his tea, put the newspaper down, now irritated with it and himself for letting a newspaper article rattle him so.

He grabbed his exercise mat and went to the gym, the next part of his normal routine after newspaper and tea. He was the first one there, he always was. He liked it that way, it gave him time to ground and center, to think upon things that needed to be thought about, and to let go of things that needed to be released. He rolled the mat out in the middle of the floor, and stood in the middle of it—the center of the center. Life was all about going to the center, and then the center of that, and then center of that, until there was only Life itself, which has no beginning and no end, so there can be no center. He relaxed his body, held his spine straight, put his rat's feet shoulder width apart, and put his hands at his sides. When he was human, having a very slight bend to his knees was part of the process, but now, his legs were bent in their natural position, it was making them straight he had to work at.

He inhaled, tensing each of his body parts as he did so, starting with his scalp, and moving down in tiny increments; his temples, jaw, end of his muzzle, neck, upper shoulders, lower shoulders, upper back, chest, upper arms, lower back, lower arms, belly, hips, buttocks, upper tail, thighs, calves, lower tail, feet, and then toes. With the completion of the inhale, all of his muscles were tensed, and when he exhaled, the tension left him, out through his breath, into the ether where it would not return to him.

He took inventory of his body, where the tension was being held, and did the exercise again. He would do it as often as he needed to, to release all the tension in his body. A tense body was not a free one. In order to fight, the body needed to be free.

His mind drifted again to the newspaper article. Americans did not take care of their women. He would not say that the Russians were the epitome of gentlemanly behavior, but they took better care than the Americans did. They walked a woman home to keep her safe, they bought her items, they kept her well dressed and beautified, women were given half of a Friday off to see to her domestic affairs. Here, in the States, a man was not looked down upon because he abandoned the search for his wife after a year and half. The man's wife had been beautiful, had given him two beautiful children, had given up a great deal, obviously to be with him. What was the matter with this Stephane Ilorsaint?

"I would not have stopped looking for her," he said to himself, as he let the tension roll out of his body.

"You talk to yourself now, Ilya Pytrovich?"

The rat looked up to see Ayah entering. After weeks of practicing together, he recognized the splay of the goshawk's feathers, an indication that the air commander was sending blood to his extremities, in preparation for their morning workout. He smiled broadly at his aerial counterpart. "I was thinking of an article I read in the paper," he replied.

"Which one?" he asked, clasping the rat on the shoulder.

Ilya shook his head, "It doesn't matter." He walked to the center of the gym, Ayah following him. They bowed to each other, then took a large step backwards, increasing the distance between them.

"If you didn't think about stuff so much," Ayah said, turning his head to the side, "you wouldn't be so bothered about things."

"Who says I am bothered?" Ilya asked.

"I do," Ayah raised his arms, and with a powerful downward stroke, his taloned feet left the floor. Each stroke took him higher up into the air, looking down at the rat moreau. "You get all broody. And obviously you start talking to yourself."

Ilya laughed, his eyes never leaving the hawk in the air. "Talking to oneself is a sign of mental health."

"I thought that was a sign of mental illness," Ayah replied. But before waiting for an answer, he swooped down, drawing his wings back, and dived at Ilya.

The rat moreau jumped out of the way, twisting as he did, whipping his tail toward the goshawk. Ayah pivoted in the air, a taloned foot reaching out to grab at Ilya's tail. It slipped through his toes, so that both opponents were once again standing off.

"That was weak," Ayah reproached.

"I had a poor morning," Ilya shrugged. "The article in the paper disturbed me."

"Your enemy doesn't care that you're disturbed by an article in the paper," Ayah replied, swooping down once more.

Ilya ducked and rolled, avoiding the space where Ayah landed. His legs hit the ground with a hard clack before he took off again. The goshawk dove at him. Ilya held his hand up, his other striking out to hit Ayah's shoulder. Ayah twirled in the air, but caught himself before he lost too much control. He landed on the ground a little less gracefully than he would have wanted, Ilya knew.

"Not bad," Ayah smiled.

Ilya stood up straight, smiling. He gestured for Ayah to continue. "You talk too much," he told him.

The goshawk laughed loudly, a sound much like a hawk's cry. "Then no more talking," he said, taking to the air once more, to spar with the rat until the Systema master's students arrived.

# Chapter 16

Finding The Garden of the Phoenix was a blessing that Céline had not counted on when she'd gone looking for cherry bark. It was run down, once a beautiful place that was now overgrown, unpruned, and abandoned. It was littered with condoms, needles, syringes, plastic wrappers, and beer bottles and cans. However, it was filled with beautiful and excellent for climbing cherry trees, surrounded by a lagoon. The place burst with wildlife, birds and woodland creatures of all kinds, the lagoon swam with fish, frogs, turtles, and insects galore.

She brought the children there to play at least once a week, to give them a different view than just the industrial warehouses that made up their home, and only a parking lot as a garden. They would run free, climbing and swinging like little monkeys, jumping from branch to branch like squirrels, and swimming in the lagoon like little fish. She loved to watch them, they all moved beautifully, but in different ways.

Ariste could climb the trees quite well, she beat all of her siblings into the branches. But her specialty was jumping and swinging. Once she was up the trunk of the tree, she could leap from branch to branch as if it were nothing. As she got older, she leapt from tree to tree, testing her distance to go farther and farther afield. She swam with passivity, not particularly fast, not particularly slow, and not particularly enjoying it. Her movements were sinuous and rippled, her tail occasionally flicking, but mostly held out to keep her balance.

Ursus was an excellent climber, but had a very difficult time following his siblings with their jumping. He was a powerful swimmer, though, using all four of his limbs to swim in a type of doggie paddle that she imagined an actual bear doing. His actions were more lumbering and slow, a careful methodical kind of movement, much like his personality.

Khenum had a more difficult time getting up the trees, but once he was up, like Ariste, he could jump up and out with little issue at all, often chasing his sister in an attempt to out-do her. His hoof-like feet did not seem suited for climbing up the cherries, but he did very well on any flat surface, a holdover, Céline guessed, from the mountain goat DNA that ran through his veins. Unlike Ariste, whose jumping was smooth and almost internally rhythmic, Khenum's jumps were exercises in pure leg muscle. He would squat slightly, his thigh muscles bunching up visibly, before springing to the next branch above his head. His swimming matched that of Ursus, a slow methodical movement, using all four of his limbs to doggie paddle his way through the water, though he wasn't as fast as his bear brother.

Naga, when she actually let go of her mother's body, was almost hypnotic to watch. She climbed the tree quickly, her body twisting its way up the trunk in some way that she didn't fall off of it. With no legs, and not using her arms to keep a hold of the trunk, Céline wasn't sure how she did it. She traversed the branches the same way, a winding motion that propelled her forward. Often, when in the same tree, she would stretch out her body, balancing on her powerful tail, to reach the next branch up or over, and then begin her twisting again. When she reached the end of the branch, and wished to go to the next tree, she launched her body in the air, looking as if she used no muscles at all, and flew like a bird to the branch, and never once missed. Her swimming was powerful, and while she could not keep up with her brothers and sister in the tree, she darted by them in the water, her body undulating from side to side, creating only a ripple in her wake.

When Céline brought them to the garden, she also brought a flashlight. It gave the illusion of the police coming, and she found that it made those people who were in the garden when they arrived, scatter. If the flashlight and call out from her did not work, a growl from Ursus usually did.

Céline kept the kids to little sections of the garden as she cleaned it up, slowly but surely. She had them all wear plastic grocery bags on their hands in lieu of latex gloves to protect them, and told them not to touch any needles, but to tell her and she'd deal with them. The kids helped her for the first ten minutes they were there, then ran off to play. They asked her about the items they found, and she felt hard pressed as to what to tell them.

"Some people," she finally said, "are hurting very badly in their hearts."

"Like when Khenum calls me nasty names," Naga asked.

Khenum huffed, but Céline answered before he could say anything in return. "1000 times more hurt than that," she said.

Naga gasped, as if such a feeling was not possible.

"Because they are hurting inside of their hearts so badly, they do things to try and make the hurt go away."

"How do needles and cans and those little rubber tubes make the hurt go away?" Ariste asked.

She took a deep breath, not wanting to explain. "It isn't the needles or the cans that make the people feel better, what is in them. And it doesn't really make them feel better, it just makes them forget."

"Why is forgetting bad, if it hurts you?" Ursus asked.

"Because you can do more hurtful things while you're forgetting," she explained, "and then you have even more hurt in your heart. You have to heal your heart, not forget."

Her own forgetfulness, brought on by trauma she supposed, haunted her at times like this, when she had to talk about healing hearts. 18 months of her life were cut out of her consciousness, and she was sure she'd done no healing from it. Whenever she thought about it, whenever she saw the date on that newspaper in her mind's eye, her heart would beat furiously in her chest. She could feel it in her neck, and if she didn't quell it, it grabbed at her head. She had to take deep belly breaths and name all the things she was grateful for, all the things that were blessings in her life, to get her heart rate to calm down. A hurt inside of oneself needed to heal, but how could you heal if you didn't remember?

"Like when I have to forgive Khenum for calling me a nasty name?" Naga asked.

Céline smiled, "That's a start," she said.

"What is inside these rubber tubes that makes you forget," Khenum held up a flaccid condom.

Céline pursed her lips together, and thought furiously of an answer. "It isn't what comes out of them that makes you forget," she said. "It's what goes into them."

Khenum put it in his garbage grocery bag, and asked, "What goes into them?"

"I'll tell you," Céline answered, "when you're older."

# Chapter 17

Ilya left his door open, so the goshawk could come in without knocking. Quite a while ago, they had decided that Ayah's rooms were much too decorated for the rat's taste. His paws itched to pick up items, and when Ilya caught himself doing so more than once, their meeting place changed from flip flopping from one set of suites to the other, to just Ilya's.

Ayah's feathers ruffled as he threw his head back and laughed, beak open. He put the rocks glass down before he spilled any of his drink. He, like Ilya, had to tip it up and pour the contents into his rigid beak. "That can't be right," he managed to get out. "You're lying."

Ilya did a poor job of holding his own laughter in. "It is true," he said. "That is why I do not understand what people tell me. I would never have told that old leather shoe that was my commander these things!"

"Oh," Ayah shook his head, "you haven't heard the doozies."

"If complaining about why he likes her and she doesn't like him is not a doozy, I do not want to know the doozies," the rat put his paws out in front of him, as if to ward the doozies off.

"You haven't gotten any of the, 'Why does my body do this?' questions?" Ayah asked incredulously.

Ilya's gray eyes went wide. "Da," he drawled. "Too many times, about too many things."

Ayah's chocolate eyes twinkled, his head twitched to the right. "A few of your troops come to talk to me," he said conspiratorially.

Ilya raised his brows. What were his troops going to Ayah for? The goshawk was in charge of the flying division, those moreaus that had been combined with birds to make up the airborne fighting force. Was he not trustworthy as a confidant? He had not told a single soul anything that any of those under him had entrusted him with. He fought being hurt by the admission and being angry by Ayah's admission of it.

"They've all been female," Ayah turned to look at the rat with one eye. "Confiding how they feel about their teacher, Ilya Pytrovich." He winked.

Ilya's mouth fell open. Had he been inappropriate any time, that his female students would feel uncomfortable toward him? He didn't think so. In fact, he worked very hard to be distant, to be a good teacher, to treat them like the men, so they would be worthwhile soldiers—soldiers that came home after battle. "I beg your pardon?"

Ayah threw his head back and laughed. "You don't know how many of your female students have a crush on you?"

The rat shook his head, "A crush?"

"Yeah," Ayah leaned forward, his head tilting to the side quickly. "It means they like you."

"Why would they tell you they liked me?" Ilya asked, his face a mask of confusion.

"Because they like you," he repeated slowly, the end of his beak extended as far as it would go in a smile, only a small curve upward toward his brown eyes. "You don't indulge, do you?"

Again, Ilya's dark brown brows drew together and he held up his drink.

"No," Ayah shook his head. It was always disconcerting to Ilya, the hawk's movements were jerky. "With women."

Blinking his gray eyes and dropping his ears to his head, Ilya chittered his teeth. "No," he replied. "That would be inappropriate."

"In what way?" Ayah asked.

"I'm their teacher. And if what you say is true—"

"—it is," Ayah cut in.

"—Then I will be their commanding officer. It would not be right for me to take advantage that way."

"It isn't taking advantage," Ayah waved a wing at him. "Not if she wants to sleep with you."

"And then what happens when it is over?" Ilya put his own drink down. "When it is the next morning?"

"It doesn't matter," Ayah said. "Because she'll be in her bed, and you'll be in yours."

Ilya tilted his head in the opposite direction of the goshawk. "Honestly?" His accent was thick.

"Ilya," Ayah said. "Have you looked in the mirror lately?"

The rat bristled. He looked in the mirror every day, and had yet to get used to what it was he saw.

"Morality is out the window. You're hanging on to some useless form of chivalry that won't serve you." The goshawk leaned forward, his avian eyes unblinking. "You aren't going to have a normal life, Ilya. No wife, no family, only brothers and sisters in arms. You might as well enjoy it."

"How can you enjoy it?" Ilya asked, his ears fully forward. "Knowing she will be hurt in the morning?"

"You don't choose the ones that will get hurt," Ayah

huffed. "You can't tell me you didn't screw around when you were human." He laughed. "You're Russian, for God sake!"

He chittered his teeth again, but stopped when he realized he was doing it. He was not going to act like an animal when he was upset. He took a deep breath through his nose, out of his mouth.

"But now you're too good to sleep with a woman?" Ayah asked, waving a wing in his direction.

Ilya blinked slowly. "No," he drawled.

"Oh, I see," Ayah leaned back, picking up his rocks glass again. "Can't sleep with an animal."

"Ayah," Ilya's voice was tight.

"Then what is it?" Ayah asked. When Ilya did not answer, Ayah laughed, throwing his head back. "Oh-ho-ho," he finally blinked. "You don't choose the women who aren't hurt in the morning. You're a softie." He reached over the table and poked Ilya in the shoulder. "Your loss, my friend. There are many a lady waiting for you, when you decide not to be so chivalrous."

"And what, pray tell," Ilya asked through a grim mouth, "do you tell these many ladies when they come to you?"

"I tell them it is normal to have a crush on your commander," he said. "And they should concentrate on becoming a better soldier."

Ilya let out a slow breath in relief.

"And now, I will tell them to put their attention elsewhere, because Ilya Pytrovich is too much of a gentleman to indulge in such things."

# Chapter 18

Though the bookstore was one of her and the children's favorite spots, Céline had to be careful about what books she read. At first, she devoured everything, all of their arms were laden with reading material of every kind. It was her escape, a way to pass the time with nothing else to do. She read out loud to the children, who listened intently to the picture books they picked up, and then thumbed through them themselves. They tore the pages when they were young, and Céline didn't mind. They already had the covers torn off of them, after all. They found them in the garbage, what difference did it make if the pages were torn by a hand that had trouble turning them? She read to herself when the children were asleep, losing herself in other people's worlds. Nightmares plagued her for years, indistinct things, with dark hulking shadows, and phantom pain coursing her body. When it occurred to her that it might have something to do with her book selection, she had to slowly eliminate genres from her reading, like an elimination diet to find out what one was allergic to.

Horror was easy to get rid of, she'd done that already.

Reading about ghosts, monsters, aliens, and just plain demented human beings was too close to real life now. These kinds of books, along with making her heart pound so loudly she could hear it in her head, caused very physically painful nightmares. She would awake to stabbing pains in her scars at her temples and in her abdomen.

Mysteries made her dream of dead bodies, or being chased, or being found out. She would be trapped in the warehouse, unable to get out without being shot by tranquilizer darts and bullets.

Science fiction and fantasy would cause her dreams to become strange, amorphous things involving children and awful monsters chasing them. Sometimes the children were hers, both from before she died and afterward, and sometimes they were just dream children, belonging to no one in particular.

When she read romance novels, she would dream of Stephane, or an old boyfriend, or some made up man conjured up from her subconscious, and wake up aching in between her legs, with a dire need for a cold shower. It did her no good to indulge in the need by herself, for it only reminded her of how she had greatly enjoyed practicing the conception of her two birth children and how Stephane had been particularly good at it. She stopped reading novels altogether, and eventually the need in the middle of the night did not return, and she was both glad and sad about it.

Any of these times when she woke up, she would sit up, cross her legs, and meditate as she'd been taught by her yoga instructor in college. She had resented it when she first learned how to do it. Her gymnastics coach prescribed it as a cure for her hurting torso and shin splints. Many of the moves were the same, save that yoga was much, much slower. She preferred the bursts of speed in gymnastics, the sweat and the burn of her muscles. She was grateful for learning to meditate now. It gave her a way to calm down, and sometimes the unbidden thoughts would speak to her, and on those nights, she considered herself lucky.

Being stuck with being able to read only non-fiction books became quite a boon, though. Plumbing for Dummies came in very handy. She managed to get the workman's shower, a tiny thing in the bathroom on the top floor, to work. They were loath to use it, though, as it had no hot water. I could have used this when I read those romance novels, she thought more than once in those early years.

The lack of novels gave her no mental escape to engage in, so Céline threw herself into Ariste, Ursus, Khenum, and Naga. As they grew, she began to think of them, not as all the same age, but stepping stones. Ariste seemed to be the eldest, with Ursus next, Khenum after him, and Naga the youngest. She didn't know if it was true or not, and, of course, they didn't either, but that is how she thought about it. When they were very small, it was easy to take up entire weeks without thinking of anything but their immediate needs. She taught them to read, to write, to speak politely and clearly. She read to them, first picture books, and when they outgrew them, she read them fairy tales and mythology, religious texts and expositions about them. When they were old enough to read on their own, she read them poetry, her own included. She made up stories just for them, having adventures among imagined foes. When she could, she practiced yoga, and some gymnastics, using the piping at the ceiling for uneven bars. Ariste would follow her about, twirling and flying through the air in a way that Céline could have only hoped for, even at her best when she was on the college gymnastics team. She meditated a lot, especially at night when she couldn't sleep.

So the years went by, and her children grew. When she passed the mirror in their living area, she saw that the furrow in between her eyes that showed when she was upset, or angry, or squinting, did not go away when she relaxed her eyebrows. The lines on her cheeks were a little deeper and lower when she smiled, extended closer to the corner of her lips with each passing year. Her hair, beginning at the temples, began to turn from its auburn to a honey blond. When she noticed, she would run her fingers through it, now extended to her waist in waves, and say to herself, "You're lucky, Céline. It could be turning gray."

# Chapter 19

**CLASSIFIED TOP SECRET**
**PROJECT SANCTUARY**

To: ██████████████████
Washington DC

From: Flayne Institute Experimental Facility
Chicago, Illinois

Subject: Request for Russian Federation Infant Transfer

The Therian Initiative sent in a request six weeks ago for the formal permission to obtain and transfer a minimum for six and maximum for 50 infants from the Russian Federation. The facilities that we have targeted are in unstable regions with highly overpopulated orphanages that are extremely understaffed. We cannot continue our experimentation of life long moreau status without the subjects to be lifetime moreaus.

Signed: Agent ████████

# Chapter 20

Dr. Montgomery had worked on this project almost as hard as he worked on his perfection of the rat transformation. Not as long, by any means, but as hard. He had personally done the research, overseen anything his staff had done, been present at all the experiments, if he was not the one performing them himself. He had controlled every stage of this particular part of the project, and he was proud, despite his misgivings, of his accomplishments.

Ilya Pytrovich was still his pinnacle, he doubted he would surpass the Russian Systemist. Earlier on in the Initiative, he hadn't realized how much the subject's psychological state really did influence the success of the transformation. In finding Ilya Pytrovich, he had been exceedingly lucky, he knew. The chances of finding another human being of his caliber would be very difficult. Finding another human being of his caliber that would be in as desperate a situation as he was to bring into the project would be impossible. He knew it.

And so there was only one Ilya Pytrovich. The rat, as a species, was too wily to be much good as a soldier without the high caliber to go along with it. Ilya was destined to be a leader, a teacher, the one who thought and made plans. For years now, Dr. Montgomery had watched his moreau do just that. He trained those under his care. He mentored those that needed it. He refined his art by bringing his body under his control, by bringing his desires under control. Dr. Montgomery was certain that given enough time, Ilya could overcome any animal instinct the rat DNA instilled in him. The man was more impressive than Agent Anchord could ever realize. That half of the equation was solved.

The other half of the equation had finally been solved, also. He hoped. Dr. Montgomery had researched many different kinds of animals, watched the moreaus he had already created, went back and read his notes from past successes and failures. His choice of hybrid was irrefutable, he felt, and as soon as he had succeeded in the 60% range with the transformations, he went on to the second phase of the plan.

Ilya Pytrovich walked up to him where he was waiting outside in the hallway. Dr. Montgomery could hear the click of his claws on the tiles, knowing that it was a noise Ilya could easily prevent if he wished to do so. He did not, he also knew, to prove the point that he was confident enough that he did not need to be silent.

"You wanted to see me, Dr. Montgomery?" he asked. Even after all this time in the US around native English speakers, his accent was still fairly thick.

"I did," he put his hand out and clapped Ilya on the arm. The rat gave no indication he could even feel it. "I have something to give to you."

The rat raised his eyebrows. "I do not think giving me anything would be in any of our interests," he said slowly.

Dr. Montgomery shook his head. "The Initiative is giving you something, then," he amended. "I am simply the one who made it."

Ilya seemed to accept this, nodding slightly.

A huge smile on his face, Dr. Montgomery opened the door, pushing down on the handle slowly, his eyes not leaving the rat moreau. With a flourish, he shoved it open and stood to the side, to reveal the something he wished to give.

Ilya's face became confused, his eye ridges forming an inverted V. His ears twisted backwards, and he stepped into the room. "Doctor," he said, his voice slightly disgusted. "These…these are puppies."

Dr. Montgomery actually giggled and entered the room after him, his body abuzz with excitement. "Not just any puppies," he said, looking from the baby gate to Ilya. "Your puppies."

Ilya looked at the doctor as if he were crazy. "Pochemu, why would I want puppies?" He looked back at the baby dogs, on all fours roaming about the enclosure and whining. They were a sort of painted coloring, golden, black and white, each one with a different variation and pattern to the coloring. Their ears, on the tops of their large heads, were bat-like, and twisting about them in a feeble attempt to hone in on whatever sound it was they had heard at the time. Each one had a white tipped tail, some only the very tip, others more than half the tail itself. When one stood up on two legs, standing straight, his paws a four fingered hand and a thumb, Ilya's face went from confused to horrified. "These are children!" He turned to Dr. Montgomery, the look of dread still on his face.

"Your children," Dr. Montgomery beamed proudly. "They are your team!"

"Moya komanda? My team? These are children moreaus!" He threw his hand toward the baby cage.

"You will get to train them from infancy," he said. "They will be your perfect team!" The Russian warrior still looked confused and appalled. "They are African Dogs," the doctor explained. "This type of canine has no hierarchical structure, so the individuals within it will not be vying for position within the pack. There is usually a set of pack leaders, a mated pair who have puppies, but that, of course, couldn't be the situation here." The doctor puffed up his chest as Ilya stared at him. "They are all male, as you requested. No sexual tension or any of that." Dr. Montgomery had tried very hard to listen to Ilya's request, he would not deny that the Russian was the expert in this kind of thing. If he insisted on no mixed gender teams, then no mixed gender teams. "They should see you as pack leader," he went on, "since they are being raised so young. You would be the male of the mated pair with puppies, just without a mate."

"They are children," Ilya said slowly.

Dr. Montgomery nodded. "Your children," he specified again.

"You have transformed babies," the rat turned his head to the side, and his face became feral.

Suddenly, Dr. Montgomery understood what Ilya meant. His own reservations of proceeding down this road, years ago now, began to creep to the surface of his memory.

"It's unethical," he had said to Agent Anchord in a meek voice.

It had been the first time that Agent Anchord had looked uncertain, ever, in anything concerning The Initiative. "These are children no one wants," he had said slowly. "We are not stealing kids out of people's homes. All of these children come from Eastern European or Asian orphanages. Do you know what happens to children in those countries?"

Dr. Montgomery had not known what happened to children in orphanages in those countries.

"They are so neglected that they develop mental illness," Agent Anchord had said, vitriol in his voice. "They come in contact with no one. They are left in a crib, crying, and given a bottle by a woman who walks away from them while they drink it. Some of them become walking vegetables, Dr. Montgomery. Girls, in Asia, are left to die." His eyes had bored into the scientist. "We are saving them from that."

Of course, Agent Anchord had been right. If left in their original situation, they would only be left to rot there, or left out to die of exposure. Even if the child died in the process, or had to be eliminated from the program for some other reason after the transformation, they were being offered a better life than could ever hope for, that they would ever get, in the places from where they'd been taken.

"These children came from an undisclosed orphanage in an undisclosed country of the Russian Federation," Dr. Montgomery told Ilya, his voice careful. "You know what goes on, or should I say, doesn't go on, in those orphanages, don't you?"

The rat was silent, still staring at the doctor. Dr. Montgomery knew from the look on Ilya's face that he did, indeed, know what did not go on in those orphanages.

"What about my other students?" Ilya asked quietly, his voice confused. "How are they to be trained if I am…training…these puppies?"

"They are puppies, not children," Dr. Montgomery said. He stepped back at the look Ilya shot at him. "They are all six months to eighteen months old," he said. "See, several of them can walk on two feet already. They can be left alone for quite a while and be safe, just like African Dogs in the wild."

"I believe pack animals are babysat by others in the pack," he said. "Not left alone."

"Be that as it may," Dr. Montgomery tried to take a more fatherly tone with the Russian. "They can be left alone and be alright, while you do your classes."

"And I am to care for them otherwise," the Russian's

voice did not sound happy.

"You need to bond with them," Dr. Montgomery said. "They need to see you as their pack leader."

Ilya Pytrovich was silent.

"I will leave you to get acquainted with your new team," said the doctor, making his way to the door, Ilya's eyes following him as he did so.

When Dr. Montgomery had left, Ilya turned back to the six puppies in the baby cage. He didn't know why they were in the barrier, there wasn't anything in the room. Dr. Montgomery spoke of orphanages where children were left in neglect and loneliness, yet here these six children were without even a play thing, in a fence, in an empty room. He went and unlatched one of the sections of it, opening it up to allow the puppies to leave the enclosure.

They poured out of it, like water out of a glass, scattering about the room. Ilya put his back to the wall, and slid down it, simply watching the children about him.

Three of them were walking upright with no problem at all, looking very much like little children in dog suits. Two were wobbling on two legs, and then falling down, just like toddlers trying to walk. One was still on all fours, not on his hands and knees, but on his four legs, like a dog, like many of the moreaus that he trained. Each had a different set of markings, albeit all the same color. Their body shapes were different, some being closer to dogs and some being closer to a human type shape. Their ears were different sizes, their muzzles were different sizes. They were each a unique individual, just as they had been unique individuals before this process.

How many had Dr. Montgomery put through the process? He tried not to think of how many had died during his own transformation. Had any others survived being transformed into African Painted Wolves, and not been chosen as part of his team? If not, what made these little ones different that they did survive? What made him different that he survived when others did not?

He shook his head and banished the morbid thoughts from his mind. It would do little good to dwell on them, just as it had done little good to dwell on them before now.

This was his team, a set of six little boy African Dogs, all between the ages of six months and a year and half. The six month old must be the one who was not yet walking upright, and the three walking with no issue must be closer to 18 months. He sighed, looking from each one, as they nipped at each other, and explored the empty room.

One of the them who could walk on two legs approached him, obviously having found the room wanting in interest. He stopped just short of the rat-warrior, his big, pale blue eyes taking in Ilya's face. Like him, this boy had retained his own eye color, for he knew that African Dogs did not come with blue eyes.

So he was to be these children's teacher, to raise them and train them to be soldiers, to follow his commands, as the consummate team? The Initiative had thought long and hard about the animals they were going to use for their purposes, he suddenly realized. A rat, crafty and wily, strong and tenacious, as a leader. African dogs, a pack in the true sense, with no pecking order, as the team that would follow the otets, the father, without question.

The little creature in front of him came closer, and Ilya remained still, as if he were in meditation. The puppy climbed onto his lap and took the rat's muzzle in his tiny paw-like hands. This child remembers his humanhood, Ilya thought. Do the others? Will this little one remember his humanity when he grows up, or will he be like all eighteen month olds and forget his babyhood in the realm of dreams?

He put his own hands on the puppy, holding his torso.

The little one leaned forward, his hands slipping to the rat's neck, and Ilya let him fall onto his bare chest, where the puppy nuzzled his fur and closed his blue eyes.

He was to create a team out of these puppies, soldiers that would fight like no other, be the elite, that would follow him without question. He hoped that would not be so.

# Chapter 21

Céline and the children were coming home from a shopping trip just as the sun poked its head over the horizon. They went the "long way around", as the kids called it, because of a gang turf war that was currently raging. The Bonecrushers, a Haitian gang, were on the warpath, looking to increase their territory. "Better to be safe than sorry," she told the four moreaus, "since we live so close to them."

This shopping trip had taken them in search of paint supplies for Ursus, his current stint at oil painting with Bob Ross had caused him to run out. They found old canvases that were already painted, and would scrape and layer them with white paint to make them bare again. Artists, it seemed, were not so careful as to empty their tubes of colors before throwing them away, and they were able to collect quite an array of colors and media. At nine years old, it appeared that oil painting was winning the media battle.

They turned the corner to the street that held the warehouse when a soft sound came from a shadow in between two buildings. Céline froze, not recognizing it as a familiar one. Her heart thumped in her chest, and visions of her nightmares came rushing into her mind.

"Hello, little pretty," said a low voice from the shadows. "I have been waiting for you to come home."

She blinked, fear wrapping its fingers around her throat attempting to choke her. He spoke with an accent, an accent she would have recognized anywhere. "Vous etez de Haiti," <You are from Haiti> she said quietly.

She heard a slight intake of breath come from the shadow, and then a moment's pause. "Oui," he replied, "mais vous n'etez pas." <Yes, but you are not.> Céline didn't answer him, well aware that her own accent was easily identifiable as American by anyone who spoke French proficiently. "I have seen you help people," he said, "with your garden."

He'd seen her? He'd seen her garden? She thought she had been careful. She was positive she'd been careful. What happened to the block being infested with demons, and keeping the vagrants away? Her gut clenched. Her breath didn't want to go into her lungs.

He stepped out of the shadows, she gasped and took a step backward. Ariste hissed, her hands dropping the bags she was carrying, and going to her mother's waist. Ursus growled low in his throat, and Naga hissed long and slow. Khenum, the only one with no warning sound, remained silent. The man was large, towering over Céline easily by a foot. The morning sun shined on him as he emerged from the alley, showing a broad torso, large arms, and an impressive frame, all covered in fur. His head was that of a cat. His body was blended with an animal, strong and feral. His fur was a dark gray, the color of heavy rain clouds. He had a white patch around one eye and ear, and his right front paw was white. He looked like he would be as comfortable on all fours as on the two legs he was standing. He was a moreau!

He held out his arm, the one with the gray paw, saying nothing. On his forearm, among matted and clotted hair, was a wide gash, writhing with maggots.

The smell of the wound alone would have sent someone retching, but in combination with the worms undulating through it, Céline had to take a hard swallow and a deep breath. "Oh," she said, and looked up at the man's face. He was still, like a statue, not even his white whiskers moving. She was torn as to what to do. He already knows where we live, she chided herself for her carelessness. Her mind was blank for a long moment, not knowing what to do. Then, her-voice-that-was-not-her-voice murmured in the back of her mind ~Heal him~

"Come with me," she said. She motioned for the children to pick up what they had dropped and began walking toward the warehouse.

Two other people came out of the shadows after him, she hadn't even noticed that anyone had been with him. One was a thin lizard, with a long neck and tiny head. The other was a rabbit, his ears extending behind his head. They all moved very quietly, slight swishes the only sound. She led them to their warehouse, and up the stairs, all of them eerily silent.

"Sit down," she motioned to a chair at the kitchen table, and the cat sank down into it. The children rallied by their mother, eying the three strangers warily, as Céline went to her bookcase and got out her medical supplies. "Ursus, " she asked, him being the tallest, "get me a bowl please, and put some vinegar in it." She sat across from the cat, and motioned for him to put his arm on the table.

He complied, and Céline took a deep breath.

She immediately regretted it, as the smell from the wound was foul. It must have been festering for weeks to get to such a state. It looked like it hadn't been cleaned at all, blood and pus clotted the fur around the gash. She instructed for a rag and a bowl of water, which one of her children provided for her on the table. She held her breath, and leaned forward to work on his wound. With a pair of tweezers, she picked out the maggots as she found them, placing them in the bowl of vinegar, making sure to dip the tip of the tweezers in it also. Then she dipped them in the water to wash the vinegar off, and returned to the cut. When the pus and blood began to flow too much for her to be able to see, she laid the wet rag on it, and squeezed gently around his arm.

He would hiss in his breath when she did it, it was the only time he indicated he was in pain.

When it was finally free of maggots and pus, she placed a compress of wild garlic on it, and wrapped it. "Is that the only wound you have?" It was the first voice that had been spoken since she started.

"Yes," the cat said, "but they have some." He motioned to his two companions.

She looked at each of them, the rabbit having a slash on his thigh. It was beginning to smell, and only needed draining, and then got the same treatment as the cat's wound. The lizard had a shallow gash from his shoulder to his breast, so that he had to take his shirt off for her to see it. It wasn't infected, but it had developed some sort of white fuzz on it, which she surmised was a type of fungus. He was given a compress of rosemary to which he had to hold to his chest, as she didn't have a way to wrap it on him.

"Is that all?" she asked, clearing her throat.

"No," he said in his low voice.

No? What did he mean, no? Dread began to creep up her spine.

"I have people who need healing," he said, standing up and looking down at her.

"You have people who need healing?" she repeated stupidly. "What do you mean?"

"I have people who are hurt," he said, "come with me."

Céline stood up, and straightened her shoulders and looked up at him. "I can't just go with you," she huffed. "I don't know who you are. I don't even know your name." She felt like she was tiny compared to these three moreaus, and wondered if she had made a mistake by helping them.

"My name is Grischat," he said, pronouncing "Gree-shah" with his Creole accent.

"Grischat," she repeated. Grey cat, very original, she thought.

Grischat made a move toward the window overlooking the garden, looking at her expectantly. "Come," he said.

"No," she felt like she was Echo, doomed to repeat things forever. "I can't go with you. Where do you want me to go?" She looked around frantically. "What about my children?"

"They can come," he said. He moved his head in a nod toward the other two moreaus. "Get the medical supplies."

"What?" she moved toward the bookcase where she kept her herbs and medical books. "You can't--"

She was cut off by a "Yes, I can," and with a speed she hadn't expected from such a large creature, she was off her feet, and looking down out the window at the garden below. For a moment she thought he was going to drop her, but then she was flying through the air, Grischat's strong arm around her waist, toward the roof of the opposite building.

She screamed and flailed, but then stopped flailing as their jumping didn't stop or slow down, and another roof was traversed, then another, then another. All she could see was the ground below her moving at an incredible rate, then a gaping hole with the sidewalk below. Each jump took the breath out of her, as she was flung half way across Grichat's shoulder and back. He ran on three legs, with his hurt arm wrapped around her waist. Every once in a while, she would smell the garlic from his compress.

She cried out when he jumped off a roof, she saw the ground coming at him and waited to hear herself splat. When they landed. He was on his feet. She was still on his shoulder. She gasped in a breath.

The other two moreaus landed next to him, and then she saw her own children fall from the sky and land, not quite as gracefully, on the ground. Had they kept up with Grischat's running? Had they jumped from building to building?

Grischat put her down. She was surprised by the gentleness of it. She looked about and did not recognize where she was. It was a short building, only three stories tall, and they were in the back, near two large loading doors. The doors were open, with sunlight and warmth streaming in. Inside, were more moreaus than Céline had thought possible, of every shape and size. And they all looked like they'd been through the ringer.

He put his hand on her shoulder and led her into the bay. It stank to high heaven, a mixture of urine, feces, sweat, and animal. The two moreaus with Grischat brought her items inside and dumped them unceremoniously on a table. "Bring Gristle over here," he called. "Do whatever she says."

Two moreaus, one looked like a badger and the other some kind of weasel, brought a pig over on a stretcher. He was bloody all over, and Céline couldn't even tell if he was breathing. He was placed at her feet and she stared at him dumbfounded. Then she felt Ariste rub up against her side and she snapped back into reality. Ursus, the largest of her kids, was half the size of most of the moreaus here, and he already towered over her. If she didn't do something, who knew what these people would do to her children, much less her.

"Put him on the table," she said.

Once on the table, she began to try and put him back together. The stretcher was filthy, the floor was filthy, the rags she requested were filthy, the bowls were filthy, the water was cloudy. She patched Gristle up the best she could, and then another moreau was put in front of her. Then another, and another, and another. Grischat had obtained a chair from somewhere and sat in it not far from her, watching her with hazel eyes, slow blinking and intense.

Annoyance began to gnaw at her as she grew tired. It seemed to her that they hadn't done simple things, like keep the wounds clean. Who doesn't keep wounds clean? After the fifth moreau, and two and half hours of being stared at, she turned to the large cat and snapped, "This place is filthy, no wonder all of your wounds are crawling with maggots! How am I supposed to work with this?" She gestured to the dirty implements before her.

"What do you need to clean it?" he asked quietly.

"Bleach!" she spurted out the first thing that came to her mind, "lots of bleach, everywhere!"

Grischat's eyes didn't leave her, nor did the rest of him move as he gave a barely imperceptible nod in her direction.

She huffed, and turned to her next patient.

Two patients later, someone said, "It's ready," over her shoulder.

"What's ready?" she asked, her face close to the wound of her patient.

"The bleached area," he replied.

She looked up from the moreau she was tending. "What?"

"The bleached area," he said, "like you asked."

Her patient was being lifted up, and her medical supplies gathered. Grischat stood up, grabbed the chair he was sitting in by the back, and began to walk across the bay. She had no choice but to follow him, looking back and motioning her children to stay close to her. She was taken to a squared area that had, by goodness, been bleached. The concrete was white, the walls were white, and it smelled so strongly that it made her eyes water. They laid the moreau she was tending down on the ground, spread her tools around her, and backed up. She knelt down and began working again.

Once all of the bad cases were done, she was able to slow down. Most of the wounds were slashes, several of them in rather uncomfortable places. She patched up several necks and groins, and not a few chests and bellies. Now she was dealing with superficial wounds, bruises, and knots.

"What happened here?" she asked as she bandaged up a moreau.

Grischat, who hadn't moved, said, "We had a fight."

"With whom?" she asked incredulously.

"With people."

"What people?" Her voice rose as she spoke.

"People with weapons."

"You're all done," she told the patient in front of her, and then looked around. She appeared to be done, too. She certainly felt it. "Maybe you should avoid people with weapons then," she stood up and the world swooned around her.

Grischat was up in an instant, his paws on her shoulders. "You need to sleep," he said. "You have been doing this for 11 hours."

Had she? She turned and saw all four of her little ones on the floor, curled up asleep, and deep tiredness overtook her. "Yes," she said, and let herself be led over her brood. She sank to the ground, cuddling with them. She felt Naga slither and begin to wrap herself around her body, now being much too big to wrap around only an arm or a leg. As she did so, and those coils warmed her body, it occurred to Céline that Grischat had not once asked her for her help.

# Chapter 22

The goshawk glanced over at Ilya's living room, the ends of his lips turned downward. With the rigid sweep of his beak, it made his frown that much harder. "You got screwed, my friend."

"Zamolchi," Ilya growled, his claws scraping the tabletop.

"If that's swearing in Russian, it sounds better in English," Ayah countered.

"It means shut up," Ilya's accent was thick. He glanced at the puppies, confined in a baby enclosure, nipping at each other happily.

"What are you going to do with them?" Ayah asked. He threw his head back and downed his whiskey in one shot, something usually meant for drinking contests with the rat.

"What do you mean?" Ilya asked, agitated, his ears upright and fully forward. "What am I going to do with them?"

Ayah's feathers puffed out slightly, waving a wing in the direction of the enclosure. "What are you going to do with them?" he repeated. "Leave them in there? Do they come out? What are you going to do with them?"

Ilya opened his mouth to reply, but nothing came out. He turned, his gray eyes looking at the six puppy boys falling over each other, on all fours, their tails wagging. They yipped, one barked, then another laughed. What was he going to do with them? Train them? To be his team? To be soldiers?

"What are they?" Ayah's voice broke through Ilya's thoughts.

He whipped his head around, his long neck muscles working. "What do they look like?" he almost yelled. "They're kittens! What are you?"

Ayah put his hands up in front of him, "I was an adult when they did this to me!" He shook his head, his feathers on his neck puffing and then settling down. "I mean," his voice became more gentle, "are they like us?"

Ilya glanced at them again, running his fingers over his head. He pressed his ears down as he did so, they popped back up as his fingers left them. "I don't know," he answered truthfully.

"Do they talk?" Ayah took the whiskey bottle and poured, filling his rocks glass to the top.

"No. Yes." Ilya shook his head. "Maybe." He looked to Ayah, who held out another rocks glass filled with vodka. He snatched it from the goshawk, and throwing his head back, downed it. He didn't even feel it go down his gullet, it was so quick. He waited for the familiar, smooth burn, but it never came. "I think they might."

One of the puppies squatted down, his tail held high, a thoughtful look on his face.

"Are they housebroken?" Ayah asked.

The evidence left by the puppy, if it hadn't smelled bad enough, answered the question before Ilya could. "No."

Ayah watched as the boy in question trotted off, leaving his odoriferous gift behind him. "This is messed up, man."

The words bounced in Ilya's head. How many times

had he thought something similar in the week since the boys had come to him? He had found that no arrangements had been made for their care. For two days, he'd left them in the room during his work day. He had trouble concentrating on his classes, knowing that the six of them were in his quarters, in a baby gate, alone. So on the third day, he'd set up the baby gate in the corner of the gym, only to find them more of a distraction to him and his students.

They cried to get out of the enclosure and he didn't blame them. What baby wanted to be kept in a cage, even if it was open on top? The other moreaus all thought they were adorable, until their braying got to the point that it was difficult to hear what Ilya was saying. He had told them to keep training, while he had Dyson help him carry the puppies back to his quarters, to leave them there once again. That had been the only day he'd taken them to the gym with him.

Ilya's glass was full once more, he didn't recall filling it. Had Ayah? He grabbed it, pouring it down his mouth again, and this time felt the sting of the alcohol which had eluded him the last shot. He slammed the rocks glass down, felt this fur bristle from the top of his head down his back, stood up angrily and waved a paw at puppies. "What am I supposed to do with them?!" he bellowed.

For a moment, Ayah looked panicked. His large, chocolate brown eyes went wider, larger circles than they already were. His feathers puffed up again, his head jerking toward the puppies, then back to the rat moreau. He flapped his wings once, then his feathers settled down and he blinked. "What did they tell you to do with them?"

Ilya bared his teeth, planting both hands on the table. "To make them my team," he snarled.

"Then you make them your team, Ilya Pytrovich," the goshawk replied. He remained seated, looking up at his friend.

"What?" Ilya tilted his head to the side dangerously.

With a click of his beak, Ayah answered, "If they told you to make them your team, then do that."

"Are you mad?" The rat looked back at the puppies to make sure he wasn't missing something. No, they were still six puppy-boys, rolling about each other, brindle tails wagging, a pile of poop in the corner of the enclosure.

"What else are you going to do?" Ayah asked.

His lips curled back in a snarl, then dropped. He felt the fur on his back settle down, as he sank into his chair. His tail whipped about behind him. His eyes darted back and forth, from the goshawk to the wall behind him. From the goshawk to the puppies. From the goshawk to the door. What else was he going to do?

"But they're only babies," Ilya muttered.

Ayah took his time, pouring the vodka from the pale blue bottle into Ilya's rocks glass. Three shots of the expensive liquor was not enough to get the rat drunk. Even as a teenager, he'd had a better booze head than that. But he wished, suddenly, that it was enough. Because, if he were drunk, perhaps all of this had just been a dream, the product of an inebriated brain, and he would wake up to normalcy in the morning.

Handing him the glass, Ayah said, "They're your babies now. Make them your team."

How was he supposed to do that? He shook his head slowly, the glass still in his hand. Ayah tilted his head, and Ilya did not need him to say what was next on his tongue. He could make them his team or they could be eliminated from the program.

The goshawk held up his glass of whiskey. "Congratulations, Poppa," he said. "You're the proud father of six bouncing baby boys." Then he threw his head back and downed his whiskey.

# Chapter 23

Céline was warm, her head laying on Naga's chest, her snake daughter wrapped around her, and the warm bodies of her other three pressed against her. She smelled bleach and....coffee.

Coffee? She opened her eyes and remembered where she was. She tried to sit up, but Naga kept her from doing so. "Curly Que," she rubbed her softly scaled body, "let go."

Naga yawned, her mouth opened huge, showing two large fangs which had not yet stopped growing, to Céline's consternation. Her forked tongue stuck out long and then whipped back in her mouth as she unwound from her mother.

Grischat was sitting in the same chair he had sat in the day before, a mug with steaming liquid in his hand. The smell was coffee--dark, aromatic coffee.

"What's that smell?" Ariste asked, sitting up and rubbing her eyes.

"Coffee," Céline crooned.

Grischat chuckled and held the mug he was holding out to her. "Want some?" he asked in French.

Céline took the coffee and shook her head at the same

time. "I don't drink coffee," she answered him. "It tastes like mud water." She held the mug to her nose and inhaled deeply. "But it smells divine!"

"Taste it," he said, "it is fine, fine coffee."

Céline took a sip and grimaced. "I am sure it is fine, fine mud water," she replied, handing the mug back to him.

"What are you saying?" Khenum asked, his voice sounding slightly offended.

Céline hadn't noticed that she had answered Grischat in French. "That this is a fine cup of coffee," Céline explained, "but I don't like coffee."

"It smells good," Ursus said, sniffing the air.

"Can we have some?" Naga asked.

She looked from face to face, each of them looking at her expectantly. "You won't like it," she said.

Grischat held out the mug again, a smug smile on his feline face.

Ursus was the first one to take it, took a sip, and stuck out his tongue. "Ugh!" His siblings gave a similar reaction.

"It is an acquired taste," Céline assured them.

"Aw," Grischat still donned that grin, "they are little still. They need to start with café bébé," his voice was patronizing.

"What's café bébé?" Khenum asked.

"It is a lot of milk, a lot of sugar, and a little bit of coffee," she explained. "It is used to have children acquire the taste."

"Mmm," Ariste piped up, "milk!"

"Can we try it?" Ursus asked. "It smells so good."

She looked at Grischat, who was waving his hand to what she thought was no one in particular. "Get me some milk, and sugar, and mugs," he called. And, to Céline's amazement, they rapidly appeared in the hands of two moreaus, and were put on the table. Grischat motioned to them, not moving from his chair.

Céline got up, fixed four mugs, and handed them out to her kids. Ariste drank hers down and she held her mug out for more. The others were slower, but they finished them. "No more," she told them, "one a day is all."

"Aw," they chorused.

"You are a harsh taskmaster," Grischat said, still smiling. When Céline didn't reply, he said, "Let them play, they were standing, watching you all day yesterday."

Let them play? Here, in this place, full of people who were hurt from a fight with who knows who? Where would they play?

"Todd!" Grischat called, "They're awake!" A fox trotted over, a boy, with silver fur and dressed in cargo pants and a vest. He seemed a little older than her own, perhaps 13 or 14, but his eyes had a worldly look to them. "Get them some breakfast," Grischat said, indicating Céline's four children. "And then you can go play."

"Come on," Todd said. The four of them didn't even wait for an answer from Céline, they all got up and scrambled to the fox.

Céline was in a kind of shock, there were other children, children for her children to play with, who wanted to play with them. "Behave!" she called after them, her gut twisting as she watched them go from her.

A moreau woman, a white rabbit, came up to them carrying a tray with a plate on it. Céline recognized her from the day before, she had been slashed on one of her lop ears which hung about her shoulders like long hair. She is...beautiful, Céline thought. She was the perfect blend of animal and human, much like Ariste. Her brown eyes were in the front of a lovely blended face. Her body was almost entirely human, save the white fur that covered it. Her hands were hands, like human hands, except for the nails at the ends, and again the fur. "Breakfast," she said.

Céline leaned forward unconsciously, the smell from the plate was inviting. It held scrambled eggs, a slab of ham, toast with butter on it, and a small apple. She hadn't seen a meal like this in years, not even for dinner, much less for breakfast. She grabbed the apple and took a bite out of it like she was ravenous.

Grischat lounged back in the chair, watching her intently. "What do you have to drink?" he asked.

"Water," she answered with a mouthful of apple, after all, it was what she and kids usually drank. It was free.

Grischat laughed outright, and shook his head. "Non," he said, emphasizing his accent, "what would you like to drink?"

Céline swallowed, the smell of the ham in front of her making it hard to concentrate. What would she like to drink? It had been so long since that question had been brought before her, she had to consider it. "Tea, please," she said, grabbing the fork on the tray.

"Get the lady some iced tea," he said to the rabbit.

"No," Céline nearly spat out her ham. She felt her face blushing, she was acting like a barbarian, but the smell of the food was so good. She covered her mouth with her hand and said, "Hot tea, with milk and sugar."

Grischat raised an eyebrow, and nodded in the rabbit's direction. "Get the lady what she wants."

The rabbit disappeared into the gaggle of moreaus who were milling about the unloading bay.

"You have not told me your name, petite médecienne," Grischat crossed one of his outstretched legs over the other at the feet.

Her name? Céline blinked. Mama, Mommy, Mom, Mother...the words ran through her head quickly, looking for a name that might have once belonged to her other than the one she'd been exclusively called for close to a decade. "Céline," she said, the name sounded strange on her tongue, like speaking a foreign language. "My name is Céline."

"Céline what?"

After a moment's pause, she said, "Just Céline. Nothing else."

The rabbit returned with a mug of tea and placed it on the table. Céline picked it up, smelled it, felt the warmth of it in her hands, looked down at it, saw the creaminess, and took a sip. It was like falling into a drug induced haze. She closed her eyes and absorbed herself in the sensation of the tea on her tongue, like her meditation, she emptied her mind and there was only the tea, sweet and creamy.

"You do not get tea much, do you?" Grischat spoke to her in French again.

She opened her eyes and smiled at him gratefully. It was nice to have adult banter with someone, not to have to explain things or be teaching things. It was nice to be the one receiving the gentle teasing, and not always giving it. Don't smile, the unbidden thought told her. It was quiet, barely audible. She lowered the intensity of her grin and said, "The tea we have all the time. It is the sugar and milk that we don't get much of."

He sat up, bringing his legs to the legs of the chair and leaned forward, a feral smile on his feral face. "You can have all the milk and sugar you like while you are here, petite médecienne."

Something in his bearing brought her up short. Her gut twisted again, like it had the day before when he'd come out of the alley. "Thank you," she said, putting the tea down. "I should check your wound, so we can get out of your hair."

"I don't mind you in my hair," he said.

She blushed and looked down at his forearm. She unwrapped it, and already the stench of it had gone away. "You'll want to keep putting wild garlic compresses on it," she told him, "until the infection is gone." She bandaged it back up, "Same with everyone else who has been injured."

He flexed his hand and stared at her with his hazel eyes.

"That is all you really need." She stood up, hoping she was showing a calmer demeanor than she felt. "Is to make sure everyone keeps their wounds clean and clear of infection."

"Alright," he said, standing up along with her and looking down at her unblinkingly. "We will be sure to do that."

She stared at him for a moment, wondering what to do next, when the unbidden thought said, Go home. She took a deep breath and turned to the rabbit who had been serving them. "Will you get my children, please?" she asked. "It is time for us to go home."

The rabbit looked to Grischat, as if for permission, and he nodded slightly. "I will take you home," he said.

"No," she took a step backwards, remembering her trip over. "You don't have to."

"How will you know how to get home?" he asked smugly.

"I know how to get home, Mama!" Ariste's voice piped up from behind her. "I remember how we came over the rooftops."

Thank whatever it was that made Ariste a cat.

"See?" she motioned to her daughter. "We will be fine."

"How will you get from rooftop to rooftop?" He seemed to be playing a game with her, trying to checkmate her arguments.

"I am sure I will figure out how," she assured him, turning and walking away. The unbidden thought came to her again and told her, Don't say it. She had taken a breath in and realized she was about to say, "You know where to find me if you need more help."

"You know where to find us if you need help," she heard Ariste's voice echo the thought she hadn't voiced herself. A feeling of dread overcame her.

"Indeed, I do," Grischat answered.

She kept her head up and continued walking away.

They went two buildings down before climbing the fire escape to reach the roof of the building. The roofs, for the most part, were close together, and jumping from one to the other didn't even need a proper vault. When they got to the first roof that she hesitated at, each of her kids, even clumsy Khenum, leaped over the space effortlessly.

"How did you all get so good at this?" she asked.

The four of them exchanged wary glances.

She had asked the question rhetorically, but the cautious glances sent off alarm bells. She stuck her hip out and put her hand on it, looking at them from across the divide of buildings.

"How did you all get so good at this?" she spoke each word firmly, her lips pinched and her eyebrow raised.

There was a moment of hemming and hawing, before Ursus said, "We practice at home."

"What do you mean you practice at home?" her voice raised an octave.

"We play on the rooftops sometimes," Ariste admitted. "We jump from one to the other. It isn't hard."

"It isn't hard?" She looked down to the ground so many stories below.

"No," Khenum bounded over the space back to her, and lifted her up off of her feet. Her son was almost the same height as she, and had little buds of horns popping out from his forehead. However, she had no idea he was anywhere near strong enough to pick her up so easily. She was more surprised when he jumped over the space while holding her as if she weighed nothing. He put her down as soon as he landed, and smiled proudly.

She shook her finger at him, "No," she said, as if to a

toddler. "No, no, no," the other three got a finger wagged at them also. "I will find my own way across." There was a moment of silence. "And all of you are in trouble when we get home."

"Awww," was chorused around her. "Why?"

"Because you were jumping over buildings," she said tartly.

"We couldn't have kept up with Grischat yesterday if we didn't know how to jump over roofs," Ariste whined.

"You did it without telling me."

"You would have said no if we told you!" Naga's voice was rising in volume.

"Yes, I would have," Céline replied. "And you did it anyway."

"If we didn't ask," Ursus' voice was soft, "then we didn't disobey you."

Céline's mind went blank. "Well," she managed to get out, "you're in trouble anyway." She pointed in the direction they were headed. "Ariste, take us home."

Ariste glared at Ursus, "Why'd you have to tell her, honey-for-brains?"

"I don't have honey-for-brains," he said, following her to the next rooftop. "You're the one with milk-for-brains."

Naga glided in the air after him, looking as if she were flying, and landing on her chest on the roof. Right after her was Khenum, and Céline followed until they got the next large gap in between buildings.

The kids got over no problem, while Céline examined her surroundings. She had to figure a way across these things on her own, there was no way her stomach or head could take being carried over them. It was nauseating. She saw the rigging for the fire escape, if she could reach that, it would get her a little closer to the other building. She leaped from the edge of the roof, watching the ground come rushing up toward her, and then her hand grabbed onto the rigging. She spun around it, using it like the uneven bars, and then threw herself up and landed on the adjacent roof.

"Woohoo!" Khenum raised a fist in the air.

"You go, Mama!" Naga slithered up to her, and curled around her body, and then uncurled in one fluid motion.

Ariste rolled her eyes and smiled. Then jumped to the next roof. Each of the kids followed her without looking back to see if their mother was keeping up.

When they got back home, she sent them all to their rooms for peace and quiet and for them to "Think on what you did wrong." She needed uninterrupted time to think. Then after that, she needed some uninterrupted time for yoga. And then after that, she needed some uninterrupted time to meditate.

Her world had been broken open. There were other moreaus out there, close by, who knew where she was, and now she knew where they were. Or, Ariste knew. That was as good as her knowing. Her children had played with other children. She wondered what they played, she would have to ask, she told herself. She had patched up at least two dozen people, if not more, and had eggs and ham and toast for breakfast. She had taken a deep whiff of coffee, and she could still taste the sweet cream of the tea in her mouth. They were not isolated anymore, their world now belonged to a different place where other people resided. She knew she would see these people again, just as she knew the poetry would come to her tonight when she wrote by candle flame after everything was quiet. A cocoon had been sliced roughly open, a cocoon she didn't even know she had made, and now she was raw with emerging from it.

At five o'clock she called the children out from their rooms, put together with scavenged pieces left over from construction projects around the city to separate out their spaces. She sat them all in front of the TV, and did something she hadn't even considered doing in the past 9 years.

They watched the evening news.

# Chapter 24

There were cameras everywhere. Ilya knew it long before his transformation. He'd removed the cameras in his suite many times and he checked them regularly to make sure they stayed removed. No one had ever said anything to him about his removal of them, but they had kept reappearing. Finally, he went to Dr. Montgomery. "I will not be spied upon in my own rooms."

"There isn't a great deal I can do about that, Ilya Pytrovich," the doctor had replied, holding one of his lab rats in his hands. "I am not in charge of security."

"Who is?" the rat-man demanded.

"I have no idea," Dr. Montgomery told him, his face twisted in confusion. "That isn't my department. You know I'm not King of the Moreaus, Ilya."

More like King of the Rats, Ilya had thought to himself. He felt a slight shame at the thought, not because he did not think it wasn't true, but because instead of realizing that Dr. Montgomery would have no pull with security, he, a rat, had gone to the doctor to complain.

After that, he tried not to go to Dr. Montgomery for

much of anything. He did what he could himself. He could find cameras. He could disable them. He could pull the wires out of the walls. He could make it difficult to replace the cameras without him knowing. Eventually they would run out of places to put them. They hadn't yet.

"Whatcha doin', Batya?" asked one of his little African dogs.

"I am taking down a camera, Nikita," he said.

"Why?" asked another one, coming up behind his brother.

"Because I do not want them here, Dmitri."

"Will we be on TV?" asked a third.

"No, Vasili, not the kind of TV you want to be on."

"I want to be on Sesame Street!" The littlest of the six came running up, and grabbed his brother by the arm. "Do we get to be on Sesame Street?"

"No, Kostya," said Nikita. "Batya said that we wouldn't be on TV, didn't you hear?"

Vasili jerked his arm out of Kostya's grasp. "Let go of me!"

"I wasn't doing anything to you!" cried Kostya.

Vasili answered him with a hard shove.

Kostya let out a growl. A pathetic thing really, Ilya noted. He then pounced on his brother and began to snap, while Vasili moved his head from side to side in an attempt to lock jaws with him. They rolled and tussled, their tails wagging, half in anger, half in excitement. Their little sounds of "Nnnnn….nnnn…." slowly breeched Ilya's consciousness, as he tried to take out the camera.

"Shhh!" commanded Ilya, turning to the four of them and giving them a stern look. They all lowered their heads and tucked their tails between their legs. This was why he needed to get these cameras out of here. All over the facility, he was constantly terrified. Terrified in a way he didn't know he could be. In the three years that he'd been bringing up his team, he was painfully aware of their developing personalities. His wish for them not to follow him blindly had come back to haunt him.

Like any small children, they fought with each other. Whenever the agents came to oversee his training with them, they always left with angry faces and stock straight backs. While in his home in Russia, that might not have been a bad thing, he'd learned here in the United States, it most certainly was. How were they not supposed to fight? They were little boys! They were puppies! Both puppies and little boys fought. If a little boy didn't fight with his brothers, there was something wrong with him. Toddlers disobeyed, they were supposed to disobey. If they didn't, there was something wrong with them. But the disobeying terrified Ilya, each mishap a tiki mark against the puppies he loved.

He loved them, and that is what made him go around in a constant terror. There were cameras in the hall, cameras in the gym, cameras outside in the grassy areas, in the little playground that had been constructed for the puppies, and many places that Ilya was sure he did not know about. Each transgression, each fight, each show of individuality was recorded for all to see, and with each passing day, the panic became more and more intense. Meditation alleviated it some. Praying alleviated it some. Taking out the cameras in their own rooms alleviated it some, but it would never go away.

The tussling boys did not obey his command to be quiet, so he turned from the wall, and picked each of them up by the scruff of their necks. Their pitiful "nnnnnn-nnnnnn-nnnnnn" of a growl continued until he tugged their scruffs each of them gently and they went limp in his hands, just as if they were puppies being held in the mouth of their mother. "You must be quiet," he said sternly. "I need to think to get this out of the wall."

"Why do we need it out of the wall?" asked Dmitri again.

Ilya put down his brothers and sighed. "Because I do not want the people to be watching us."

"The people in the glass box in the gym?" asked another of the puppies.

Of all of them, Evgeny was the most perceptive. He did not talk much and often Ilya would forget he was even there. He played quietly, was not inclined to tussle with his brothers as much, but when he did, he was vicious in his fighting. "Da," said Ilya quietly, putting the other two down. "They do not need to watch us in our home."

"Why do they watch us in our home, Batya?" asked Nikita, his eldest.

The rat was at a loss as to how to respond. He was silent for a long moment, not an uncommon occurrence in and of itself, but obviously longer than normal, because it was Evgeny who answered. "They're bad people."

It felt like a knife to his chest when the little boy said the words. He was three, at the most four, and already he knew the answer to Nikita's question. Was the air here so oppressive that they noticed, or was it his growing terror that alerted the boy? "Why do you think they are bad people, Evgeny?" he asked.

"They never smile," Evgeny said.

"That does not make them bad people," he replied, sitting down on his rump instead of staying in the squat he was positioned in. "Many people say I do not smile much."

Maxim, his quietest, yet most rebellious, snickered, his own smile wide.

"But they don't feel good," Evgeny said. "They shake their heads and they say mean things to you."

Ilya picked the boy up, what could have given him the impression that they said mean things to him? "What do you mean?" he asked gently.

"They tell you you're a bad daddy, Batya." The little boy looked into his father's gray eyes with his great big chocolate brown ones.

The memory of what the boy was probably talking about came to him, and the panic tried to grip at his heart.

"Ilya Pytrovich," Agent Anchord had said, "Your team seems to be coming along…slowly." He spoke as if he chose his words on the fly, as if they were unthought of previously, that they had just come to fruition at this observation.

"They are babies," Ilya had said, all six of the puppies tussling with each other at his feet. "Babies do not come along quickly."

"It was my impression," the agent had replied, unsmiling, "that children come along much faster than adults do, especially when learning a new skill. That was my experience with my own children."

"Your children must have been exceptional," the Systemist had tilted his ears to the side, so they were both facing out. "All of the children I have ever been exposed to have not been such a quick study with complicated subjects."

The agent had frowned at this, and raised an eyebrow. "Do the Special Forces come in contact with many children?"

"As many as government agents, I would imagine," had been his response.

"Independent agents, Godspin Leschyov," said Agent Anchord.

"I am under no illusion as to what kind of agents you are," the rat had replied, gesturing to the puppies. "Soldiers are run by governments. You are making soldiers. I am training soldiers, I decide at what rate they go."

"The Initiative decides at what rate they go, Ilya Pytrovich," Agent Anchord had raised both of his eyebrows, as if he were surprised by the rat's announcement. "And they are businessmen. Businessmen want to see a profit." He leaned in closer, and tilted his head to the side. "So far, they have seen very little profit from this," he gestured to the puppies, "venture."

"And what would you have them do?" Ilya did not back up as the man invaded his personal space. "Bite the enemy to death with their milk teeth?"

Agent Anchord had cleared his throat, "It is the Initiative that decides these things, not I," he admitted, his tone of voice not changing at all. Ilya had seen the statement for what it was. It was not an apology. It was an abdication of responsibility.

"The Initiative cannot make children grow any faster, can it?" Ilya had asked, beginning to walk away, stepping over a pair of rolling puppies as he did so. The "nnnn-nnnnn" of baby dogs had come to his ears, which he had tilted backward, almost subconsciously, to keep an ear on the boys. One by one, their pitiful, playful growls stopped. He turned his neck to see the agent from one eye, and saw the little puppies crawling over themselves and their brothers in an effort to get back to their father and pack leader. The heat from their little bodies soon engulfed his feet as they returned to him. "If it can," he said, "then I am, indeed, impressed." He had walked away, leaving the agent without an answer, and not inclined to give him a chance to come up with one.

At the moment, his ears were pointed slightly backwards, his eyes soft, yet worried. "You do not think I let them get to me thinking I am a bad batya, eh?" he asked the little boy.

Evgeny did not smile, but shook his head. "No, Batya," he said. "You are a good daddy."

"Go play," he put the boy down, and shooed the five others away with him. "While I destroy the camera."

They did as they were bid, with no complaining at all,

heading into the living area.

You are a good daddy, Evgeny's words echoed in his head. What kind of father was he, letting his little children know that they were surrounded by 'bad people'? What kind of father was he that he could be here, and allow, at any moment, for any of the six of them to be eliminated from the program? Everyone knew what that meant. It meant that you summarily executed, and no one knew how. It could be a bullet to the head for all they knew. Ilya doubted that The Initiative cared about humanely putting a moreau down.

He tore the camera out of the wall, a rage engulfing him suddenly. He brought the camera to his mouth and bit into it hard, cracking the plastic casing, shattering the lens. He had not expected to ever become a father once he knew he was being turned into a moreau. He didn't particularly want to be a father. His team was supposed to be full grown adults, people who had some sort of idea of the world. He was not supposed to be training little children to be killing machines. That was not what Systema was.

He turned to look at the six little ones behind him, his mind a storm of anger and fear battling it out to overtake him. He became aware of his breath, always returning to the breath. His breaths were shallow and in his chest. Inhale, exhale, his muscled stomach expanding and retracting. His body was tense, he breathed away the tension, breathed away the fear, and clarity came to his mind.

# Chapter 25

Elias Montgomery swept into his lab, slamming the door shut behind him. He had not turned his music player off when Agent Anchord had called him to an urgent meeting. The Nutcracker Suite still played in the background, as if it was taunting him with melodic fingers wiggling in his face.

Ilya was gone! Ilya, and all six puppies, were gone. Poof! They had disappeared into thin air, as if they had never existed. Dr. Montgomery had only been able to stand in shock when he was told.

"How the hell did they get out of here?" Agent Anchord had yelled at the Head of Security.

The Head of Security just opened and closed his mouth, as if doing so would make some words come out. It didn't.

"Seven people!" Agent Anchord bellowed. "Seven people are gone!" He pointed an accusing finger at the Head of Security. "Under your watch!"

"It wasn't my watch," the man managed to get out. "I wasn't even on duty!"

"You are in charge of security," Agent Anchord's voice

cracked with rage. "How did he get out?!"

"I don't know," the man said quietly.

Not being able to get anything out of the Head of Security, Anchord turned to Dr. Montgomery. "Your prize!" he snarled out the last word. "Your prize has disappeared with his entire team!"

Dr. Montgomery had only shaken his head, it couldn't be possible.

But it was possible. Not only was it possible, it was so. The rat man had disappeared from their surveillance, along with the six puppy boys, and was nowhere to be found. They had no idea how long he had been gone. He could have been gone two hours, he could have been gone 12. He had disabled the last set of cameras in his rooms a few days before, and they had not yet been replaced. When the Systemist had not shown up for practice in the morning, the first time ever, one of his students was sent to check on him. No answer had come to the knocking at the locked door. When it was torn off of its hinges by a bear moreau, the place was empty, like a ghost room. The bedroom, however, sported a hole, large enough for a man to crawl through. The guards who followed the tunnel, which they reported was made by chewing the parts of the building out of the way, said it ended at the exterior of the building. After that, there was no sign of any of them.

No footprints.

No broken branches or bent blades of grass.

No smell of rat or dog.

No nothing.

No Ilya.

Dr. Montgomery let out a scream of frustration and swept his desk with his arm. Everything on it fell to the floor with a loud crash and he lay prostrate across the empty surface. Tears came to his eyes, he squeezed them shut in an attempt to block out the world. This couldn't be happening.

Everything he had labored to accomplish through the years, the pinnacle of his work, had abandoned him, without a reason, without a trace.

He had put his all into Ilya Pytrovich Leschyov. He had put his most precious research into the man, making him a thing of perfection. He had combined him into the two greatest species on the Earth, having the benefits of both and the drawbacks of neither. He had searched far and wide for an animal that would make up the perfect composition of his team. Then he had used dozens and dozens of subjects to get his six boys, just like he had asked.

How did the man repay him? Dr. Montgomery felt heat rising in his throat, dripping down into his chest, and wafting upward to his brain. Ilya had repaid him by kidnapping his team and disappearing into the night. How dare he? How dare he?!

The doctor pushed himself up and grabbed the side of the desk, with the intent to throw it over. He hefted it, the great, oak thing didn't move. He screamed again and kicked the desk, only to feel the blow to his toes. He spun around, leaning against it, holding his foot, facing his large, multi-storied rat cage. The beautiful things in it stared at him compassionately, as if to say, "Yes, we understand. The wretched man left you, left you here to rot, without a backward glance." Dr. Montgomery felt tears coming to his eyes again.

He could replicate the transformation. There had to be someone out there who met the criteria. There had to be! He slumped his shoulders, and dropped his hurt toes to the floor. It had been almost ten years since Ilya had undergone the moreau process, and Dr. Montgomery had not yet been able to make another rat-man. Each additional try had ended up in the death of the subject, either from them not surviving the transformation process or process producing something deformed and deranged. There was no one else.

The tears in his eyes began to fall down his cheeks, hot and filled with despair. He looked at the little white and brown rat that stared at him from the cage and pushed himself off of the desk. Opening the cage, he took her out, and held her to his chest. "What am I going to do?" he asked. A teardrop fell on her fur.

She looked up at him with her black eyes, and blinked compassionately. She licked his hand.

"I know," he said to her. "You don't know, either."

She squeaked. The little, high pitched squeak that she had always made Dr. Montgomery feel better. Now, however, it did not. Another tear fell on her and she twisted her head to lick it off of her body. The music of the Nutcracker Suite played and Dr. Montgomery could think of nothing except the answer to his question.

His stomach turned and he had to swallow to keep from retching. After all of his years of service, all of his expertise, all of his adult life, there was no way the Initiative would let this slide, not when he had fought so hard for the stubborn Russian rat. He held the rat in his arms up to his face and kissed her head. She was a beautiful thing, a hooded rat. Her little brown head extended in a stripe down her back to her pink tail, the rest of her little body was a bright white. "Ilya was my greatest creation," he told her. "He did not deserve the honor I bestowed upon him."

Clarity, bitter and too late, came to his mind. "I am the one who deserved it."

Elias Montgomery had taken the various testing very early on in the program and had not gotten past the second level. He'd failed both the genetic test and the psychological test. He hadn't administered either of them, as an honest researcher, he did not want the results skewed. But those giving him the test could not have known everything that was inside of his head, everything that was in his genetics. The tests had changed over the years, as he had perfected the transformation process. He hadn't taken any of the newer tests, in fact, he hadn't taken any other than the original ones. Surely by now, the process was perfected enough that he would survive the transformation.

Carrying the rat with him, he left his office, into the small lab that adjoined it. This was not where he changed the other moreaus, those rooms were filled with monitoring equipment. He didn't need monitoring equipment. He had everything he needed right here, an IV bag, some rat moreau serum, and a needle. He put the rat down and she propped herself up on the table, looking at him curiously. He tied off his arm and inserted the needle. It pinched, but he got it in the vein. He went to grab the IV bag, and realized he didn't need it. He could inject the serum right into his body, without it being diluted by salt water. That was only to make the process slower, so they could monitor it easier, see where they might have made mistakes, if they made any. He took the little bottle of serum and glanced at the needle in his arm. He should have put the needle in his arm last, but it was already there, so he took a syringe and drew out the serum. He placed the needle on the syringe in the cannula tube meant for the IV bag.

He stared down at the needle in his arm, then up at the rat. She blinked at him and seemed to nod her little brown head. "Yes," he said. "It will be alright."

He pushed the plunger and fell to the floor, screaming.

# Chapter 26

**CLASSIFIED TOP SECRET**
**PROJECT SANCTUARY**

To:
Washington DC

From: Flayne Institute Experimental Facility
Chicago, Illinois

Subject: The Therian Initiative Update Report

It is with great regret that I have to inform you that our chief geneticist, , is no longer with The Therian Initiative. He has expired from a non-prescribed hallucinogenic medicine overdose. However, we still have his notes, formulae, and remaining blood samples from and are able to carry on his research without his supervision.

It appears that the shock from the death of his close companion has caused the rat moreau to lose his grip on reality. The transformation process, as we know, already makes the psychological make up of the subject unstable. It appears that subject ██████ was unable to endure the stress of ████████████ absence. He killed six African wild dog moreaus, subjects ██████, ██████, ██████, ██████, ██████, and ██████ in his care and then committed suicide.

While we understand that these setbacks will cost the Initiative a great deal concerning our budget, both past and present, we are confident that we can make that up in training the other moreaus we have and utilizing the sale and rental of moreaus as discussed in the several past round table meetings.

Signed: Agent ████████████

# Chapter 27

Their encounter with Grischat and his group had left Céline and her children in a buzz of excitement. Splayed on the couch after their adventure, the four of the children recounted their morning.

"We played baseball, Mama, have you heard of that?" Khenum asked.

"Yes," Céline answered. She tried to be happy for them, but the nagging pull at her chest on all of them made it difficult. She wanted to hug each and every one and not let go.

"I did excellent at tagging people out at the bases," Naga bragged.

"And I did excellent getting to the bases," Ursus said.

"What about you, Ariste?" Céline asked. "What were you excellent at?"

"I wasn't excellent at any of it," she said. "I didn't really like the game all that much. All it is, is hitting a ball with a stick and running. What's the fun in that?"

Céline chuckled and ruffled the top of her head, "I have always thought the same thing."

"I think Todd is cute, though," she said with a giggle.

Céline thought her eyes were going to pop out of her head and was glad she wasn't facing the couch at that particular moment. "Cute?" her voice sounded much too high as talked. She cleared her throat and turned. "Cute?" she said again.

"Don't you think he's cute, Mama?" Ariste twisted on the couch back to better face her mother.

"I...uh..." she blinked. She couldn't tell if he was cute or not! He looked like a fox in a person's body to her. How does one know if a fox is cute or not? She thought all of her children were beautiful, in a mother's way, and she knew it was a mother's way. Ariste's fur was shiny, with beautiful markings around her eyes and down the back of her head, disappearing into her shirt, only to reappear on her tail. Ursus was fuzzy, like a bear should be, a wonderful shade of brown. His paws were big and if one looked closely, one could see a slight streak of paler brown hair going down the middle of each of them. Khenum was wide, he would have very impressive shoulders when he grew up. His fleece was still downy and white, even though he was beginning to get some black down his back and near his hooves. Naga was the gorgeous dark green of the tropical forest from which Céline was sure she'd originally come. She had diamonds of even darker green running up her back, and then twisting to her front, to twist back around until they ended at the top of her head. Two diamonds came down around her eyes, like the fangs she had grown. Her thin arms had never thickened and they still looked like they would break easily, but Céline knew better. They were strong, like the rest of her. If she stood up to her full height, as high as she could get on her tail, she was already over six feet. She had no way of gauging whether any of them were considered good-looking in any other standard than the one she'd set, very much like a dog groomer sets up for animals. The thought almost made her blush, she was ashamed of it. "I didn't notice, honey. I was busy patching people up."

"You patched a lot of people up, Mama," Khenum said.

"I like his fur," she said dreamily. "He likes baseball and

carting."

"Carting?" Céline was feeling quite out of her element.

"They're like cars, but they are so small they only fit one person," Khenum said.

"You mean a go-cart?" she asked.

Ariste giggled. "Yes," she said. "He said the next time we come over, he'll take me riding."

Céline blinked, "I thought it only fit one person," she said slowly.

"I don't know," Ariste said, "maybe he can fit two in it."

Not if I can help it, she thought. She took a deep breath, wasn't this kind of thing supposed to start at a later age than 9?

"Do you know they go out into the city by themselves, Mama?" Naga said.

"They said they knew a great place for art supplies," Ursus told her.

"They?" Céline's mind didn't seem to be working right. "How many were there?"

The kids all exchanged looks, "Maybe 7," Ursus said.

"They were all Todd's age?"

"Yeah," said Khenum, "I think so."

"There wasn't anybody younger?" The next youngest of the children at the Cargo Bay had to be five years their elder.

"No," said Ariste, swishing her tail back and forth as she lounged on the back of the couch.

"We finally have friends!" Naga threw her arms into the air.

"You've always had friends," Céline fought a wave of guilt welling up in her. "You've had the roach farm, and the ant farm, and the alley cats, and that cat that lived with us for two years--"

"She left," Khenum interrupted.

"I told you," Céline explained, "she went off and married that black cat who kept visiting."

"It isn't the same thing," Ursus said. "They can't talk back to us."

"You have each other," Céline said, "and you have me."

Ariste laughed, almost derisively, "Oh Mama!" Céline braced herself for 'You're not our friend," and was filled with adoration when she said, "You have to be our friend. You're our Mama."

She doubted very much these moreaus were children. They might be children in age, but she suspected they were in a whole other category from her own. Worldly in a way that frightened her for her kids. Céline hadn't realized how much she'd sheltered her four children from the world of humans. She thought that shopping in the alleys and helping homeless men and women was showing them the world around them. They read books voraciously. Didn't that teach them about the human world?

The news and their encounter with Grischat's group showed her that it didn't. She had confused the human world with the world of humanity, and in so sheltering her little ones, they had not been aware of what people were capable of doing. They were shocked at the violence the news portrayed, and asked her question after question as to why someone would do such things. She had no answer for them.

It gave her a way to talk to them about people's intentions, however late the talk might have been.

"Why would people do that?" they asked, over and over.

"Because they are hurting," she told them. "People who are hurting hurt other people."

"So we have to help them," said Khenum.

"When we can," Céline answered.

"Can't we always help them?" Ursus asked.

Céline was quiet for a moment, as she thought of how to answer. "No, Teddy Bear," she said finally. "Sometimes, you can't help people. If they don't want to be helped, there isn't anything you can do. If they are abusive to you, then it is important to take care of yourself."

"I thought it was important to take care of others," Naga repeated a phrase that Céline, in her naivety, had told them.

Her heart beat fast in her chest, what she was about to say seemed to go against everything a parent was supposed to teach their children. She was telling them not to help people. She was telling them it because she was afraid. "You know, when we go out shopping sometimes, and I give homeless people medicine?"

The children nodded.

"Well, there are some people who don't take it, right? I don't give it to them anymore. Not because I don't want to help them, but because they don't want help."

"But what if someone does want help. Aren't we supposed to help them?"

"Not if it is to do something wrong. Or that will hurt the other person."

"Like when you give people vinegar tinctures instead of alcohol ones, because they're alcoholics!" Khenum announced proudly.

"Yes," Céline nodded. "Exactly."

"How do you know when to help someone and when not to?" asked Naga.

"If I knew the answer to that, Curly Que," Céline said, "I'd be queen of the world."

# Chapter 28

The hardest thing Ilya had to do in his life was keep his six puppies quiet. If it had not been for the crepuscular tendencies of their species and insulation between the basements and the buildings, he wasn't sure he'd have been unable to manage it at all. He had gotten them all to sleep during the day, waking up at dusk, and staying awake through the night, and falling asleep as dawn was approaching.

He had taken refuge with the puppies in the old basement of an office building. In modernizing the structure, some of the original basement had been abandoned. It was simply left open, a relic left behind from a bygone era. It was separated from the more modern basement by only the supporting joists and cinder block walls. For five days, he and the puppies had huddled in a darkened corner during the day, and he prayed to every saint he knew that they would not be discovered, that the puppies would be quiet, that no one would come down the basement for anything. It looked as if God had heard his prayers, because in those five days, no one found them.

While they lay hidden in the open space during the day,

at night they went out on 'supply runs'. He had never dreamt that his Spetsnaz training would come in handy hiding him, not once, but twice, in his lifetime. He stole sheet rock, drywall mud, tape, and paint from the hardware store. Doing so was more frightening than any hostage situation he had been involved in, more frightening than any fire fight, more frightening than not following orders, more frightening than knowing the Russian government had been after him to kill him for what he knew. The entire time he was coming to the hardware store, near the hardware store, in the hardware store, or leaving the hardware store, he was utterly terrified that a camera would catch a glimpse of them. Or more accurately, catch a glimpse of him. He was never 100% sure that he'd avoided the security cameras as he carried out supplies to build a wall to hide their den from the rest of the basement. He would have the puppies carry the mud and the tools while he carted sheets of drywall to their new hiding place. He built the framing the first night, and for the next four, erected a wall that matched the other walls in the basement as best as he could. He would have noticed that the wall was put up later than the others. He would have noticed it was not put in by an experienced construction worker. But office workers who came down to the basement would not know, he was sure, and once it was fully constructed, he was able to breathe a little easier.

The inside of the den was much less stressful to put together. He worked on the other side of the drywall first, gathering wooden pallets for wood and taking them apart. He built another frame for the wall and used empty soda and water bottles wedged in place with plastic grocery bags, in the space for insulation. Now he could relax that they wouldn't be heard so well on the other side. He then used pallets to make a wall paneling, for each of the walls throughout the entire space, which consisted of three rooms. Over the years, the walls made the place look like a real house, if one did not look up at the ceiling, or at the hole in one of them that led into the dirt beyond the wall.

He and the boys hollowed the surrounding ground out, making a burrow of types, with separate 'rooms' where they slept. It began with only one nest, a hole that was large enough for the six of them to sleep in. They piled up, using blankets for the bottom of the nest and nuzzling into them. He finally got tired of the dirt in his fur, and to keep it out, he put a floor made of pallets. It seemed silly to just have a floor, so he paneled the walls. Then the hallway that led to the nest. As the children grew, each wanted their own 'room', a new nest area, which also ended up paneled from floor to ceiling, so that Ilya was finally alone in the original nest, curled in a circle in a slew of blankets, dark and warm.

He felt safest in a nest, settled with his sons about him, away from the light of the world and the sounds of human voices. He hated himself for it. That is what a rat does, he told himself, stay hidden during the day in a hole in the ground. But then, what else was he to do? He and the boys could not go up in the light of day. Even when he went out with them at night, which he forced himself to do regularly and often, he was terrified of being caught. Even if one person saw them, and told someone else, The Initiative would find out, and it would only be a matter of time before they found them. As it was, they were living on borrowed time. Their lives belonged to The Therian Initiative, and the lives they lived now were stolen. He tried to console himself with the thought, Wild dogs spend the days in holes, too, waiting for the sun to set. It was one of the few things that he could bring himself to think that would comfort him.

He continued to teach the six boys Systema. One of the basement rooms was converted into a type of rink, simply an empty room with a wooden floor. The hardwood pallets were also excellent for an absorbent surface of the gym. He sanded them smooth, and he and the puppies oiled them with any oil they could find from their supply runs. The floor was shined to a burnished gold. For his Systema teaching, Ilya did not need any equipment, only the bodies of himself and his sons. It made the transition for the little ones from the Flayne Institute Campus to this new place much smoother. At least their training was the same.

He taught them to breathe. He taught them how to realize where their bodies were in space. He taught them to recognize their fears, and he taught them to trust in Spirit that their fears were unjustified, no matter what they were. The only thing in the room was a painted icon of "The Seeker of the Lost." He had painted it himself, and while he wasn't impressed with his artistic skills, it was close enough to what was shown in church that it was recognizable. The Queen of Heaven held the Divine Child in her arms, where he whispered the names of those lost and in danger of perishing into her ear. Each day, before training, even though his own Systema teacher would probably have been appalled by it, he said to the icon, "Seek us who are lost, O Queen of Heaven, do not punish us for our wrongdoings, but in your love for your children, have compassion and rescue us."

"Are we lost, Batya?" Evgeny asked one day after the prayer.

"We are all lost in one way or another," Ilya responded.

"How are we lost, Batya?" Dmitri asked, scooting closer to his father. "We know where we are."

Ilya was quiet for a long moment, looking at the icon that leaned against the wall on a shelf. "We are lost," he said, "because we are not like other people."

"Like the people on TV?" asked Kostya.

"Da," Ilya nodded. "Because we are different, we have to remain hidden," he said.

Nikita knelt next to the rat, pressing his body against Ilya's knee. "We have to be hidden to stay safe," he said, echoing Ilya's own words.

"Da," said Ilya again. He looked down at his eldest son, the boy's pale blue eyes gazing back.

"But what does staying hidden have to do with being lost?" asked Evgeny.

"Because if it is hidden," Ilya replied, "it might as well be lost."

# Chapter 29

Ilya put the newspaper, the top article "5 Bone Crushers Killed, Turf War Continues" in bold next to the picture of a murder scene, on their little kitchen table, to be waiting for him when they awoke in the morning. He still read the entire thing, cover to cover, with his morning tea, every day. He told himself it was to keep him abreast of what was happening around him. He knew, though, it was for any inkling that The Therian Initiative might be looking for him and the boys. Currently, he had seen nothing to indicate the need to be worried. However, he would stay out of the Haitian district for the time being, no need to be caught in the middle of a turf war with humans shooting at each other at night. Even if the police wouldn't believe them that a rat man with six puppy boys were out and about, the Initiative would believe them immediately.

The puppies put their bags of supplies from their run on the kitchen table also, and began to meander to their nest, except for his youngest, Kostya, and two in the middle, Vasili and Maxim.

Kostya pulled on Ilya's tail, "Come, Batya," he said, his

voice sounding much like his father's. "It is time for bed. The sun is rising."

Ilya flicked his tail out of the little boy's paws, "Go to bed," he said, none too gently. "I need to talk to your brothers."

The five year old sighed dramatically, as if a great burden had been put on his shoulders, and began to meander toward the hole that led to the nest. His theatrical skills were out in full force, he was cute and he knew it. This morning, however, the cuteness factor was not enough to make his father capitulate and come to bed with him. "Alright," he drawled, as he disappeared through the dark entrance to the bedroom.

Ilya crossed his arms and looked down his muzzle at the two boys that stood before him. They were the two that he figured were flat out in the middle of the pack in age, based on their body coordination and development when they were very small. He considered them both about six months older than Kostya, who, being the only one who could not walk when they came together, was his measuring stick. That would make them just over six, old enough to be out unattended with their father close by, but also old enough to know to follow orders. He said nothing, his face impassive, but his ears facing backwards.

Vasili, with his ears pressed to his head, looked at the floor, at the table, at his feet, at his hands, at the air about him, but not at his father.

Maxim's dark green eyes looked at Ilya unabashedly, his ears standing on end.

Neither said anything.

Ilya could wait them out.

When he felt his impatience rising, Ilya found the physical tension in his body, and released it with his breath. Like a flow of water, his breath drained from his ears, his eye ridges, his muzzle, his cheeks, his neck, his shoulders, his arms, his torso, his hips, his upper tail, his lower tail, his thighs, his calves, then his hands and his feet. With his body relaxed, and his breathing steady, he would continue to wait.

Vasili was the first to break.

"I am sorry," he said with a whine.

Ilya raised an eye ridge. "Sorry for what?" he asked.

The boy looked about the room again, as if something in it would give him the answer that his father was looking for. His white tipped muzzle, which made his black nose seem all the more black, twitched as he thought. "For not doing what we were told," he said.

Ilya sighed. Such a general explanation was to be expected from Vasili. He often could not pinpoint what it was he had done, either good or bad, when asked, only the general essence of the thing.

"I'm not sorry," said Maxim, his deep voice, even at the age of six, rumbling in the air about him. "We got what you wanted."

"You disobeyed me to get it," Ilya's voice matched his son.

Vasili's ears were glued to his head, and he leaned away from Maxim a little, as if his brother was exerting a force around him, pushing him away. Ilya saw it from the corner of his eye, and turned to him. "We did what you wanted, Batya," Vasili said, his voice still a whine. "We got the jam."

The rat said, exasperated. "I didn't tell you to go get it."

"But it was easy!" Vasili explained.

"Hvatyt!" Ilya said. "Enough." He turned to Maxim, who unlike his brother, could probably tell exactly why what he had done was wrong. Also unlike his brother, he probably wouldn't admit it. "Why am I angry?" The rat-warrior heard his voice rising, and put his attention back to his body to find the tension in, and breathe it out.

"Because you're scared!" Maxim yelled back.

Vasili inched away from his brother.

There was a silence in the room, a physical thing that one could grab and touch. Ilya stood stock straight, his stomach muscles showing against the lighter dusting of fur on his belly, his arms across his chest. Maxim looked up at him, his ears pointed forward, a scowl on his little muzzle, and his hands in fists by his side.

"Vasili," Ilya said, his eyes not leaving Maxim. "Go to bed."

Vasili wasted no time before running for the hole that led to the nest.

Ilya bent down, his breath coming in hard puffs, as was Maxim's. He put his muzzle up to the boys, his gray eyes glaring. "Do you know why I was scared for you, Maxim?" he asked, his mouth barely moving.

"You are scared of humans," the boy said. "You do not have to be scared for me. I can take care of myself." The defiance in his little, dark green eyes shined.

Ilya could see his own nostrils flare at the end of his muzzle, as well as feel them. "Do you know what the humans will do to you if they find you?" he asked very slowly. He knew his voice was vicious, a harsh parody of what it should be, the voice a commander and not a father.

The little boy continued to stare at him defiantly.

"Maxim," Ilya drew his name out, "when a human sees you, they will scream. Not scream like you and your brothers when you are playing, but scream like they do in the movies on the television. If they have a gun, they will shoot you, and kill you. If they do not have a gun, they will run away, and tell someone who does have a gun. If you are lucky, the gun will kill you right away. If you are not, then the bullet wound will cause you to fall. While you lay on the ground, you will have trouble breathing."

The defiant look began to fade from the boy's face. He looked at the rat as if he were crazy.

The Systemist knew that he shouldn't be saying what he was saying, the way he was saying it. He seemed to be unable to stop himself from talking to the puppy as if he were a soldier and not a little boy. "As you try to breathe, you will feel the blood running out of your wound. You will see the ground beneath you turn red, and you will know in your heart of hearts that is your life draining away."

The boy began to look scared.

Good, thought Ilya, he is beginning to understand.

"You will begin to burn," he continued. "You will be unable to get air into your lungs, and you will be so hot you will feel like you are on fire. Pain will shoot up your body from the gunshot. Then, when you cannot get any breath in you at all, you will suffocate and die."

He stared into the boy's eyes, which shone in horror.

"Do you understand, Maxim?"

The puppy gave a little nod, much like one Ilya would have given him when he was angry, but defeated.

"Jam for tea is not worth that," Ilya's voice became tender, and he drew the boy to him. Maxim nuzzled his head in the crook of Ilya's neck, where it was especially warm. The rat could feel him blinking rapidly, and knew it was to keep tears from coming.

"But you want jam for your tea," he whispered.

"But I want you more," Ilya picked him up, and walked toward the hole in the wall. He nestled down with the six puppies, all of them piled upon each other for warmth and comfort. Ilya kept his arm about Maxim, his hand holding the little boy's shoulder to keep him close.

It took little time for the boys to fall asleep, their different breathing patterns identifying each one in the dark.

# Chapter 30

From The Desk Of

Dear

I would think that after all this time, you would think that by now you would be above petty rumors, . I would also think that you would have come to me or if you had any real questions involving the Initiative and not rely on the grapevine to get your information.

There has been no change in the otter team. It is, and always will be, one of our most powerful teams. All of the members are healthy and in full working order, for eldest to youngest. If you had ever once bothered to visit the facility, you would know that.

Dr. Theedy is a disgruntled employee, nothing more. You, of all people, should know about disgruntled employees and the damage they can do. She is upset that she did not get position upon his death, and was not promoted on this last round of promotions. Obviously, this is her form of revenge.

If you want to do something constructive for The Therian Initiative in particular, or Project Sanctuary in general, you can advise me on how to proceed with Dr. Theedy, rather than get on my case about matters that don't exist.

I know you have a lot on your plate, we all do. Of course, I will write up an official report about this, which will arrive shortly. But next time, pick up the damn phone and ask some questions before you send over reports like that last one.

Your friend,

██████████

# Chapter 31

He slept curled up, his back cold and wet from the dampness of the sewer tunnel. He could feel the other rats all about him, bits of warm and cold differentiating their little bodies against his fur. Their familiar smells, mixed with the stench of the sewer, gave him great comfort. Curled under his thick neck, the little brown hooded rat, she told him she liked the name Evangeline, slept soundly, warm and safe.

If it was not for Evangeline, he was sure he would have died on the lab floor. The pain in his body had been more than he thought was possible for a body to bear. It ripped him into pieces, severed him in places that should have killed him instantly. It merged him together, burning his muscles, his skin, his organs. When the great agony of the transformation stopped, still pain lingered in every cell of his body. His brain was on fire, like someone had reached into his head and placed hot coals on his gray matter. Through the fog of torment, he felt words, soft and beautiful.

"You must get up," it said. "You must get up and run."

It was more of a sensing of words, than of actually hearing them. Almost as if he were being given information, and his brain was translating it for him into words that he could understand. "I can't," he thought back to the words. "I can't move."

"You can move," it told him.

He felt something soft and warm on his nose, wet and lapping.

"You must open your eyes, and run, or we will have to leave you alone. We cannot stay here."

The word 'alone' made his already pained body clench, a stark contrast to the warm, wet lapping on his nose, and on the front of his lips. He opened his eyes, and the world swam in front of him, wavy and blurred, like looking underwater. He moved his head back, and tried to push himself up. The pressure on his arms made needles shoot through his limbs, and he moaned in discomfort.

"You must come," said the voice.

He looked down, and saw the little brown and white hooded rat who had been with him when he injected himself. She was propped up on her hind legs, her black eyes looking at him expectantly. He closed his eyes as a wave of nausea joined the pain in his body. When he did, sounds, small and far away, bombarded him, so that it was difficult to distinguish any of them. A loud bang made him start, the movement aching.

Someone was banging on the door to his office.

More than one something was banging on the door to his office.

"Montgomery!" he heard someone shout, he couldn't recognize who, "open the door!"

Another bang resounded from the far room, loud and strong enough that he managed to get to his feet. He looked down at them, and they were a twisted parody of claws, a tripod of long toes on an even longer foot. His trousers had been torn open during his transformation, to show short and thick legs covered with white drizzled dark gray fur. He saw the little white and brown rat scurry to the window in the room, clawing at it frantically. When he didn't move, she looked at him, compassion in her little black eyes, and she bolted behind the bookcase.

The door shook as someone tried to kick it in.

Dr. Montgomery got his deformed feet to move, barely, and made his way to the window. He was on the second story of the building, bushes and flower gardens adorned the edge of the building below.

"Jump!" said the voice in his head.

He knew if he jumped he would make it. He knew, deep in his being, that he would land, and he would run. He backed up, and crashed through the glass, falling, falling, until the hard ground hit his arms and legs, jarring his joints. But he had made it. He was on his feet, his hands served as feet too, he noticed. His fingers, like his toes, were a tripod of digits ending in claws. He felt his back bend and straighten as he ran, and the little brown and white rat was by his side.

He needed to get somewhere dark. He needed to get somewhere close. He needed to get out of the open. The little brown and white rat had run for a storm drain, and he'd followed her, all but overtaking her. She disappeared through the space in the grate. He grabbed it with his hands, three fingers and thumb, and threw it off to the side. He was down the storm drain, running, running in the dark, until his body would not hold him up any longer and he collapsed on the filthy concrete. Pain still wracked his body, but he felt the soft, wet lapping against his nose and his lips again. Opening his eyes, he saw the little white and brown rat licking him affectionately. "You're safe now," she said.

He sighed, and closed his eyes again.

When he opened them, the pain had gone, but the noise in his head had worsened. He could hear impressions of all kinds of things. Noises came to his ears, some voices, some not. Impressions of others speaking to him, as the little brown and white rat had, also bounced in his brain. He sat up, and saw there were many rats about him, most of them gray or brown sewer rats. They sniffed him, and licked him, and rubbed against him, and he heard their voices so clearly that he put his hands to his head.

Only, his head was shaped wrong.

Where his ears used to be, it was now only head, rounded and furry. With the tips of his elongated fingers, he could feel the ears on the top of his skull, moving as if by their own volition to hear the things about him. When he touched them, he noticed they were small, and the feeling reminded him of the ears of his sea otter moreaus. He moved his hands to his face, seeing they were bright pink. He did not have a muzzle, he felt, but rather just an elongated nose that seemed to twist down onto his lip. Underneath it, he felt two giant teeth protruding from his blunted mouth.

He looked down at his body, the ghostly noises in his head not abating. His legs were short and curved, like a rat, and he stood on his toes, his ankle now sticking out behind him. His body, however, was long, with stretched shoulders and a straight back. At the base of his spine, he curved, as if he needed to do so to accommodate the short, thick legs. His coccyx did not end at the curve, it kept going, and split, and split again, so he had nine segmented tails, each moving independently of the others, a caricature of the lovely hind end of a rat.

Nine tails. All he needed now was a nutcracker, and he would be The Rat King.

"The Rat King," rang in his head in hundreds of different voices, each a phantasmal utterance. All around him rats began to flock, rats in all different colors. Brown rats, white rats, gray rats, black rats, spotted rats, hooded rats. "The

Rat King," he said to him, each and every one.

And he knew that was who he was.

# Chapter 32

"Don't move," Ilya told his boys. Since Maxim and Vasili's little 'adventure', he had been very deliberate on his instructions to them when they were out and about. They were in a series of dumpsters behind a grocery store and a bakery, on a supply run for food. He had found early on that human beings dumpster dived also. Most of them were homeless or poor college students. A few of them went food diving to get food for their urban farms, he'd overheard. The Systema Master had had to breathe away some envy upon hearing the conversation while hidden in the shadows. On a small urban lot, the people had chickens, vegetables, two apple trees, two plum trees, and many berry bushes. It was something he could have done, he had all the time in the world to do it, if he could see the light of day. But he hadn't been out in the daylight for years.

Tonight, however, it was not homeless people or poor college students, he could tell by their footsteps. They were not the sound of soles hitting the asphalt, but the soft slap of bare feet and the scrape of claws.

Moreaus.

There were moreaus out in the city at night. Why would there be moreaus out? The entire Therian Initiative was to train soldiers. Were these moreaus out to hunt him? When still at Flayne Institute, he had heard that other moreaus had escaped, especially early in the program. Had The Initiative now decided to send people after those who had escaped? Ilya knew more than most moreaus about what was going on in the compound, about what the Initiative was up to. Did he know enough that he was worth going after and trying to find?

He smelled squirrel, pig, dog, and sea otter. Sea otter?

"I hate food duty," someone said. "These boxes get heavy."

"I don't like that we have to go back and then go out again," said someone else.

Ilya could hear their footsteps come closer to the garbage can where he and the boys were hiding. He motioned for them to bury themselves in the rubbish, and as they wiggled, he heard, "What's that noise?"

There was a moment of silence, and Ilya knew that the moreaus were sniffing the air. "Rats," said one of them.

"...and dogs?" another added.

"Dogs in a dumpster?"

"Rats and dogs?" a different one asked. He dropped his voice, so it was very soft. "Are you sure, rats and dogs, in that dumpster?"

"Yeah," answered the voice that had indicated the dogs.

Again, there was a long moment of silence, and Ilya relaxed himself, breathing out his tension, as he got ready to strike.

"Ilya Pytrovich?" a voice called gently. "Is that you?"

At hearing his name, the first time in five years, the rat felt his heart jump to his throat. He had to breath three times to get the tension out of his body, he was so coiled. Whoever it was, he did not recognize the voice, knew him and knew he had puppies.

"Subzero," whispered one of the voices. "What are you doing?"

"Ilya Pytrovich?" Subzero said again.

Ilya was still, relaxed and his mind at ease. He heard claws gently touch the lip of the dumpster before he saw the tips of the fingers of a sea otter. A wedge shaped head with small ears perched on the top emerged slowly from the lip of the garbage dump, a dark brown against a dark night. The Systema Master wasted no time, as soon as he saw the ears emerge, he jumped out of the dumpster, landing behind the sea otter. With a quick grab, he threw the moreau across the street, so that he rammed into the wall of the opposite building. The other three moreaus recovered from their surprise quickly and came at him, teeth bared, knives and claws drawn. Ilya's tail dispatched the dog, he appeared to be crossed with a doberman pinscher, with little trouble, one swipe crashing against his arm and sending the knife skidding, and a return whip smacked him the in the ribs, causing him to slide to the side, curled in a ball. The squirrel had jumped in the air, and was coming at him in an arc from above. He grabbed one of the squirrel's outstretched arms as he fell upon him, and deflected his attack by using his momentum to flip him over and behind him. The pig was charging him, his head down low, his shoulder's clenched. Just as the pig reached him, he heard Subzero shout, "Stop! This is Ilya Pytrovich!" But the pig had reached him. He strafed out of the way, brought a relaxed arm down on the pig's back, and the moreau collapsed, his own propulsion making his fall that much harder.

"Stop!" said Subzero again. The sea otter was up, and had his hands outstretched. "Ilya Pytrovich, it's me!"

Ilya regarded the sea otter through the learned relaxation that lay behind the adrenaline of the fight. He recognized him.

"Teacher," said Subzero, almost pleadingly.

"Dyson," the sea otter's name came to the forefront of his mind. He consciously softened his body, ready for another attack from any of the downed moreaus.

The sea otter smiled at him, with his tight muzzle it looked like a small mouthed grimace, the tips of his eye teeth showing. "Yeah," he said, pushing himself up off the ground. "You still pack a punch."

In his peripheral vision, Ilya could see the other moreaus moving, but none of them were getting ready to come at him. Their bodies were not the tense of an attack, but were the slight tense of confusion.

Dyson's smile faded as he saw that Ilya was not changing his attitude. He put his hands to his back and arched it, "When you escaped, we thought that your puppies wouldn't be able to survive, they were too little."

"Why are you here?" Ilya asked harshly.

"To get food, man," said the squirrel, rolling his head in circles to stretch it. "We gotta eat, same as you."

"We escaped too," Dyson explained, slowly coming closer, as if he were approaching a wary animal.

But then, he is, isn't he? thought Ilya.

"When?" he demanded.

"Before you," said the pig with a grunt, getting up off of the ground. Once he was up, he straightened the denim vest he was wearing.

"You're quite the famous one," the doberman said. He was wearing a white sleeveless undershirt and jeans tailored to his body. When Ilya didn't answer him, he said, "You gonna leave your dogs in the dumpster?"

Ilya felt the situation around him, suppressing the anger that threatened to bloom in his chest at the words "your dogs". It sounded like he was making them pets, that he was making them servants. They were children, not animals. But beyond his own anger, and the wariness of those about him, he felt no danger in the situation, and no lies in what any of them were saying. "Vykhodit," Come out, he called. The rustling in the dumpster preceded six little puppy heads popping up over the lip.

"They're all still alive," Dyson said in amazement. "I don't believe it."

As they climbed out, Ilya retreated so that he was standing near the dumpster, his six little puppies gathered around him. "Why not?" he asked. "You think that my sons would be fodder for The Initiative?"

Maxim raised his nose in the air and sniffed them, Evgeny held firmly onto Ilya's leg. All were silent.

The look on Dyson's face changed to one of concern, "No. They were just so little…"

"Little does not mean defenseless," Ilya said.

The squirrel laughed. He took a few steps forward and put out his hand. He was about four and half feet tall, and very squirrel-esque, the human in him manifesting mainly in his chest, shoulders, and arms. "I like you," he said, rubbing his head, "you know you're stuff. I'm Bullwinkle. Subzero here, and few others, have told us a lot about you."

Ilya looked at his paw for a moment, before extending his own. He gave the squirrel a firm handshake, and said, "I am Ilya Pytrovich Leschyov. These are my sons," he gestured to each in turn, "Nikita, Dmitri, Vasili, Maxim, Evgeny, and Kostya."

Bullwinkle smiled down at them.

"We can tell the Medicienne that someone's got more kids than her," the pig said, putting his own hand out. "I'm Gristle."

"I'm Comet," the doberman said. "She might not like being one upped." He winked at Ilya in a conspiratorial manner.

"Children…?" he said, looking from the other two to Dyson.

"La Petite Medicienne," he explained. "She's our doctor. She has four little ones of her own. They're older than yours, though. She keeps a tight rein on them."

"I don't blame her," Ilya said cautiously. There was another moreau out there with children? He only knew of the making of the puppies for his team. Had some of the other puppies somehow escaped? "She is French?" he guessed from the name.

Subzero shook his head, "No, our leader is Haitian." He gestured grandly, "That's why we're near Englewood. It's part of our turf."

"You have turf?" the rat asked. He had actively avoided Englewood, West Englewood, and Gage Park for the New City neighborhood so that he wouldn't come in contact with any of the Haitian gang members or their enemies. Yet, here he was, on someone else's turf, once again. Only this turf, next to what the Bone Crushers claimed, was claimed by a bunch of moreaus.

"Everybody's got turf," said Bullwinkle. "Some people just defend it better than others."

Ilya nodded at him, a slight nod, almost just of his muzzle. The squirrel was correct, his den would be his turf, wouldn't it? The places he frequented, like here, he would be sore to give up and have to move on. "You must protect your turf?" he asked.

"Sometimes," Comet said, his voice a little suspicious.

Ilya could see him tensing his shoulders a little, the dog did not trust him. Good. He shouldn't. "Against whom?"

"Whoever decides they want to encroach on it," Subzero said, coming up to Ilya and clapping him on the shoulder, his smile still wide. "Do you have anyone else?" He looked about, as if to emphasize his words, "Is it just you and the pups?"

"It is just I and the puppies," he said, putting his arm around the nearest one to him. He could tell by the feel of the fur it was Nikita, his eldest, who had just turned seven.

"Come on then," Subzero motioned with his head, "Grischat will be thrilled to meet you."

"Who is Grischat?" Ilya asked, not moving.

"He's in charge of the Grey Cats," Gristle said. "You don't have to be by yourself anymore. There's a whole bunch of us."

Ilya looked at him confused. "A whole bunch…?"

"Dozens of moreaus, Ilya Pytrovich," Subzero said. "People who have escaped, some of them a long time ago."

Fear reached for the Russian, touching him gently with its fingertips, trying to roll his heart closer so it could grab him. Dozens of moreaus who had escaped…other people. He shook his head, pulling Nikita closer to him. "No, we are fine," he replied. "We have a home, and we have each other."

"We have a doctor," Gristle said.

"I do not need a doctor," Ilya turned only his head to face the pig. "I have been able to handle whatever has come along." He looked to each of the moreaus in turn.

"But you can't—" Comet began.

"This is part of our turf," Subzero interrupted him. "If you want to find any of us, we'll be around here."

Ilya nodded again. "I heard you were on a food run," he said. "This dumpster is a good catch." He motioned to the boys to go ahead of him in the direction they had come, then turned.

"Aren't you going to take anything?" Subzero asked.

The rat shook his head, "It is all yours," he gave him a wan smile. "We will get something on the way home."

"You're welcome to come with us whenever you want," Bullwinkle assured him as he walked away. "We've all been in the same boat."

Ilya twisted his head around, and nodded once again. "Thank you," he said. "I will remember that."

# Chapter 33

Two days after their stay at the Cargo Bay, as Céline and the children were tending their little garden, she was clipping some juniper branches, she heard "Hey, Medicienne!" The young voice said the word with no trace of a French accent, so that she giggled. She had never heard the old fashioned word for a female doctor butchered in such a way, and it was refreshing to hear a young person speak with so little self-reservation. Moving the ivy that grew on the chain link fence aside, she saw three of the 'children' from Grischat's place passing the garden on the sidewalk. Their arms were laden with bags.

The kids began to climb the rope that hung down from their top story window that led into their garden, which was inaccessible any other way, unless one jumped the high fence. They scrambled up quickly ahead of her, her own progress was always much slower. She had to use the knots they'd tied in the rope, the kids didn't seem to need it. Even Khenum, with his large, stout frame could do it faster than she. And to be honest, she didn't think she did it all that slow.

The kids were already headed down the stairs when she

climbed in the window, calling out to the kids on the street. They were like normal children, receiving their friends when they asked to come out and play. For some reason, she didn't like it.

She stayed in their home, and waited for the kids to come up. She could hear them all chattering, both hers and the others. When they emerged from the stairwell, Todd who was beaming a smile at a beaming Ariste, turning it Céline. "Hello, Medicienne," he said. "We've brought you some stuff. Grischat says if there is anything else you want, to let us know, and we'll get it."

She took a deep breath. "That's very nice of you all," she said. She wasn't going to ask Grischat for anything. Being in his debt did not seem like a good idea to her.

They put the bags on the table, and her kids began taking the items out. "Mama," Ariste exclaimed, "milk!" She held up a gallon jug.

"And sugar," Naga said, "and flour."

"And tea!" Ursus gasped, taking a canister out of the bag, "and coffee!"

"And honey," Khenum took out a great big jug of it. Ursus "mmmm"ed and reached for it, Khenum swatting his paw away.

"Grischat wanted me to give this to you," Todd handed her a small shopping bag. "He said it was for you by yourself. Not to share."

She opened the bag, and in it was a chocolate bar. A chocolate bar...she hadn't had chocolate in...how long?

"Of course it is to share," she said, smiling as she opened the package. Todd and the others of his group looked shocked as she broke off the little squares it was divided into and handed one to each child. It left three for her. "You can tell Grishcat that I had more than everyone else, and thank you."

Todd's group ate their chocolate slowly, obviously knowing what it was. Her own, however, gobbled the little square once they put it in their mouths. "Oh, Mama," Ursus crooned. "That is good."

She chuckled, "Yes it is, honey."

"We can stick around for a while," one of Todd's group said. "Wanna go out?"

"Can we, Mama?" Naga said pleadingly. "Pleeeasssseee?" All four them drawled out the word.

She sighed. She didn't want to let them out of her sight, her stomach clenched and the sweet taste of chocolate was suddenly bitter. She didn't know anything about these moreaus. They were all a bit older than her children, many of them had been patched up from the fight that caused so many injuries. But she couldn't think of any good reason why she could refuse the request.

"Who is the oldest?" she said, looking over the moreaus in front of her.

"We're all 14," Todd said. "Except for them," he pointed to a boy squirrel and a girl ferret moreau. "They're still only 13." Both of them smiled.

Five years older than her own…that seemed like such a big age difference. She didn't want to let them go. She wanted to tell them to go home, that her kids couldn't come out to play today. But why? Because she didn't know these children? Fourteen was still a child, they still played. Didn't they? Who was she to deny them playing with people closer to their own age than she was? "Alright," she managed to squeeze out. They all rushed toward the stairs, "but stay in the block, and don't let anyone see you!"

"OK!"

"I mean it, only these four warehouses!"

They were already down the stairs, and she didn't know if they heard her or not.

She began to put the food on the table away, placing the cold items in the old fridge that worked so well, they had to keep items from the back of it or else they froze. She held the box of tea, it was Sephisa Breakfast Black Tea. A gourmet tea. A cup of sweet, creamy tea, she thought. Don't mind if I do.

Her four little moreaus were gone all day. The warehouse was eerily silent, the only sounds the knocks and scuttles of the old building expanding and contracting in the heat of the day. She drank her cup of tea slowly, with her eyes closed, but when she was finished, she was still alone and all was quiet.

She hoped that they were staying within the block. That if a human being came into view they'd hide. How did Grischat's people deal with humans? They obviously had no issue with her. But then again, they had all been beaten to hell and needed someone to doctor them.

She looked at her bookcase, noting she didn't have any books on birds. She needed some books on...birdology. That wasn't right, what was the study of birds anyway? On the top of the bookcase sat the vase of juniper branches, a stoneware white with a chip in the back. Her tribute to the bird in her life that she'd lost, and had no need to learn how to care for. The top of the bookcase had become an altar of sorts, an unintentional place to put precious things. A small bowl of the children's milk teeth, the ones that hadn't been swallowed, sat at one end of the shelf, and another small bowl on the other side with her wedding and engagement ring in it. Photos in frames of her and the children, taken with an old, discarded Polaroid camera were on either side of the vase. The photos of the kids were when they were younger, still little children and not something in between a child and a teenager. She had always thought the 'tween' movement was idiotic, but now she could see why parents sectioned it out.

She thought of the previous conversations she'd had with the kids, and of Ariste's question of "Don't you think he's cute, Mama?"

She made her way to the work out room, a purposefully set up gymnasium with a makeshift jumping horse, a balance beam, a platform to give her some height to able to reach the ducting nearer the ceiling that she used for the uneven bars, a section of the concrete covered in an area rug for floor exercises, and a section covered in wood flooring for practicing yoga and for dancing. While everything would have made another gymnast cringe, Céline loved her homemade gym. She'd made it with the children, and was proud of them all for having done so. She did some cursory stretches and then jumped to the rafters.

She would tell Ariste that "Of course he's cute, Kitty Cat."

She vaulted, and twirled, and twisted, and spun, and still couldn't get her mind to quiet. It was not until the sun began to go down and her four precious things came back up the stairs that she was able to feel even remotely calm.

Sitting at the table, all of them eating sandwiches from items in the many bags brought to them, the kids talked over each other trying to tell her what happened during the day.

"We showed them all the warehouses."

"And introduced them to the alley cat."

"They taught us how to do power kicks!"

"I tried to teach them to do back flips!"

She listened to them tell about their day, an ordinary day of children playing. Why did it bother her so much? Nothing they said indicated anything awry, no reason for her to feel uneasy. It is just different, she told herself. You don't like that you're not in control. But that reasoning seemed hollow. She had allowed them to play without her supervision for many years now, keeping the boundaries to the four warehouses and their large lots that made up the block and become invisible if a human happened to come into view. They had never been caught by a human while within their little kingdom. She knew they did things that she would not approve of, but she also knew they did not often directly disobey. She knew they had broken things, on purpose, in the other warehouses, and in this one. She knew, now, that had been jumping over roofs for some time. She knew they had a little workshop in the adjacent warehouse that they built secret things in, that they had a TV in there where they watched shows of which she would not have approved. She knew that if a human did come into their space, they stealthily scared the wits out of them, again in ways of which she would not agree. They kept things from her, she knew this, but they were innocent things. And they knew they were innocent things, for when they felt guilty about doing something wrong, all four of them would confess.

She recalled a few years ago when someone had left a car just at the edge of their block. They had bounced and begged to explore it, and she told them they could, after she was done in the garden so she could go with them. She was too afraid that the car as in full view, and an abandoned car was probably stolen. She didn't want the police to come by looking for it, and find her little ones instead. They had gone off by themselves, taken huge amounts of it apart, taken the parts back to their warehouse, and carried them up the stairs all so quietly, she hadn't heard them come by the garden wall. Before she had finished with the garden, they had all come down the rope and stood by her, their eyes wide and their mouths pouted. "Mama," Ariste said, "we went to the car."

Céline put down her spade, and raised an eyebrow. "Oh?"

"We took some stuff off it," Ursus said, looking everywhere save at his mother.

Céline raised her other eyebrow. "Oh?" the word was drawn out slower.

"We took the stuff upstairs," Naga told her.

"Oh?" she crossed her arms in front of her chest. She looked at each of them in turn. "Why did I ask you not to go to that car by yourselves?"

"Because a human might see us," Ariste said.

"But humans see us all the time, " Khenum whined.

"Lamb's Ear, those humans aren't..." she searched how to put it nicely, "aren't reliable witnesses."

Khenum looked at her quizzically.

"She means they're crazy," Ariste elucidated. "No one will believe them if they say they saw us."

"Oooooh," Khenum nodded his head knowingly.

"If a human sees you, it is dangerous," she told them. "They may take you away, or they may hurt you because they're scared." She looked each in the eye again. "I do not tell you to do something to be mean. I do it to keep you safe."

Each little face had looked so remorseful, she didn't have the heart to punish them properly. Instead, she made them stay in her sight for three days.

Watching the four of them now, eating their sandwiches on bread that was not stale, on cheese that did not have to have the mold cut off of it, with meat that didn't have to be picked through to take out what was rotten, poured the feeling of inadequacy into her soul like it hadn't for a long time.

She thought she had done so well. Going from knowing nothing, to being able to provide them with food, shelter, clothing. They had things that other, normal people had. They had beds, and mattresses, and sheets and blankets, and dressers and desks, and a kitchen with a stove and a fridge…yet compared to these simple sandwiches made with food that did not come out of a dumpster or behind a grocery store, none of that seemed to compare.

After they were finished, Céline's thoughts kept swirling, so that she clapped her hands to summon the kids to her, and said "Let's dance!" They made their way to their little makeshift yoga/dance floor, Ursus put on the radio, and Céline tried to lose herself in the music and movement.

Dancing was her drug of choice. When nothing else worked to quiet her mind, when she was overcome with feelings of guilt, or inadequacy, or the intense loneliness that sometimes came upon her, she would turn on the club music station, and move her body in whatever way it wanted to move. She would lose herself in the music, and time would go by without her knowing it. The kids would start out dancing with her, each of them moving their bodies in a way that was natural to their species. There had been many times, however, that when Céline had returned to the here and now, her body shining with sweat, her hair sticking to her forehead and neck, and the kids were asleep on the edge of the dance floor or on the couch. Hours had gone by, and her body was numb. She would collapse into her bed, and before the morning, all four of her children would be in bed with her, Naga wrapped around her, Ariste curled into a ball at her thighs, and each of the boys on either side of her.

Tonight was no different. The kids stayed with her as long as they could, then exhausted they bedded down around her, dance music still beating through the warehouse.

# Chapter 34

"Batya," asked Kostya. His gray eyes, the color of ocean water, were wide. "What does turf mean?"

The seven of them were curled up together in their nest, now buried in different degrees in the blankets and each other. The hardwood floor made of pallets helped to create a pocket of air between the ground and the floor, keeping it warmer than it had been.

"Turf," the rat replied, "is territory. It is a place that one claims they own."

"Like your house?" asked Dmitri.

"A little," said Ilya. "But more than that."

The puppy waited in the intense dark of the nest.

"Like what, Batya?" Kostya asked.

"Territory is a piece of land that someone thinks is theirs. Just like a toy that you feel is yours and not your brothers."

"Like my pookah?" Ilya felt Kostya wiggle in what he knew as a hug with the little boy's small stuffed bunny.

"Yes, exactly like that, but with land."

"How do those moreaus own land?" Nikita asked.

"Wouldn't the humans kill them like they would us?"

Why did children have to ask such hard questions? "Yes, that is why they were out at night. They were on a food mission, just like us."

"But how can they have land?" Nikita persisted.

Ilya sighed, "My guess is they kill humans they find."

"Good," said Maxim.

"Maxim," Ilya drew the boy's name out. "That is not good."

"The humans would kill us," he said. "Why shouldn't we kill them?"

The rat was silent for a moment. "Killing people is wrong," he said.

"Then why do you train us to fight?" Dmitri asked.

"If the situation ever comes up that someone is going to try and kill you, I want you to be able to be the one who walks away."

There was a moment of quiet, and Ilya thought the conversation was over, when Evgeny said, "I saw you defeat those other moreaus." His voice was very small, as if he did not want to wake anyone up who might have fallen asleep with his talking.

"Yes," Ilya answered just as quietly.

"You were so fast," he whispered.

"One day, you will be that fast," he said, a little louder. "And when you are that fast, you do not have to kill anyone."

"Because you can run away faster?" Vasili asked, the only one who had not spoken so far in the conversation. It was a question he would have expected from Maxim, asked in contempt.

"Nyet," replied Ilya. "Because you can knock them out before they get to you."

"Why didn't you knock out those other moreaus, then?" Maxim asked.

"I didn't need to."

"Because one of them knew you?" Nikita asked.

"No," Ilya answered honestly. "Because they were not a threat enough to knock unconscious."

"What's unconscious mean?" Kostya asked.

"It means to knock out," Evgeny answered before Ilya could.

"But one was your friend," Kostya said to his father. "Why would you knock him out?"

Ilya was quiet, trying to think of an answer the boy would understand.

"He's your friend, isn't he?"

"He may have been once, a long time ago, when we lived at the research institute."

"Is he your friend now?" Evgeny asked.

"I don't know," was all Ilya could think to reply.

The room fell silent again, and Dyson came to his mind, as did many of his former students. He had gotten to know about them on such a deep level, they shared things that he would never have dreamt of sharing with a commander, but he did not know if they were ever his friends.

You abandoned the one true friend you had at FSRI, the thought seemed to come from outside of him, the voice wasn't his. It had its own distinct individuality, separate from him. It was smooth and deep, almost hypnotic sounding.

He watched out for you. He protected you from those who wanted to hurt you. He loved you, like his own son. But you abandoned him.

He shook his head slightly, the chastising voice was still in his mind, though. He could feel it there, like someone was reaching inside of his thoughts and wiggling their fingers around.

Why should anyone else befriend you? You are only out for yourself.

No, Ilya thought to the voice, panic beginning to rise in him. I am not only out for myself. I look out for the boys.

Do you look out for them, for them? asked the voice. Or for you?

The answer did not come to him. I do it for them! his mind yelled.

They are your team, the voice said.

Yes, Ilya replied with relief.

Do you care for them to make up for your lost teammates back in Russia?

The relief was whisked away by the harsh wind of the thought, making his heart race. Was he going insane? Hearing voices in one's head is what happened to crazy people, wasn't it? Perhaps he was dreaming, and this dream was only sound and no vision. But as soon as the thought occurred to him, the memory of his last mission before his team had left the military assaulted him.

The seven of them were gathered together, fear beating in their chests. The walls and roof of the canvas tent billowed in the harsh wind, and they could see their breath as white clouds floating away in front of them like smoke.

"You don't have to come with me," had said his commander. "You can still follow orders of the mission. I won't blame you."

None of them had said anything in answer.

"If you do come with me, you can always say you were following my orders. Even though I'm not giving you any. I'll take the rap if you choose to stay with me."

They were a Spetsnaz team, some of the finest military elite in the world. They were a family. They stuck together. They didn't follow unethical orders.

"You know we're with you," said one of his teammates.

His commander had nodded. Two days later, he'd been killed.

Is this what you want for your boys? said the voice.

"No!" Ilya sat up, feeling two of the puppies fall off of him as he did. It was dark, complete darkness, as was normal in the nest. Not even his night vision could pierce the blackness.

"Y'OK, Batya?" Kostya asked sleepily.

The Systemist took a deep breath, and then laid back down. "Yes, Kostya," he answered, closing his eyes again. "I had a nightmare."

The little boy cuddled up with him, Ilya could feel the stuffed bunny he always slept with in between them. He put his arms around his youngest son, and the word filled him with comfort. My son, he said, squeezing him to his chest. Not my teammates. My sons.

# Chapter 35

"Please can we go play at the Cargo Bay?" Céline's children asked.

She had fobbed the question off quite a few times, taking them to play in The Garden of the Phoenix or going on foraging in some of the overgrown places in the city, allowing them to run and play in a different abandoned section than their own. But the enticement of other people, people like themselves that weren't themselves, was too much for Céline to keep away. Finally, she consented.

She only needed to be directed by Ariste once and she used her new trick of swinging on the fire escape rigging to catapult from building to building when the space was too wide for her to jump. Someone must have seen them coming, for Todd and several of his peers were waiting on the top of their building. Her children left her in a rush, no longer waiting for her to catch up, and then disappeared down the building with their friends. Friends whom she wished would disappear, leaving only she and her children again.

She walked down the fire escape to the loading bay, to find Grischat waiting at the bottom of it for her.

"We get a visit from la petite Medicienne," he said.

I came to check on my patients, the unbidden thought said, whispering. If it was not for her search for a response other than "Bonjour," she would not have heard it. "I came to check on my patients," she told him. Your patients? she thought to herself, you're getting kind of high and mighty, aren't you, now, Céline?

"Oh, a house call," he overly-pouted, leaning against the building. "Not a social call."

"No," she informed him, glad to have that understood between the two of them. Her uneasy feeling around him had not diminished from the last time she was here. She couldn't pinpoint exactly what it was that set her alarm bells off, and that unnerved her. Was she just misreading him because it had been so long since she'd been around other people? "Do you have somewhere I can check everyone?" she asked. "That's clean?" She chided herself for being snide, but his reaction was grating.

"Ah, oui," he replied, chuckling. "Your emergency room is still up and cleaned to your instructions." He led her into the bay toward the back where she'd been before.

While the emergency square was still up and clean, the rest of the place hadn't been cleaned up any. It smelled strongly of animal, decay, and infection. "People are still hurt," she stated.

"Oui," he answered.

"Perhaps if you cleaned up the rest of the place, they'd heal faster," she didn't chide herself for her tone this time.

"Ah, la petite Medicienne, I am not the only one who lives here. I can control much, but not all."

"I am not une medicienne," she said. "I haven't had any medical training at all."

"You fix wounds," he said, "you give healing agents. I have seen you with the people on the street and you have helped them like a doctor would. You are our la Medicienne."

Céline held out her hand, "Can I see your arm, please?" Grischat held out his hurt appendage, still bandaged. As she unwrapped it, she heard his words in her head again, 'I have you seen with the people on the street...' He had been watching her, following her, for there were no people in her block of warehouses. The kids had made sure of that. How long had he been doing that? How in the world did he do it without her knowing? What was left of her assurance that she'd been careful evaporated as she checked his arm. "This is healing nicely," she said. "I think you can put something like comfrey on it to heal the cut and be fine."

"Something like comfrey?" he repeated mockingly.

She sighed, and took out a small jar of salve that she had brought with her in her messenger bag. "This," she put it on the table. "Comfrey is a plant." He stretched his arm closer to her. She understood what he wanted and she sighed again, opening the baby food jar she'd found in the trash that was now the pot for her healing agent, and rubbed some gently on his wound. When she was done, he simply stood in front of her, looking at her intently with his hazel eyes. After a moment of silence, she asked, "And the others?"

His smile was derisive. "La petite Medicienne is here," he called, still looking at her, "come get your check up!"

Several moreaus came up to the table, but Grischat did not move. Céline simply turned from him, so she used the other side of it.

Some cuts were still infected, some hadn't even had the original wrapping removed. "You need to change the dressing," she said over again to each person. "You have to keep the wound clean." She would get a "Yes," or a grunt in reply

Many of the splints that she had applied had been taken off, and she wasn't entirely sure how many of the moreaus were functioning without them. She told a moreau that looked like a cross between an egret and a seagull, "Your wing…uh, your arm is going to heal crooked if you don't keep the splint on."

He only shrugged.

Her mind was calm as she worked, she concentrated on what was at hand. She was able to push the revulsion that tried to creep upon her away. Some of the moreaus were downright hideous, they could easily be called monsters. Most of them smelled atrocious, strongly aromatic of the animal they were. More than half had scowls on their faces when she dealt with them, and she couldn't determine whether they were scowling at her, or whether they scowled all the time and that was just their regular expression. She seemed to know intuitively what to do with most of the wounds, despite her having only dealt with anything major a week prior to today. The unbidden thought did not come to her, but it reminded her of writing poetry, when the unbidden thought became her own, and there was no difference between the two. She would have described it more of a feeling, but there was no emotion attached to the knowing.

When she was done with everyone who came up, she put the lid back on her various salve jars, and saw a black hand with pale gray stripes place a mug on the table. She looked up to see a female...was she a badger...a convoluted looking cat or dog...smile slightly and then walk away.

Grischat was still standing by the table, or had come back to the table, she wasn't sure which. He motioned to the mug with his head, "Drink," he instructed.

She picked up the mug, it was sweet, creamy tea, piping hot. It reminded her of the tea she had at home now. "Thank you for the groceries," she took a sip. "And for the chocolate."

"It isn't anything," he waved his hand dismissively. "If you need anything else, ask."

"Actually," Céline said slowly, "I would like a book." Why not use the offer of a gift to get some information she needed?

"A book?" he asked. "Any book?" He looked incredulous.

She managed to smile at his confusion. "No, a book on birds."

He raised one of his eyebrows, the whiskers sticking from it making it very apparent.

"I don't know much about birds," she explained. "If I had a biology book of some kind on them, I would be able to help them better." She looked around the Cargo Bay at all the moreaus milling about. "When they need a 'checkup'."

Grischat nodded slowly with an "Ah." He leaned against the table with a large gray paw, and looked down at her, that derisive smile back on his face. "Anything else?"

She paused for a moment, and then asked, before even thinking about it, "Where did all your people come from?"

He looked about him and then at her with a confused look. "The same place all moreaus come from," he said.

"Where is that?" Céline asked.

He was silent for a long moment, watching her with those hazel eyes. He turned his head gracefully, as if to get a different angle to look at her. "You don't know?" He chuckled. "The Flayne Institute."

"I've never heard of it," she said.

Grischat's look became incredulous. "They have a large compound in the city. They are an animal testing facility." He shrugged. "At least, that is what the world is told."

"What is it really?" her heart beat in her throat as she asked.

"They make monsters, mon amie." He held his arms up to show his chest off.

Her mind went blank for a moment. That was not the

answer she was expecting. "Why?" she managed to choke out.

"To frighten," he said as if it were self-explanatory. "Why else would you make monsters, but to scare people?"

She shook her head, she didn't like that he kept using the word monster to describe them all. "Why in the world would a research facility want to scare people?"

"Non, non, non, la petite Medicienne," he clucked his tongue. "You do not know much about business, do you? The facility doesn't care what it makes. Only that it gets paid for what it makes."

Her mind was fuzzy, she couldn't get what he was saying into focus. "I don't understand."

"You frighten people," he leaned in close, so his pink nose was close to hers, "to control people. So that they will not fight you when you try to control them."

"Who would make…" she searched for a word that wasn't monster, "…animal people to frighten other people? Who are they supposed to frighten?"

"Je ne sais pas," I do not know, he replied. He looked at her closely, his hazel eyes blinking slowly. "How did you become a moreau?"

She blinked, surprised. "I'm not a moreau." Couldn't he tell that by looking at her?

He smiled derisively again, "Ah, oui, of course not. Then, how did you come to be the caretaker of moreaus?"

He hadn't mentioned anything about the men in black suits or the scientists in lab coats or the glass-like cages she and her children had been trapped in. He hadn't mentioned anything from the kind of experience that she remembered from all those years ago. "A lab," she said finally.

He nodded, "All of us came from laboratories," he said. "Many of us are accidents. Many of us came from misfortune." He smiled, baring his teeth and looking very feral. "But with misfortune comes benefits."

"Yes," she put her now empty mug down on the table. She was thoroughly unsettled, her mind didn't seem to want to come up with any clear trains of thought. "I am sure it does." She took her bag and slung it over her shoulder. "I need to go now," the words came out quicker than she intended. "Could you send for my children to meet me on the roof?"

"Oui," he replied.

"If anyone needs anything else," she said, "they can come to me." She didn't plan on making house calls to this place a common occurrence.

Grischat only nodded.

"Au revoir," she told him.

He returned her goodbye with a chuckle. "Adieu, ma petite Medicienne."

The word 'ma' my was not lost on her.

# Chapter 36

Training started each evening with the rat moreau and his puppies laying on the hardwood floor. With their heads toward the center, they laid in a circle, their bodies the spokes of a wheel.

"Breathe," he told them, from when they were small enough to listen. "In through your nose and out through your mouth." He would come to each of them, taking their arms and their legs and shaking them gently to get the children to relax. "You must be soft," he said in Russian, his voice deep and warm. "So soft that an angel could land upon you and mistake you for a cloud." He listened to them breathing, a sweet sound, much like the sound angels must make.

Occasionally Vasili would fall asleep, none would know it until they were told to do something else and the boy continued with his breathing. In his slumber, the boy breathed in through his nose, out through his mouth, a wave of air going and in and out of his body. "That," he told Vasili's brothers once, "is perfect breathing. That is what you want to do. Everything that you need is already inside of you. Always. Even in your sleep."

"But he isn't supposed to be sleeping now, Batya," Nikita said.

"And you are not supposed to be talking."

Nikita had been quiet after that.

"In the beginning," Ilya began the story that his teacher had told him, many years ago in Russian. He was Russian, the story was a Russian Orthodox one and though he was by no means considered himself a righteous or religious man, it was still the story of his people. The story of his children's people. It was the story to relate the teachings of the Universe. "God made the heaven and the earth. But they had no form, there was nothing but water. So, the Spirit of God breathed upon the water, and the Universe rippled into existence." So he tried to instill the importance of breathing, that breath instills all things, big and small.

As they grew older, he told them small things, that he did not know if they understood or not. "Your breath is everything," he told them. "Without it, you are not alive. Without it, your body cannot work, your mind cannot work, and therefore your spirit cannot work. You can only go three minutes without breath before you begin to damage yourself. You want to breathe always, never stopping, and you want your breath to go through your entire body."

"But what if you're underwater, Batya?" asked Dmitri. "You will breathe in water."

The rat breathed in himself. "No, then you do not want to breathe."

"Or what about if it smells really bad?" Kostya had asked. "You don't want to breathe that."

"Yes, you keep breathing," Ilya said.

"What if it's poisonous?" asked Evgeny.

"When will you be breathing in poisonous air?" asked Ilya.

"If the aliens come down and infect the Earth," he

answered. "Like in that movie we saw the other day."

Ilya had thought the movie tame enough to let the boys watch it. Apparently he was wrong.

"No," he said, "if the air is poisonous, then you wouldn't breathe it. But the air will not be poisonous."

"How do you know?" asked Maxim.

"Because I know," he replied.

"Do you know everything, Batya?" asked Kostya.

"Yes," he said, his calm, soft voice giving way to a rather irritated one.

"You can't know everything," Evgeny said. "No one can know everything."

"God knows everything," Nikita muttered.

"God's not a person," Maxim retorted. "God is…God."

"You don't know what God is," Nikita said, sitting up.

"Lie back down," Ilya commanded. The boy did as he was told. "Breathe in through your nose and out through your mouth. Don't stop breathing." He looked to Dmitri, "We are not underwater." His gray eyes then went to Kostya, "The air is fresh." His steely gaze landed on Evgeny, "There is no poison." He then regarded Maxim and Nikita. "And the Lord formed man of the dust of the ground, and breathed into his nostrils the breath of life," he quoted from Genesis 2:7. "You do the same. Breath in through your nostrils, and out through your mouth."

All six of his pups do so.

# Chapter 37

Todd appeared at The Haunted Warehouse, he and his peers loaded down with books. "We have a gift for you, Medicienne," he called as he came up the stairs.

Ariste ran over to him, stopping short of actually hugging the boy. Was he a boy or a young man? Céline didn't know how to categorize him. He beamed a smile at her daughter and put the books down in front of the bookshelf.

"Please don't call me Medicienne," she said. "My name is Céline."

Todd nodded, "Céline the Medicienne."

Céline sighed. "No, just Céline." She went over to the stack of books, there were at least 15 of them, all of them on birds.

"Apparently, what the Medicienne wants, the Medicienne gets," Todd said with a smile, backing away so she could get a better look at the new addition to her library. He turned his smile again to Ariste, who twitched her tail, before saying, "I can't stay. I have to get back. Grischat wanted me to give you these." He waved, and then was gone down the stairs.

Ariste giggled, "Look at all the books, Mama."

"You'll certainly know about birds now," Ursus said.

"It would appear so," Céline replied, beginning to put the books on the bookshelf in a neat row.

"The news is on, Mama," Naga announced.

They all sat down on the couch facing the little TV set to engage in what had become an evening ritual. The top story was about a break in that had occurred the night before at The Strand, one of Chicago's premier book shops. The front windows had been broken, and all that was taken was the cash register and their entire section of ornithology books.

Ornithology. Céline knew the word as soon as she heard it. The study of birds.

She looked over at the row of books she'd placed neatly on her medical bookshelf. She felt slightly sick to her stomach as she came to a realization, all of the behaviors exhibited by the people at The Cargo Bay.

They had an hierarchy, with a supreme leader at the top. She had never seen or heard of anyone going against anything that Grischat had ever said. He enforced his rule ruthlessly, and she had seen other moreaus almost groveling for his approval.

The group had assistant leaders, Coney and Jive, whom she'd only seen defer to Grischat, everyone else deferred to them.

They must have a chief enforcer, who kept unruly moreaus in line. They obviously had some sort of outside connections, illegal ones, because Grischat had mentioned doing work.

Quickly, the unbidden thought and her own were the same one.

Grischat's group wasn't a group. It was a gang.

# Chapter 38

Dmitri was Ilya's best fighter, his technical skill was superb. He was not naturally inclined to moving his body, however. He had to think too much to get his body to move in the way he wanted it to. He was tight, he had to stretch more and warm up longer than the others. Ilya did not mind, as he would warm up and cool down for longer than the boys. He needed to be massaged occasionally, especially his shoulders and legs, to loosen his muscles. It occasionally frustrated the boy, especially when the others had all seemingly mastered something and he hadn't. His determination, however, outshone any one of his siblings, it rivaled his father's, so that if the boy put his mind to something, it was going to get done, no matter what stood in his way.

So Ilya was not surprised to find him with his eyes closed, moving about the hardwood floor and falling. He had trouble with his falls, he wanted to tense up when he did it. Ilya was on him for it, he had to be relaxed. It was being relaxed that gave one the softness to fall uninjured. By having his eyes closed, he didn't know when he was about to hit the ground, so he had to remain soft throughout the entire roll. He could see the boy tense up after a few moments, still within the roll, so that his strikes to the ground with his shoulder were harder than they should be. The boy was going to hurt himself.

"Dmitri," he said gently. "You should go play with your brothers."

The boy opened his eyes, the color of tea after it had been properly brewed. "I played with my brothers all evening," he said, sounding much older than his eight years. His ears, one half white on top, the other mottled black, gold, and white, craned back toward his head. "I am practicing now."

He had played with his brothers. All of their training was play for the most part, wrestling, tumbling, running. Even their strikes and kicks were done mostly in play. Dmitri, of all of his boys, was the most aware of the subtle difference between practice and play.

Ilya came further into the room. "Aren't you tired from your playing?"

Dmitri rolled again, his eyes closed again. "No," he said.

Ilya sighed, taking him by the shoulders. "You are angry," he said. "That is not going to allow you to be soft."

The puppy jerked out of his father's grasp. "I can be soft!"

Ilya chuckled at the force of the statement. "I know you can be soft," he said. "But it is difficult if you are angry." He paused. "Especially if you are angry because you can't do it."

"I can do it, Batya," he insisted, his voice a whine. "Nikita can do it. Evgeny can do it. Even Kostya can do it!"

"Kostya is very good at being soft," Ilya agreed. The youngest of his children still saw this as play. "But there are many things that you are good at."

"I can't be good at anything if I am tense," he said petulantly.

"No, none of this anyway," the rat motioned

throughout the room. "But you don't want to be limp, either."

"I can't even get limp," the boy said, frustrated. "All I get is more tense."

"You can do it," Ilya insisted. "You do it when you wrestle. You do it when you run. You can do it here, too."

"Whenever I close my eyes," he shook his head. "I can't do anything."

"It doesn't look that way to me," the rat sat down, urging Dmitri to do the same. "But you tense up, because you don't trust your body," he said.

The puppy looked at him like he'd just said something in Martian.

Ilya smiled. "When I was learning Systema," he said, "I was older than you. I had to unlearn all of my tension." He put his arm around the boy and drew him close. "It was a habit that I had to break, even if I trusted my body. I had to unlearn how to be limp, because that is what my body seemed to want to do when it wasn't tense. I had to trust my body again. Your body, especially when you are young, knows what to do. We just convince ourselves that it doesn't."

Dmitri pouted.

Ilya pulled him closer, bending his head down closer to the boy's ears. "You are waiting for the floor to meet your shoulder," Ilya's deep voice was calm. "You have to know that floor is there, and that your shoulder knows when it will hit it."

"How do I do that?" a definite canine whine in his voice.

"You have to not think about it," he said. "You have to trust your body, that it knows what to do."

The boy had tears in his eyes, and with his ears back, it made him look utterly pitiful.

"You remember," Ilya said, starting at the beginning, "when you learned baby rolls?" Dmitri nodded. The rat got to his knees and his son followed suit. "When you do a baby roll, you put your arms out in front of you, da?"

"Da," Dmitri agreed.

"Why?" his father asked.

The boy was quiet a moment. "Because your instinct doesn't want you to hit your face on the floor."

Ilya smiled and nodded. "Da," he said. "Because your face knows the floor is there. What happens if you tell your face that the floor isn't there?"

Dmitri stared at him.

"Try to roll with your hands behind your back."

The puppy clasped his hands behind him, schoolboy style, and from his knees tried a forward roll.

"What does your face do?"

"It moves to the side, or it moves down to my chest," Dmitri explained.

"Why?"

"Because it's going to get smooshed!" The puppy was obviously getting frustrated. His ears were no longer stuck to his head, but rather pointing out behind him in a gesture of annoyance.

"How do you know?" his father asked.

"If I fall on it, it'll get smashed," Dmitri shook his head.

"Your face knows it will get smashed, da?"

Dmitri nodded slowly.

"So it automatically moves to the side or your chin to your chest," he continued.

The boy nodded again.

"How should you move it, then? To the side or your chin to your chest?"

"To the side," the practiced answer spilled out of the Dmitri's mouth almost before Ilya was finished with the question.

"Why?"

"So we don't hurt ourselves."

"What do you do with your arms?"

He took his arms from behind his back and spread them out airplane style. "We twist our arm at the shoulder and then follow the twist back to the roll."

"Why do you think you do that?"

"So that we can hold a knife and roll at the same time," Dmitri answered.

Ilya laughed and ruffled the boy's head. "Very practical," he said. "And yes, eventually. But for right now, it is to do something with your arms when you fall. Because what do they want to do if you leave them to themselves?"

"They want to catch you falling," Dmitri replied.

"So they are not happy behind your back?"

"No," he shook his head, "they want to come out."

"So we give them something to do, da?"

"Da."

"And they are happy?"

Dmitri smiled a tiny smile. "Da," he agreed.

"Why are they happy?"

Again, Dmitri just stared at him.

"They know the floor is coming. This way, they get to do something about it."

Dmitri pulled his ears back against his head again and breathed in deeply.

"Your shoulder," Ilya said gently, "knows too. So you must breathe, and trust your body that it knows what to do, just like your arms know what to do, and your head knows what to do. Everything you need is already inside of you." He touched the boy's chest.

"I wish tumbling was already inside of me," he pouted.

Ilya kissed the top of his head. "It is," he promised.

# Chapter 39

The very next day, Céline had a patient come to her warehouse for a checkup. It was the lizard she had treated the very first day, the one with the infection and what she thought might be a fungal growth. He was alone and looked rather sheepish, glancing around the floor in a way he had not when he had come with Grischat.

"Are you alright?" Céline asked him, after she had said hello and he'd only answered with a hello in reply.

"I--" his voice cracked and he cleared his throat. "I need help."

She was struck by the plaintive tone of his voice. "Alright," she replied. She had to get over this uncomfortable feeling that welled inside her whenever she was in the presence of one of these people. Again, she told herself it was the newness of the situation, the invasion of her space by strangers, the knowledge that she'd been watched for some time without her suspecting a thing. "Are you here by yourself?"

"Yes," he said.

She immediately felt better. Her children were out playing, and knowing he had come alone helped to set her at ease. "Let me see your wound," she instructed, remembering his gash on his chest.

It was healing nicely, just like the last time she had seen it. The fungus was completely gone, there was no infection present, and it had sealed over. She could even see new scales beginning to form on the top and bottom edges. "It looks fine," she said, "does it hurt?"

"No," he said.

There was a moment of silence as she waited for him to elaborate. When he didn't, she asked uncertainly, "Is something else the matter?"

He looked at her and said nothing, shame radiating off of his reptilian face in waves.

"I can't help you if you don't tell me what's the matter," she tried to make her voice gentle.

"You cannot tell Grischat," his voice was low. "Don't tell him I was here."

"Why would I tell him?" she said indignantly, suddenly feeling protective. "It isn't any of his business who comes here and what they do when they are here."

He looked at her with black eyes, they were very similar as Naga's, and nodded slowly. He then began to unbutton his pants. She stood up, her eyes wide, and put her hands out in front of her. "Um," she felt her cheeks getting hot, and she backed up. She looked around wildly, and grabbed a plate that was still on the table, holding it up in what she hoped was a threatening gesture.

The lizard shook his head. "No," he said, plaintively. "My thigh..."

Céline let out a deep breath, and put the dish down. "Oh," her cheeks were hot for an altogether different reason now. "Alright."

He slid the pants down, to reveal a series of puncture wounds in his upper thigh and lower hip. They were still weeping slightly, not having scabbed over completely. She looked down at his pants, and saw they were bloody. How in the world had she missed that?

She came back up to him, all of her fear vanishing. "What happened to you?"

He sighed, "I was hurt."

Bending down, she examined the wound, gently touching the edges of each mark. "Is this..." no, she had to be wrong, "is this a bite?"

He didn't answer.

She looked around, thinking she needed him to lie down, but when she saw that the back of thigh also had marks, she changed her mind. "When did this happen?"

"This morning," he told her.

"And you're just getting here now?" she admonished with a click of her tongue.

"I couldn't get away sooner…" he almost whined.

She stood up, went to the sink, got salt and hot water, and a bag of bandages made from torn t-shirts that she and kids had found and bleached. As she tended the wounds, cleaning out each with salt water, placing a bandage with pressure on the holes that were still bleeding, and placing bandages with salve on those that were not. "What is your name?" she asked, trying to make small talk. He did not give any indication of pain when she tended him, not even a jump of his muscles when she put the salt water on him. Her face at his groin certainly put her ill at ease, and she suspected from his posture, it did him also. A little place in the back of her brain hoped her children did not come home quite yet. Seeing her kneeling in front of a lizard-man who was naked from the waist down was not a picture she wanted etched in their minds.

"Jive."

She wondered how he got that name. "Well, Jive, I think we can get you fixed up." When he did not reply, she kept talking, unable to take the silence. "How long have you been a...uh..." she felt stupid having started the question.

"A moreau?" he finished.

"No," she said. "I was going to say, how long have you

been with Grischat?"

"I've been with the Grey Cats for 9 years," he said.

The Grey Cats, Céline thought derisively. That's as original as Grischat. She cleared her throat, "Why...uh...what..." she took a deep breath. "Why did you become a Grey Cat?"

He was quiet for a long time, so that Céline thought he was not going to answer her. "I had another choice?" His voice was derisive.

She looked up at him from his leg, unable to come up with a response. Turning back to his wound, and being unable to think of anything else to say, she asked, "Do the Gray Cats often break into bookstores?" Her ears pounded as she waited for his answer.

"Not usually," he replied, "but the Medicienne seems to get special treatment." Céline didn't know what to say, so she said nothing. "We haven't had a doctor before," Jive went on.

"I am not a doctor," Céline told him. "I am not a medical professional at all. I am an amateur herbalist."

His leg moved as he shook his head, "We haven't had an amateur herbalist before."

When she was done, she washed her hands at the sink, and when she turned back to Jive, he'd pulled his pants back up and buttoned them. "You need to keep the wounds clean," she told him.

He nodded.

"Can you do that?" She had serious doubts after yesterday.

"Yes," he said. He looked down, and then back up at her. "Thank you," his voice was very low.

Céline smiled. "You're welcome," she replied warmly. She felt a sudden and strong urge to reassure him. "I promise that I will keep your visit between you and I."

He nodded, and then turned around and walked out of

the warehouse.

# Chapter 40

Ilya was not surprised to find Nikita in front of the icon of The Queen of Those Who Are Lost after this evening's training. Of all of his boys, he was probably the one who needed to meditate and pray the least. He seemed to be born with a quiet and contemplative mind, all on its own. However, of all of his boys, he was the one who seemed to speak to her the most.

"What do you talk to her about?" he asked, sinking beside the boy.

Nikita shook his head, his black tipped ears flopping slightly. "Nothing, Batya."

Ilya pressed his knee against the boy's. From his profile, Ilya could clearly see the black that descended from the tip of his ears, down the outsides of them, to come around on his cheeks and encase his muzzle. "One does not look at The Queen of Heaven so intently without saying something to her."

"I asked her to help me with my wrestling," he said, his voice sounding very small.

Ilya felt his chest tighten. "That is what she is there for," he replied. "To answer you when you ask for help. Are you upset because you didn't win any of the sets with Dmitri?" He had slowly started counting the competitions between his two eldest boys, transitioning them, his plan was to do it slowly, to a more mature form of teaching.

Nikita nodded. "He has gotten a lot better," he said.

"He's been practicing," Ilya told him.

The boy nodded, his eyes still on the icon. "Does she ever answer you, Batya?" he asked.

"She does," he answered.

"What does she say?"

"She doesn't say anything," the rat explained. "She speaks to me in different ways. Sometimes," he shifted his position so that he was sitting crossed-legged, "I see pictures when I meditate. Sometimes I will smell something when I am out, and I will know it was her that sent the smell to tell me something. Or sometimes I will see something."

"I don't get any of those things," Nikita answered.

"I don't either," he said, "unless I am very good about listening."

The puppy turned to his father, "But I do listen to you," he whined.

Ilya smiled. "No, not to me. To Spirit."

"I try to listen to Spirit, Batya," he said, finally turning to face Ilya. His bright blue eyes were imploring. "But I don't ever hear her."

"Spirit will speak to you in different ways," his father tried to explain. "Sometimes, it will just be an urge to do something, a knowing that it is the right thing to do."

"How do you know it is a knowing and not just what you want to do?" Nikitia leaned his head into Ilya's side, and the rat put his arm about him.

"You will eventually get a feel for it," Ilya said. "You…Spirit's guidance, for me, comes from a different place in my body."

"I don't understand," Nikita said.

The little boy wants to be grown up so badly, Ilya thought, he is too little to want to understand grown up things. "Each thought we have does something in our bodies," he explained. "We feel every thought. It is important to know where you are feeling a thought. That is why I have you pay attention to your body before we have class. When an urge comes from me, from my mind, I will feel it in my shoulders, or in my back. When something comes from God, I feel it in my heart, deep in my chest. But it is not like fear, it is like a calm." He kissed Nikita on the top of his head. "It may be a different feeling for you."

Nikita didn't answer, but turned his eyes back to the icon.

Perhaps I should begin to teach him about tension in his body, Ilya mused. He didn't want to. He didn't want the boy to have to be old enough to need it.

# Chapter 41

She had a steady stream of visitors, as if she were a proper doctor and her place a proper clinic. Her kitchen turned into a combination restaurant/emergency room. Her table was used more than once as a doctor's bed. The thought of eating on it after these people had been lying on it was so unappetizing to her, that she began to look for items with which to make an entirely separate clinic area.

After trying several places in the upper story where they lived, she decided she didn't want all these people in her house. Many of them were unsavory, many of them gave her the willies, many of them made her want to just run. So the second floor, far enough away from the top to not be home, and far enough from the bottom to not be easily accessible, became the clinic.

By asking questions as she worked, she discovered that all moreaus were humans before they were changed and that all of the moreaus she helped were originally part of the prison population. She tried not to think about that—what had they done to be in prison in the first place. What had children, like Todd, done to be in prison that they were taken to be made moreaus? She found that line of thought even more frightening.

In the evenings after these visits, she would watch her children, and wonder how they had become moreaus. They were not born animal beings, apparently none of them were. That meant they were human children, no, babies, before their transformation. Where did they come from? Where were their birth parents? Did they worry about what had happened to their infant? How did they come to be in a position where they could be transformed? Then, she would tell herself it didn't matter and she'd pile them all into the double mattress that they all shared and sleep surrounded by warmth and soft breathing.

Finding out where these people came from, whether she knew the crime that put them there or not, she curtailed social visits to the Cargo Bay and insisted that her children stay within their block. She even encouraged them to build things in their secret workshop in an attempt to keep them home, going on 'shopping' trips to acquire items for them. They were surprised she knew about it, and even more surprised she wasn't upset about it. She suggested they move the workshop to the floor below their home. They would be close that way, she figured. A floor below their living space and a floor above the clinic. She could keep an eye on them, or at least an ear. If any Grey Cats came over to play, they would be supervised, sort of. The kids readily agreed and they moved their items over.

She was impressed by what they had already constructed and by the amount of items they'd collected. "Where did you kids get all this stuff?" she asked as they carted things from one building to the other. She was afraid of the answer.

"It was in the warehouses all around," Khenum said.

There were cardboard boxes of nuts and bolts, of nails,

of washers, all used, most of them rusted. "We will have to find some sandpaper," Céline said, "to clean a bunch of this stuff up."

All four of them beamed smiles at her. "Will you help us make stuff, Mama?" Naga asked.

"Of course," she told her, a wave of gratefulness soaking her. It was a way to keep them close, and they still wanted her close, even after meeting other people.

She knew a few hours walk away there was a military-industrial complex. "They must have a dump. After all, the military produced a lot of trash," she said, presenting a plan to the kids. "If we leave in the afternoon," she told them, "and keep to the shadows, we can reach the dump at night. If we're careful, we can get some stuff that you might find useful for your projects."

"Seriously?" Khenum's eyes went wide. "We can get stuff from a military dump?"

"As much as we can carry across the city," she laughed. She might find something for her clinic, too.

The trip was the farthest that the little family had ever been from their warehouse. The walk there during the daylight was not bad at all, but as the sun began to set, they had to keep hidden more and more often, as more and more humans came into alleys. Aren't the back streets supposed to be less populated after dark? she thought. The people were wearing dark clothing, had their heads covered with hoods or hats, and spoke in low voices.

The five of them turned a corner quietly, and came face to face with four young men. They were dressed as all the other young men were dressed, dark clothes, heads covered. Céline's mind started to blur at a mile a minute. They're going to see the kids. How do I hide the children? They can't see the kids, I have to keep them distracted. I never should have taken them out here. I should have just told them no, you can't play with a bunch of criminals, even if they are animal people like you. The one closest to them smiled upon seeing Céline, "Well, what have we got here?"

The other three began to laugh, but stopped suddenly when Ursus came out of the shadows and growled.

"What the--?" the one in front backed away, his eyes wide.

No, no, no, Céline's mind was still running. He can't see any of the kids. They'll tell the police. The police might believe them. They aren't crazy homeless people, they're dangerous people. The thought hit her like a physical thing. They're gang members.

Then Ariste, Khenum, and Naga followed suit. Khenum made a strong huffing sound, while the girls hissed, Ariste high pitched and forceful, Naga beginning low and building in intensity.

With an exclamation of curses, followed by screams, the four young men ran out of the alley.

There was a moment of no sound, not even the city seemed to make any, as if Chicago herself was holding her breath.

Ariste broke it with a laugh, "Did you see them run!?"

"That was fun," Khenum said.

"Does this mean we don't have to hide in the shadows anymore?" Naga asked, still hissing slightly.

"No," she said, rubbing Ursus' head, "we still need to be careful." She kissed him on the temple. "Thank you." Then, Céline was smiling, even though she knew she shouldn't have been. Adrenaline was still being flushed through her blood, and the danger was now over. She had no other way to deal with it. "But," her eyes twinkled. "That was fun."

It took them all night to get to the dump, rummage through it for treasures, and get back to their warehouse. The sky was just becoming gray when they got back, their arms aching with their haul, and their legs aching from the all night walk. They trudged up the stairs, dropped their items on the workshop floor, then went up the stairs to their home. They all collapsed onto their bed and slept until well past two in the afternoon.

Despite orchestrating adventures and projects for them, the kids still begged to go to the Cargo Bay. So, when a messenger came asking for Céline to come to doctor someone who he claimed was unable to make it to her, she agreed. She sent the messenger on before them, and then sat her kids down.

"Do we take things that belong to other people?" she asked them.

All four of them shook their heads. "We only take things that others have discarded," Khenum said. She smiled, when he was little, he was the one she had to repeat that to the most.

"Do we accept things that have been taken from other people?" She hoped they knew the right answer.

"What's the difference between that and taking something from someone?" Ursus asked.

"Because we didn't take it," Khenum replied. "So we aren't thieves."

"It makes you an accomplice," Ariste said, "so it is the same thing."

"Yes," Céline nodded at each of them. "It is just as bad as if you took it."

"And we're good!" Naga announced. "Because the world needs more kindness."

Céline smiled, reassured that some of her attempted teaching had sunk in. "Yes," she said. "Let's go."

The kids waited for her as they traveled the rooftops until they saw their playmates in the distance and then left her in their wake as they sped up to meet them. Céline could keep up with them a little better than she could in the beginning, but she would not be able to catch them if they chose to lose her.

She was all business when she emerged from the fire escape, her messenger bag on her shoulder. Grischat was waiting for her, his chest bare in the summer heat. "Where is my patient?" she asked.

"What, no bonjour?" he asked.

"Bonjour," Céline said without feeling. "Where is my patient? If he couldn't make it to me, he must be very hurt."

"Oh," Grischat put his arm around her shoulder and veered her into the Cargo Bay, "she is hurt."

Céline moved out of his grip. "She?"

"Oui," Grischat led her to a far corner of the bay, her emergency room had long been dismantled. "She is. Perhaps you can help." He didn't sound very concerned.

Laying in the corner was a ferret woman, her clothes torn to pieces on her body, chunks of her fur torn out, fur that was still on her was clumping together with clotting blood. Céline gasped and dropped down to her, putting her hand on her cheek. The ferret turned her long neck toward her, her brown eyes filled with fear. "What happened here?"

"There was a fight," Grischat told her. "She lost."

"She lost..." Céline was having trouble comprehending.

"Oui," Grischat said. "But I like her," he waved his hand at her dismissively. "You can fix her, non?"

She turned to Grischat and glared at him, "What happened to the person who did this to her?"

He laughed, "She has a mouth full of fur."

"If she'd kept her mouth shut, then maybe she'd be in better shape." The white lop-eared bunny, the one who had given her the mug of tea that morning she'd stayed at the Cargo Bay, sauntered up and leaned against Grischat. Her mouth still had blood on it, her large front teeth a pale pink.

Céline turned away from them, to look back at the ferret, fighting down horror. "She is not a robot," she said, ignoring what the lop-eared bunny had said. "I am not a mechanic, I do not fix people."

"Ah, Medicienne," Grischat said, bending down next to her, almost pushing the bunny away from him, "I know you will do the best that you can." His hazel eyes looked at her with that intense, eating look that made her feel like her skin was crawling.

"Then go away," she said hotly, "and let me work." She felt his breath on the side of her face and neck, but then she was left alone to deal with her patient.

# Chapter 42

The boys ran off as soon as they reached the Chicago Municipal Waste Management Landfill. It was a treasure trove of goodies, they could find almost anything there. If they couldn't find it, then they could find the pieces to make it, and that was just as good. There was no particular reason that they were at the dump, they needed nothing in particular. But the children were getting antsy, they were still puppies after all. The landfill was a safe place to let them run free. The chances of meeting a human being there were slim and the ones that they might meet would not be likely to tell anyone that they had seen a giant rat man with six puppy boys.

He was startled, therefore, to hear voices talking, indicating more than one person being in the landfill with them. Ilya whistled a bird call, a nuthatch, that signaled to the boys that they were to find him—quickly and silently as possible. All six boys were at his side in only a few moments, and frozen around him.

Ilya swiveled his ears and tilted his head, so they faced the sound. It took a moment, but he recognized some of the voices that were speaking.

"That's those moreaus we met that time," Nikita whispered.

"Who have the turf?" Kostya asked.

"It would appear we are not the only ones who come to find things at the dump, da?" Ilya said, raising his eyebrows.

"Can we go see them?" Vasili asked. "They aren't bad are they?"

"They aren't good," said Nikita.

"Net," Ilya agreed, giving his eldest son a hard look. "But they aren't bad, either. We just need to be wary, that's all."

The boys all nodded, following close beside their father as he made his way over to the voices. "Dyson," he called before they came into view.

"Ilya Pytrovich!" the sea otter came trotting over to his former teacher. A group of four moreaus was behind him, a boar, a brightly colored red parrot, a lizard, and a dog. Dyson smiled, his pointed canine teeth showing. He looked down at the puppies gathered about Ilya's legs, "Hello, there."

None of the boys said anything.

"Say hello," Ilya told them in Russian.

"Zdravstuyte," the six of them said in unison.

Dyson looked up at Ilya confused, who laughed. "In English," he said.

"Hello," again the six said together.

"They're bilingual?" asked the parrot. By the sound of its voice, it was male. His clothes were makeshift, hardly even sewn together.

"Da," Ilya said cautiously. "I see no reason why they shouldn't be, if I am."

"DeShawn," Dyson motioned to the parrot. "This is Ilya Pytrovich." He said as if he were introducing one of the Romanovs.

The parrot blinked in surprise, otherwise it had little

expression. "I thought you were dead."

Ilya drew his brows together, "Izvinite?" he asked, "Excuse me?"

"At the Institute," DeShawn explained. "They talk about you all the time. But they told us you were dead."

"He escaped," Dyson said proudly. "With all six of those puppies, they were still tiny."

DeShawn whistled.

"What is he talking about, Batya?" Nikita asked.

The rat shook his head. His chest constricted, so that he consciously had to breathe through his nose and out of his mouth. "Go off and look for your things," he said to them.

"Awww," whined Kostya. "Are you going to come?"

"I'll be there in a little bit," Ilya almost snapped. He sighed. "There is this entire place to explore. Go explore."

Evgeny grabbed his brother's hand and led him away, tail wagging.

The dog and the boar had joined them at this point, Ilya nodded to them. "They talk about me at the Institute?"

The parrot nodded. "They say you were one of the best warriors they had. You had control over your body like no one else they'd seen."

"I never went to war for them," Ilya said firmly. "So they would not know what kind of warrior I am."

The parrot's enthusiasm died a little at the reply.

"They talk about you outside of the Institute," the boar said. "They have for a long time." He put his hand out, "I'm Gristle. It's nice to finally meet the legend, Ilya Pytrovich."

Ilya felt suddenly uncomfortable, like he was being examined, like he did when he was under Dr. Montgomery's care. He shook Gristle's hand and nodded.

"This is Toaster," Dyson motioned to the dog, a golden blonde haired man with little triangle ears on the top of his head and a messy looking muzzle. The dog nodded in Ilya's direction, smiling broadly. It was the most human smile, despite being on a muzzle, that any of them probably had.

"This is part of your turf?" Ilya asked. "Your arms stretch far if it is."

Dyson shook his head, "Oh no. The Grey Cat's turf ends way over that way," he pointed. "We just needed some stuff for DeShawn," he threw his head on his long neck in the parrot's direction. "This is the one stop shop." He winked. "But you already knew that."

"Da," he nodded his head. He looked over, sniffing, identifying where each of his boys was. It was hard to smell them through the stinking refuse, but he did. "Tell me," he turned back to Dyson. "About these…Grey Cats." He looked the little group over and raised an eyebrow. "None of you are gray and none of you are cats."

Toaster chuckled, a barky sound. "That's because the group is named after our leader—he's gray and he's a cat moreau."

"There are many of you?" Ilya asked.

"Quite a few," Toaster said. "Our numbers go up and down, sometimes things happen to people," he shrugged. "Our population is a bit more stable, now that we have a doctor."

"I was telling you we have a doctor," Dyson said to the rat. "She patched DeShawn right up!"

The parrot moreau lifted the leg of the pants he was wearing to reveal a bare patch on his thigh. There were dozens of tiny wounds, as if someone had stabbed him over and over again, each one meticulously stitched up. Ilya did not smell any infection coming from it, he hadn't even detected the wound with his nose. Not only that, the man was braving coming to a garbage dump! These people have a lot of faith in a doctor, Ilya surmised dubiously.

"So many of you live together?" Ilya asked. "How do

you do that without..." his voice trailed off.

"The Institute knowing?" Gristle finished for him. "We stay quiet."

"For the most part," Toaster added.

"We live in one of the abandoned districts." He smiled, showing the gums where his large tusks attached to his mouth. "We do a pretty good job of keeping people away."

"How do you do that?" the rat asked.

Toaster bared his teeth, then laughed. "That's how."

That was not how Ilya wanted to keep people away. "You have a leader," he asked, glancing at Dyson.

The sea otter nodded. "We do," he said. "His name is Grischat, apparently that's French for gray cat." He rolled his eyes. "He's been a moreau longer than us."

"Twenty years," Gristle said. "We were all around the same time as him, Toaster and me." He reached out and grabbed the dog by the shoulders. A fond smile passed between the two of them.

"Twenty years," Ilya repeated slowly. So much time had passed. So much time, and so little progress. Progress toward what, he wasn't sure, but they were all in the same situation they were in when they escaped the Institute—in hiding.

"Come back with us, Ilya Pytrovich," said Dyson, putting his hand on the rat's shoulder. "The Grey Cats could use someone like you, and you'd have other people. They'd have other people," he motioned to the puppies.

Yes, Ilya thought bitterly. They will have other people. Moreaus, garnered from the destitute and the deviant. "Nyet," he said. "But thank you for the offer." He gave a sharp whistle and the six puppies came running toward him, all of their tails wagging. "Good luck on your hunt," he said, gathering the boys up to come back the way he came. "I am sure you'll be able to find whatever you need."

"It's getting used to the smell that takes effort," Gristle

said to the parrot, clapping him hard on the back.

After they walked a while and were hiding in the shadows on the streets, Nikita asked, "What was he talking about, Batya?"

"Yeah," asked Dmitri. "What's The Initiative."

"It is why we stay hidden," he said quietly. "It is why we are lost."

"Those people didn't seem lost, Batya," said Kostya.

"They may be even more lost than we are, little one," he replied.

# Chapter 43

"Huh."

"Hah!"

"Rehwr!"

"Thhhhsssss."

Céline looked up from the notebook in which she'd been writing, a birthday present from Ariste, judiciously erased of all the pencil marks of the math student to whom it once belonged, to make it empty again. The four of her children were play fighting, arms, legs, and tails being swung and avoided. I have to do a better job of supervising them at the Cargo Bay, she thought, putting her pencil down and standing up. Time to change the subject!

"Let's play Catch the Monkey!" she called.

They stopped their fight and cheered, all running to the workout area. "How many warm ups do we get before we start timing?"

Céline pretended to give it a lot of thought. "Two," she said. "Sound good?"

Four heads nodded in agreement.

She stood in the middle of the area, her feet shoulder

width apart, her arms at her sides. Each of the children stood at the four cardinal directions, where the edge of the room would have been if it was separated from the rest of the floor. "Ready," she said. "Set. Go!"

All four mutants rushed at her as she ran to the vaulting horse and jumped to the rafters. Each of them took different positions trying to catch her, Ariste and Naga and headed up the rafters after her, and Ursus and Khenum followed on the floor for when she came down. She twisted and flipped and vaulted and swung, sometimes on the floor, sometimes near the ceiling, and sometimes somewhere in between, while the four young ones tried to catch her.

When she had first thought up the game, she had done so out of desperation. Naga was teething, her fangs were coming in. She cried, a pathetic sound, "Mama, make the hurt stop, make the hurt stop." Céline had no idea how to make it stop, other than giving her ice in a bag to chew. Her gums were a livid red, and she could see the sharp points just underneath the surface of the gum.

"Let's play Catch the Monkey," she had said on that day, her voice slightly manic. "I'll be the monkey and you try to catch me."

And so the game had been born. She had grossly underestimated how quick and how strong her children were, for even as little as they were at the time, they caught her much more easily than she would have guessed. As they had grown up, they had only gotten stronger and quicker, and they had also developed a strategy.

The two girls would head to the rafters to drive Céline down the floor, where the boys had a better chance at catching her. Céline's strong suit was in the air, not floor exercises, so her speed decreased dramatically when on the ground. Once on the ground, the girls would stay up the rafters and follow her in an attempt to close any gaps that would give her a chance to get back up in the air again.

They had become so good at it, that Céline began to time them, in an attempt to help her get better. Losing after a minute or two was getting old. Her strategy became solely evasive, look for holes in their formation and jump, slide, skip, flip, run through them. She had gotten pretty good at finding holes.

Her best time was one hour and forty two minutes. Her worst was 2 minutes, 17 seconds. This game, her time was 47 minutes, enough that they forgot about their play fighting.

Khenum, at 10 years old, had begun to work on mechanical things and with wood. His carpentry skills were impressive; he was currently building a set of uneven bars, but had not yet figured out how he was going to round the bars themselves. He had already re-framed the door to their floor, made a new set of dining chairs for them from bits and pieces of other chairs they found dumpster diving, made a bed frame for their double mattress, and when he realized that it needed something to keep the mattress from sagging, he built a box spring.

Then, while shopping one day, they found a twin mattress, and he said he wanted to take it home.

Céline's heart sank and her throat tightened. "Why?" she asked, but she already knew the answer.

"Because," he looked away from her, "I want to sleep in my own bed."

"What'd you want to do that for?" Naga asked, slithering out of a dumpster, holding two expired canisters of coffee.

"Because," Khenum's voice was soft, "just...because."

Céline took in a deep breath to keep tears from her eyes. "Of course we can take it home, Lamb's Ear," she said.

Khenum looked up at her and smiled. She noticed that his horns were long enough that they had begun to develop some curvature to them and he did not have to look up very high at her any longer. One more growth spurt, and he'd be taller than her.

"And you shouldn't call me Lamb's Ear anymore," he said.

She took another deep breath. "OK."

After that, he began to frame himself a bedroom. She was quietly impressed and dismayed at the wonderful progress he made. Watching the framing come up, the building of the walls from discarded pallets, the door being mended from the sorry shape it was in when they found it to be placed in the door frame. He made himself a bed frame and box spring. He would still end up in her bed with the others, but as the year went on, he would come to her room less and less, until he didn't come at all.

Ariste asked him to make her a bedroom, which he did. Ursus was not to be left out, and even Naga, who did not particularly crave a bed of her own, insisted on a bedroom. Sheets, pillows, and blankets became a prime look out item on their shopping trips, and Céline began to sew together bits of material from discarded clothes to make quilts for them. The warehouse floor began to look more and more like a house, with spaces divided off by walls and doors, so that her own sleeping space needed only one wall and a doorway to become a room. So for their 11th birthday, Khenum framed her one, and the children painted it a pale blue and put a juniper branch above the door.

Somehow the Grey Cats found out when their birthday was (Céline strongly suspected Todd had told Grischat, and that Ariste had told Todd), and she was graced with a visit from Grischat and his left and right hand, Jive and the rabbit that had been with him the first time she'd met them, whose name she now knew was Cottontail Coney. She didn't even bother to ask how he got that name.

"Bon Anniversaire, ma petite Medicienne," he said, swinging in from the garden window, apparently not bothering to get off the roof of the building to take the stairs. "I come to you on your birthday, since you will only come to me when someone is hurt."

Todd and several of his cohorts jumped in after the adults. They were now firmly teenagers, looking more like adults every time she saw them. He made a beeline to Ariste, who swished her tail slowly from side to side and smiled broadly at his approach.

Grischat, Jive, and Cottontail Coney saw her gaze follow him, and then come back to them. "They grow up so fast, n'est pas?" Grischat grinned.

Céline chose not to answer. "Our birthday is the only thing that brings you here? The only other time you've come is when you've been hurt."

"I cannot come to visit a friend?" he asked. She motioned for the three men to sit down, and they did. "I have brought you a birthday present." He motioned to Jive, who stood up and took a small package out of his shirt. "For you," Grischat nodded toward her.

Céline moved a strand of honey colored hair from her face and took the package. It was obviously a book, and a stray thought made her smile. It's on ornithology, I bet. But when she unwrapped it, she saw that it wasn't, it was a copy of The Aeneid. And it was new.

"You stole this," she said flatly.

"I did not," Grischat looked at Jive, then at Coney. "You think I cannot come by anything honestly?"

"No," Céline didn't even hesitate to answer.

"Ah, I am offended, ma petite." He put his hand to his chest and gave her a pouty face. "I asked for it for payment for a job."

"The job was illegal," she said, holding the book out to

him.

"Getting paid for work well done is not illegal," he said.

She blinked. Had she heard him right? "What work can a moreau do?"

He motioned to the book, ignoring her question entirely. "Take it."

Céline looked at the book, it had an orange cover and gold edging. In gold inlay it read The Aeneid in fancy script. She still had an uneasy feeling about it, but the book was beautiful. She liked The Aeneid. "Thank you," she said cautiously. "It was very kind of you."

"You do not ask for anything, la Medicienne," Grischat motioned for her to sit down at her own table as if he owned it. She remained standing. "I have to guess what you want."

"I don't want for anything," she told him. "I have everything I need."

Grischat looked around doubtfully. "Ah, oui, I can see."

Ariste came over with Todd at her side. "Look what I got for our birthday," she said, holding up a jug of milk.

"A perfect birthday present," Céline said, smiling at Todd.

He beamed a smile back at her and then Ariste.

"I will stay until the morning and give you a perfect birthday present," Grischat purred.

The comment took Céline by surprise. It had been so long since someone had spoken in such a way to her, that she couldn't think of a reply. "Don't you have things to do?"

Grischat chuckled, "Always, mon amie." He stood up and motioned for his crew to leave.

"Can we go with them, Mama," Ariste asked, "it's been so long since we've played."

"No," the words almost came out before Ariste had finished saying them. "But," she tried to soften it, "Todd and his friends are welcome to come here whenever they can."

"I'll come back soon," Todd told her quietly, "Happy birthday."

Ariste swished her tail. "Thanks."

"You don't have to come with us," Khenum said to his mother. "We can go on our own, we know how to get there."

"No," she answered him faster than she meant to. "You're not old enough."

"How old is old enough?" Ariste asked.

"13," Céline told her. "You can go on your own when you're 13."

# Chapter 44

The sewer was quiet, except for the dripping and occasional scrabbling of a rat. The lack of noise was a blessed relief, especially in the middle of the day after the nocturnal activity of the rats that attended The Rat King. With the quiet, he could concentrate on the absence of chatter, or he could stretch out his mind and fill his head with the voices of beings near and far. Tiny voices spoke to him, to each other, to themselves, and he could hear them all.

Sometimes they would be too much for him, and he would curl in a ball on himself, his nine tails wrapped about him, and feel the tears running down the sides of his short muzzle. At those times, and many others, Evangeline was at his cheek, her tiny pink paw stroking him, her little rose tongue licking his nose. The physical touch of her helped to bring him out of his head, out of the sea of voices that flooded him so that his own could not be heard, even by himself. She would not speak to him at these times, only touch him, small rubs on which he could concentrate.

He could not have asked for a better companion.

He had realized, through his time trapped in his mind,

trapped in the comforting closeness of the sewer, that Evangeline was a most astute rat. Rats, in and of themselves, are intelligent creatures, but he had been blessed with the company of Evangeline. She was intelligent enough that she could carry on conversations with him, real ones. She could understand, albeit rudimentary, abstract ideas. Most of the other rats chattered in his mind and his ears, only nouns and verbs, pictures accompanied by sound in his brain.

"How can you stand it?" he had asked her at the beginning.

"Stand what?" she'd asked.

"The voices, the constant noise in your mind?"

She tilted her head to the side, her black eyes mild. It was then he realized she didn't hear the voices in her head, that is not how she communicated with those around her. Of course not, he chided himself. Did he not know more about rats than almost any other person on the planet? They weren't telepathic, despite what children's cartoons would have their viewers think. Even the words he heard in his head, they were not words, exactly, but rather ideas or feelings that his mind translated into words for him.

So when he heard actual words in his mind, he was taken aback.

He stretched his mind out, late in the day, before the chittering of rats filled his thoughts. There were a few chatters of those early risers or rats that were prisoners in people's homes. Then, he felt another presence that wasn't quite a rat. It felt subtly different, like the taste of a dark brewed coffee compared to a medium roast. The thoughts, the feelings were not simply nouns and verbs. They were not even the basic abstract thoughts that Evangeline could understand. These were ideas that came from no rat, how to build things, the emotional wellbeing of children, the contemplation of the Divine. The Rat King snapped his eyes open, they took only a moment to adjust to the dark of the sewer, and the thoughts were gone.

Real thoughts.

Thoughts of a rat tinged with humanity.

He felt he should know who it was, who had such thoughts, cognition so close to his own.

So he stretched out his mind when he felt that he could. Evangeline would sit on his lap, or his shoulder, nuzzling his muzzle when she thought he had been gone inside of his mind for too long.

But eventually, he was able to make out a word.

"Initsiativa."

He did not know what it meant, but he knew the accent in which it was thought.

His heart soared.

# Chapter 45

The summer of their 12th year was a particularly hot one. The temperature rose in small increments each day, no stop seeming to be in sight, as the day of their birthday, the day their new life began together, approached.

The year had been a busy one for Céline. Todd and his friends came over on a regular basis, especially when the weather began to get hot. The children would piddle in the workshop below, until it became too hot to work and then come up and lounge in the living room watching TV. She would put them to work in the early mornings, the only time that they could garden with any kind of comfortability, weeding and digging and splitting and cutting. The juniper bush had sections of it die off from the heat, and Céline worked especially hard to keep it alive.

She meditated a lot that summer. Meditating was still, it got her mind off of the awful heat, and it was a great way to trick the kids into thinking she was occupied so she could eavesdrop on them.

She loved to eavesdrop on them! Sometimes she would even sneak to the middle of the stairs and listen as they talked in the workshop. They talked about what they were working on, what they liked and didn't like, the latest music, or movie, or movie star. They spoke like little grown-ups, and Céline had to remind herself more than once that grown-ups is what they were becoming.

One afternoon her brood and their friends gathered around the TV to watch the VHS tape of Harry Potter and Sorcerer's Stone they'd found. ("Look, Mama!" Naga had said, "It's brand new, still in the packaging with the price tag on and everything!") Her kids had waited until their friends arrived to watch it together. They were riveted to the screen, but Céline walked away after only 15 minutes. The book was better, she thought, and she hadn't thought the book was all that great. Rowling stole too much from Tolkien. Now, when they found the VHS of Fellowship of the Ring...

She went to her little yoga floor at the opposite end of the house, sounds of little wizards echoing through the rafters, and began to stretch. She noticed that her yoga practice was much longer these days, the stretching eased her muscles which seemed to ache a little bit more after a vigorous game of Catch The Monkey than they used to. She sat down in the lotus position, placed her hands on her knees, and began to breathe. The sounds of the outside world began to fade away, and she was alone with just herself.

Her voice echoed in her head, as it always did in this stage of her meditations. Today the words were lazy, almost slurred from the heat of the day. Cut some juniper, the unbidden thought told her. She hadn't cut any recently for fear of stressing the plant. She would cut some when she was done. Consider the floor, said the unbidden thought.

Consider the floor? What a silly thing to think. For the first time ever, after decades of hearing this voice of hers tell her to do things, she answered it. "What does that mean?"

Consider the floor, the unbidden thought said again.

"It's just a floor," Céline answered in her head. "We made it ourselves. We gathered the wood from a construction site. We sanded it smooth so we wouldn't get splinters when we did our floor exercises. We rubbed it with the only mineral oil we could find until it shone like a mirror, and filled the entire floor with baby smell."

Consider the floor, the unbidden thought said once more.

Céline brought a picture of the floor up in her mind. It materialized slowly in front of her inner vision, as did her knees below her. From her seat, she saw lines emanating from her in all directions. They looked red, and then they were blue, and then gold, and then white. Looking at them all around, her eyes fell on one, and the unbidden thought said, That one.

She touched it with a finger, and it felt very much like a soft fishing line. She followed it with her eyes, and it seemed to twist and turn in her vision, until it disappeared through the outer wall of the warehouse.

Follow it, the unbidden thought said.

"But it goes out the wall," Céline protested. "I can't follow it past there."

Follow it.

She stood up, and began to walk alongside the line. It began to glow white, and stayed that color, so bright that everything around her faded away to darkness, so there was only she and line. She would touch it occasionally, and it almost made a sound, like a piece of a tune she didn't recognize. The smell around her changed into the cool soil of the underground, so that when she looked up, she found herself in a dark tunnel.

The light from the line, which she held in her hand, faded, and she could see she was in a curved channel. Dirt, packed and cool to the touch, arched over her head. In the distance, she heard a deep voice, accented. What was the accent? The words were slurred together so that she could not tell one word from another. They carried on the cold air that hung the tunnel, as if emanating from far away.

"Mama," she opened her eyes, to see Ariste looking at her with a concerned expression.

The abrupt return to reality made her head spin, so she had to blink several times to steady her head. The smell of the earth disappeared, the coolness of the underground was replaced immediately by the 90 degree heat of Chicago on this summer day. The deep voice was gone.

"Mama," Ariste put her hand on Céline's shoulder, "are you OK?"

"I'm fine, Kitty Cat," she said, stretching her legs out in front of her. "I was just startled, that's all. Go and watch your movie."

The children behind her looked concerned, Todd and his friends hanging in the back. "The movie's over, Mama," Ursus said, putting his hand on Ariste's back. "You've been meditating for hours."

# Chapter 46

There were many days when Ilya and the boys did not come out of their dens at all. The cool, dark of the ground slowly turned into the hot dark of the ground, compared to the intense heat of the living area. The puppies rolled languidly on the floor, their tongues lolling out of their mouths. Ilya imagined that he could see the water vapor of their breath rising into the already saturated air, as some of their saliva dribbled on the floor below their mouths. They kept their eyes half closed when they were awake, and they dozed when they were not actively doing a chore.

Ilya felt as if his tail was on fire. He knew that a rat's body cooled itself by sending blood to the tail, so the body heat could disperse into the air. He wasn't entirely sure, however, how his body attempting to ignite his tail in flames helped to cool him. He blew on it, the movement of hot air doing little to cool him. He dipped it in water, a higher than room temperature liquid that was almost painful when it touched him. But when it evaporated, it gave him a modicum of relief, so he kept using it, despite the initial sting.

"Get off me, Kostya," Nikita breathed, pushing at his

brother with his foot on the floor.

"I'm not on you!" Kostya replied, sitting up, baring his teeth.

"You're practically on me," Nikita did not get up, but only rolled over. "I can feel your body heat."

"How can you feel his body heat?" Evgeny asked. "The air is hotter than his body heat."

"He's adding his body heat to the air," Dmitri rolled over also.

"Shut up, you two," Maxim sat up also, his own teeth bared.

Kostya growled.

"Hvatyt!" Ilya barked.

Instead of standing down, the order seemed to drive the six of them forward in their agitation. Nikita's fur on his neck stood on end, his eyes squinted hard at Maxim. In return, the volatile puppy moved to a prepared crouch, one leg folded under him and the other.

Ilya was in between them in an instant, his hand on Nikita's scruff. He shook him angrily, the boy's head bobbing about as he did so. The drill instructor, the teacher, Ilya Pytrovich came out in full force. The heat from his tail seemed to engulf him, ending at the tip of his nose. "Up," he commanded. "All of you!"

All five of the other puppies immediately popped up to their feet, their hands at their sides like little soldiers.

"You want to fight, eh?" His voice rang like a deep gong, thunderous and heavy. He all but threw Nikita to the far end of the room, and then grabbed Maxim by the ear. "You fight, then." He stood back, his muscled arms across his broad chest.

Both boys stared at him as if he'd gone insane.

"You will fight," he said. "The first one who cannot get up is the loser."

"But, Batya," Nikita said. "You said—"

"It does not matter what I said," he interrupted. "It matters what I say. I say to fight, until one of you cannot get up." When neither boy moved, he came between them. "You use your fists," he curled each of their fingers into their palms. "No teeth, no claws, only legs, feet, and fists." He backed away, his arms still across his chest.

Dmitri had taken Kostya's hand and led him toward the wall. Vasili and Evgeny joined him, all of them looking concerned at their father.

"Go," Ilya said casually. "I do not see you fighting."

Both boys, fists ready, relaxed. Nikita even smiled slightly.

"Fight!" Ilya bellowed.

Both boys jumped, Maxim staring at him with wide, dark green eyes.

"You are so eager to fight each other, fight!" Ilya physically pushed Nikita into his brother.

That was all the provocation that Maxim needed at the moment. The youth swung his fist at his older brother, striking him smack in the middle at the side of his muzzle.

Nikita growled once he recovered from the strike. He brought his own fist up from his waist to collide with Maxim's ribs. The younger puppy crouched to protect his torso, which left his head completely open. Nikita slammed his paw into Maxim's ear, wrenching a howl from him as he fell to the floor.

The older puppy backed away. Ilya stood with his arms still across his chest, a scowl on his face. The boy thinks that the fight is over, he thought. The heat that he felt in his body was not only the temperature of the air, but his anger rising to the surface of his skin. Had not taught his sons well enough? Just because an opponent is down does not mean they are out.

And Maxim was not out. He shook his head, then jumped up with a growl, teeth bared, claws out.

"No teeth!" Ilya called. "No claws!"

The Systemist felt a rush of satisfaction when Maxim curled his fingers into his palms, and twisted his body so that he would not land on top of his brother. Instead, taking Nikita by surprise, he landed at his side, and brought a foot out to kick him across the room.

Nikita recovered quickly, leaping up from a crouch, his strong canine legs springing him across the room. He hit Maxim full on, his palms striking at the shoulders, knocking him down. Nikita flipped as his brother fell, landing on his feet at Maxim's head.

Maxim grabbed at Nikita's ankles, pulling him toward his head. Nikita's feet fell out from under him, the sound of his claws scraping on the wood loud in Ilya's ears as he watched. His eldest son hit the floor on his shoulder blades, the air being audibly knocked out of him.

Both boys were fighting horribly. He had taught them better than this. They knew better than this. Why were they not fighting better than this? His body felt like it was going to burn up, his tail flapping slightly in an attempt to cool it.

Both boys were on the ground now, wrestling with each other, getting closed fisted blows in whenever they could find an opening. Growls emanated through the little room, then a whimper.

Ilya looked toward the sound to see Kostya clinging to Dmitri's arm. Dmitri, himself, stared at the fight, his eyes, the color of coffee, wide with concern. The rat looked back at his two sons on the floor, and realized that this was no longer a sparring match, if it ever had been. It had deteriorated to a proper fight, between siblings. The cold that ran through his body did nothing to cool his tail, but it did his heart. "Hvatyt!" the cried.

Both boys stopped immediately and stood up, facing him, their back straight, their hands at their sides. At least I taught them that right, Ilya mused.

"Are either of you hurt?" he asked in a tired voice.

"No, Batya," both boys said in unison.

"Good," he dropped his hands to his sides loosely. "You are ready to stop fighting?"

"Yes, Batya," they said.

"Good," he repeated. "Nikita, go refill the water bowl for my tail. Maxim, get another towel to put on the floor so we don't ruin the wood with the water."

They nodded, and ran off to do as they were told.

"Are you alright, Batya?" Kostya asked quietly, still clinging to Dmitri.

Ilya glanced over at him, annoyance welling in his tired body. "I am hot, child," he said tersely. "I have no patience for your brothers' antics today."

Evgeny nodded, but Dmitri put his arm about Kostya, who still clung to it, and pulled him closer to his body.

"Lie down," Ilya told them, crumpling to the floor. "Try to stay cool."

The boys did as they were bid, the air in the room more tense than it had been before he had ordered his two sons to fight out their heat induced anger. He dipped his tail in the newly delivered water, taking it out to lay it on the towel. Parenting was always full of choices, he had thought more than once. It appeared this time, he had made a poor one. It isn't the first time, he tried to console himself. It will not be the last.

# Chapter 47

The heat of that summer seemed to affect Khenum the worst. At least, Céline thought it was the heat. He was constantly at odds with his siblings, especially volatile Ariste, and when he was not, he was in the workshop working on something. He was amicable when Todd and his friends were around, even if he and Ariste still dueled it out. Todd was savvy enough to stay out of it, and only subtly take Ariste's side.

A meditation session was interrupted by a loud, high pitched hiss, followed by several loud bumps. Opening her eyes, Céline saw Khenum running at Ariste, who had jumped on the kitchen counter. She jumped just before he reached her, easily flying over him as he rammed the counter top. Céline leaped up, running across the warehouse floor. As Khenum made another run toward his sister, Céline managed to reach her, she grabbed Ariste's ear, giving it a hard pull. Khenum' head was still down, his horns in front of him, curling around his head. With her free hand, she caught his ear also. Twisting it, he came to a quick halt with a yelp.

"What is this?" Céline asked. "I have to tweak your ears

like little children?" It had been years since she had to employ this form of disciple. "What is the matter?"

"She started it!" Khenum pointed at Ariste, wincing from Céline's pressure on his ear.

"I didn't," Ariste twisted in an attempt to get out of Céline's grip. She pulled harder on her little triangle of an ear. "He is the one who tried to ram me."

"Stop!" Céline thundered, also in a way she hadn't done in years. Both of them froze in position. She let go of their ears, and they each stood up, glaring. "What is going on?"

"She won't help to clean up," Khenum said. "She always goes off with Todd, and leaves the mess for us. I'm tired of it."

"You're the one who makes all the mess," Ariste wailed.

"No, I'm not, you help. And you're the only one who doesn't help to clean up!" Khenum's voice cracked when he spoke.

Ariste hissed.

"Stop!" Céline yelled again. "To your rooms!"

Ariste was gone in a heartbeat, and Khenum stomped out and slammed his door.

Céline looked at Ursus and Naga, "What was that about?"

Ursus shrugged. "They started arguing about cleaning up..." He motioned to Naga, who had already begun slithering to the window. "We'll be outside."

Céline made herself a cup of tea, the expired aspartame giving it a slightly bitter flavor. She had to stir it quite a bit to get the expired powdered creamer to fully disperse. She drank it slowly, taking deep breaths to calm down. She had no doubt that Ariste had somewhat provoked Khenum, she was good at that, however ramming things in the house was not acceptable.

After she finished the tea, she went to Khenum's door,

and knocked on it slightly. Then, she opened it, to find him splayed on his bed, face is his pillow.

"Go away," he said.

"No," she said firmly. He had never told her to go away before.

He didn't say anything, so she went to his bed and sat down on it. She admired the craftsmanship of the frame. He had begun to carve into the bedposts and headboard, she couldn't tell what they would be, but he could see what was in the wood, and was bringing it out. She put her hand on his back, and began to rub it. "Oh, Lamb's Ear..." she crooned.

"Don't call me Lamb's Ear," he said into the pillow.

"Khenum," she said, in the same crooning way. "What is the matter? Surely Ariste not cleaning up didn't make you that angry."

He flipped around with such speed and ferocity, that it frightened her, and she jumped slightly. His jaw was thrust forward in anger, his eyes animalistic. "What would you understand?" he huffed.

She was quiet for a moment. "Because I've been here the whole time?" she asked gently. "But I can't read your mind, Khenum. You have to tell me what's the matter, or I can't help you."

He sat up and huffed again. "I don't know," he sounded defeated. "She just makes me so...angry. They all make me so angry. Everything makes me angry!" He threw his hands in the air barely missing her.

"What about everything makes you angry?" Céline felt at a loss.

"I don't know," he huffed again. "If I knew, I'd fix it."

Céline wracked her brain. She had no antidote for being angry without knowing the cause of the anger, so she grasped at the only thing she could find. "If them not cleaning up after themselves is a problem, would you like to have your own workshop?"

"That's just mine?" he asked.

"Yes," she nodded. "And no one can go in except you."

"Even you?"

Céline considered for a moment. "No, I get to come in."

Khenum considered for a moment. This surprised her, he was not, by nature, the considering type. "OK," his voice cracked, and he cleared his throat. "OK."

She stroked his head in between his horn and his ear. He looked so pathetic. "You could build a car." Did she really say that?

"A car?" His voice was incredulous. "How are we going to get the stuff to build a car?"

"I bet we could find most of what we need around here, with all the abandoned vehicles just between us and the cargo bay. And there are mechanic shops all over Chicago that do not dispose of their parts in the proper manner. Their dumpsters are probably a gold mine."

"When would we drive it, Mama?" He looked disappointed. "Where would we drive it?"

"You could drive it all along the warehouse district. I doubt if some person who is here after dark tells the police that a giant ram boy is driving a vehicle that they'll get much of a consideration." When Khenum finally smiled, she went on, "You can drive at night, especially in the smaller places. They don't have such a strong police presence." She opened her arms, and he fell into them, putting his head to her chest like he did when he was little.

"The police aren't good people, are they?" he asked.

"They do the best they can with what they have," she said.

"Then why do you always tell us to never let them see us?"

She had explained this already, she was positive she had, but she did it again anyway. "Because they do not understand." Khenum nodded into her breast. "That's because people don't think you're real. They think you are part of a fairy tale. If they saw you, if they saw us, they wouldn't understand. And when people do not understand something, they are afraid of it. When they are afraid of it, they try to get rid of it to make themselves feel safe again."

"Is that what The Grey Cats do?

"Not exactly," she answered. "But I would strongly guess that people do it to them, and this is how they retaliate."

Khenum sat up, looking at her he said, "They wouldn't be afraid of you. They wouldn't try to get rid of you. You're like them."

She reached up and put her hand on his cheek. "Oh, Khenum," she crooned. "I wish it worked that way."

# Chapter 48

He had left the boys in the living room of their den, retreating to his own personal burrow. It was dark, a few degrees cooler than the other room due to the lack of extra bodies and the drop in temperature that always happens just before sunrise.

The picture of the Our Lady of Lost Souls, holding The Divine Child, stared at him from the icon he had in his room. It was much smaller than the one in the practice room, and different colors, but it was still the same presentation of the famous icon. The Lady's eyes, soulful and knowing, looked out at the world with compassion. Did her compassion extend to them?

On his knees in supplication, he lowered his head and closed his eyes. Seek us who are lost, O Queen of Heaven, he prayed. Do not punish us for our wrongdoings, but in your love for your children, have compassion and rescue us. He knew his compassion had been lacking. He blamed it on the heat, burning him from the inside out and from the outside in. The thought had occurred to him that if he bit off his own tail, then the heat would stop, and this slowly rising fever from outside of him would cease to consume him. He had never felt a compulsion like this as a human, at least not caused by the temperature. By pain, yes. This was not pain, he had endured hurt far worse than even if his tail had actually been on fire. He was one of the best in the world, The Russian Elite, the Spetsnaz. The heat should not be affecting him this way.

He repeated the prayer in his head, trying to bring the feeling of compassion into his heart, to push the heat and the anger out of the way. It was able to wiggle in, only a small tendril, but it left exhaustion in its wake, the bone weariness he had experienced as an soldier, as a Systemist, as an escapee from the Therian Initiative, he should not be feeling it because it was a hot summer and his tail felt as if it were on fire.

He emptied his head, meaning to fill it with cool blackness. The dark was anything but, it was stuffy and warm, like breath, reminding him of the inside of a mouth. Perhaps he was a tooth, his tail was the tongue, and he had swallowed some steaming tea.

Seek us who are lost, he began again.

"I have sought you since your beginning," came a voice from the dark.

Ilya snapped open his eyes. He looked to the icon, visible to him in the low light of the candle only because of his rodent enhanced vision. He was expecting the mouth of the Lady of Those Who Are Lost to begin to move, to speak to him, like he had heard what happened to monks in the middle ages when such icons appeared. But she only looked back at him, her gaze steady and settled.

He closed his eyes, breathing deep, bringing his heart rate back under control. The heat was beginning to get him.

"It is the fire of greatness, Ilya Pytrovich."

He gasped, putting his hands on the wooden floor below him. The claws that extended from his dark pink fingers hit the oak planks with a clink. He looked up at the icon in front of him. The candlelight wavered slightly at the movement, making it seem as if the Lady and The Child were blinking at him from their prison in the painting. The voice speaking to him was not his own, but he could not identify whose it was.

"I am your brother in heart," the voice said, "your brother in soul, Ilya Pytrovich."

His brothers in heart, his brothers in soul were all dead, slowly picked off by a government that no longer wanted them, but that thought them too dangerous to leave them be. The family he had made for himself as a youth, as part of the most elite, had been stolen from him, either by the bullets of the enemy or the bullets of the very institution they were sworn to protect. Each of the other six of his brother-at-arms, gone.

"But I am not gone," was the reply to that thought. "I am here. I have been here. I was here when you had no one else in the world…"

He shook his head hard, feeling his lips slap against his gums. He was going insane. The heat had done something to him, he wasn't sure what. The loneliness of staying hidden underneath this business building, keeping his puppies quiet, trying to feed, clothe, and shelter them had worn him down so that he was breaking. The hiding had made him crack.

"Then why remain hidden?"

"Because showing ourselves would be suicide," he whispered to the icon, wishing their lips would move, would block out this other voice that was speaking to him. He knew it could not be from either of them. If they were urging him to suicide, then they would have done it long before now.

"Then show yourself to me," the other voice suggested.

He could not show himself to a disembodied voice. He couldn't show himself to a broken slice of his own psyche.

"You flatter yourself, Ilya Pytrovich," it said. "Have you

been alone so long that you do not know your own brother in soul?"

He put his hands to his temples, pressing his palms inward. "Get out of my head," he hissed.

"You and I share the same heart, now that we are together, I cannot leave you."

"You will leave me." The rat curled into a ball, bringing his flaming tail around to wrap his head. "Get thee behind me, Darkness."

The image of a sewer rat, gray bodied, black eyed, pinked toed, flashed in his mind. Behind it, tails lashed in slow motion. He counted them, 1, 2, 3, 4, 5, 6, 7, 8, 9. His chest seized, he couldn't get air into his lungs. A nine tailed rat? No child in Russia could mistake that picture—The Rat King.

"Lord, have compassion to me as one who offends the Highest Love," he prayed. "O Queen of Heaven," his voice was high and desperate, "rescue me."

There is no one to rescue you," it replied. "Only I can do that."

"Rescue me," Ilya repeated, "O Queen of Heaven."

"Batya?" Nikita's voice broke through Ilya's thoughts, the voice of the other speaking to him, his own prayers.

The rat looked up at his eldest son, the boy's pale blue eyes shining in the dark of the room. Ilya's mind went blessedly quiet. "Thank you," he breathed. "Lady, who will not let me be lost."

"He's not a lady, Batya," said Kostya, who was at his side. The puppy's eyes, the same color gray as his father, were wide, his brows drawn together.

"No, Kostya," Ilya said, breathing heavily and standing up. "He isn't a lady at all."

"Batya was praying," Nikita said, in almost a whisper.

He put an arm about each boy's shoulder, the heat of their bodies intense against him. "And my prayer was answered," he said, kissing Nikita's head. "Come, let us play a game."

Kostya jumped, "You haven't played with us in a long time, Batya."

"Batya is busy doing other things," Nikita scolded.

"Net," Ilya replied. "I should not be too busy to play with my boys. Ever."

# Chapter 49

It is a well known fact that crime skyrockets when the heat maintains 90 degrees for over a week. That statistic was apparently no different for the moreaus who resided in Chicago, for Céline had more patients to deal with, and a slew of nastier injuries, than the past three years combined.

What made her most angry, though, was they were doing it to themselves.

At least if The Grey Cats were fighting some other gang, she could feel sorry for their casualties and injuries. Infighting rankled her.

"This is a waste of my time," she muttered.

"Then leave him," Cottontail Coney said. "He doesn't mean anything."

Just as Grischat seemed to go nowhere without accompaniment, usually Jive or Cottontail Coney, so Céline was always in attendance by one of the three of them when she was at the cargo bay. She wasn't entirely sure, even after almost three years, why that was, but she chose to think it was for her safety. Her safety from what, she hadn't decided on yet.

"I can't just leave him," she huffed. Her own patience was wearing thin, she'd been at this for hours. "Can't you all get hurt by someone else instead of yourselves?"

"Do you have someone in mind?" Cottontail Coney asked, his own voice on edge.

Céline wiped sweat from her eyes with her shoulder. She was wearing shorts and a tank top, both of which stuck to her damply, and exposed several of the matching, round scars that always showed on her temples. "Who do you normally fight?"

Cottontail Coney chuckled. "Whoever stands in our way."

Céline finished up with her patient, and told him to rest and stop being stupid. The Grey Cats were very good at deflecting her questions, even though she'd been able to glean a great deal of information from them, they stopped short on letting her know too much about the outside world. She knew there were other moreaus out there, how did they live? Were they in gangs like this one? Did they live all alone? Did they have someone to take care of them? Oftentimes, when she felt this way, she would think of the other hybrids in the cells with her all those years ago, and wonder what happened to them all. Did they wonder what happened to her and the kids?

Grischat came over, and motioned with his head that Cottontail Coney was relieved of his babysitting. He was shirtless, the hair on his rather impressive chest damp from sweat. He held out his hand to help Céline up. She took his paw, tired from the heat and the tedious work of people patching. The fur was soft, like alpaca wool, and his grip was strong. He looked her up and down appreciatively, and she was so hot, she didn't even care. "You look overheated," he said slowly.

"It's hard not to be overheated in here," she snapped. "It must be 110 degrees with all these people. Those fans don't cut it. You need to steal an air conditioner or two."

Grischat laughed tiredly. "You, who will not take a gift taken from someone else, tells me to steal an air conditioner."

"The heat makes people crazy," she sighed.

"Come," still holding her hand, he led her to the side of the bay, "I have already stolen an air conditioner."

Céline was too hot and too tired to argue. She let him lead her to a small room, which may have once been an office. Opening the door, two moreaus, both dogs, were in a compromising position. Céline turned around quickly, but Grischat did not let go of her hand.

"Sortez!" Get out! he growled.

The two of them scampered out of the chair, grabbing clothes, and running by Céline without looking at her.

Grischat led her in the cool room and closed the door. The room was not cold, but the coolness of the loud air conditioner tingled the tips of her ears and her toes where they peeked out of her sandals. "Ahhh," she closed her eyes and put her head back.

"You see," he said, "I am not all bad."

Céline sank into a chair by the door, leaving the previously occupied one for Grischat. "I never said you were all bad," she replied.

"You do not agree with my business dealings," he said.

"Because they aren't business dealings," she told him. "Stealing, extortion, assault, battery, and attempted murder are not business dealings."

"You forgot successful murders," he added.

She opened her eyes and glared at him.

His pupils were round with the lack of light, he blinked his hazel eyes slowly. "You do not understand the nature of my business," he said in French.

"I understand it fine," she said. "I do not agree with it."

"There is a place in the Southwest Side," he said, leaning

over his long body to the small fridge at the side of the room and opening it up. "Englewood, you know it?"

Céline nodded, taking the Coke he offered her, "The big Haitian neighborhood."

"Oui," he opened a Budweiser, took a swig. "I have ties to this place," he nodded

She nodded back, "Is your family there?"

"I have ties to this place," he said again. "There is a group of people there. They make it difficult sometimes." He took another drink of his beer. "I have ties to this place, and if I am compensated for helping to make it less difficult, where is the crime in that?" He sounded genuine, as if he was honestly asking the question.

"Because what you do to make it less difficult is illegal," she was quite sure it was, even if he hadn't gone into detail. "Why can't the police handle it?"

Grischat laughed, a little less tiredly than earlier. "The police?" He leaned forward, "The police do nothing, ma Medicienne. The police are useless. We," he clapped his bare chest, "we are not useless."

She didn't say anything, but she looked at him dubiously.

"Do you know what would happen to you if you were out there, on your own, without your children?"

She blushed.

"Do you know how much, even as little children, they protect you because they are monsters?"

"They are not monsters," her ire began to rise again.

"Non, that is where you are mistaken, ma Medicienne. We are all monsters. You," he pointed at her, "are the mother of monsters. It is because of those monsters, us, that you are safe."

Céline shook her head, "No," she said vehemently, "no, we don't have to be monsters." She stood up, "Being a monster is a choice, not what you look like."

"You tell that to the monsters out there, ma cherie," he stood up also, towering over her. "Tell that to my people, and see what they do to you." He leaned down, his face close to hers, "Like it or not, we are not humans, ma petite Medicienne. We are freaks, abominations, monsters. Do not forget that."

# Chapter 50

The sun began to set, the temperature getting a few degrees cooler. Céline asked for her children to be brought to her. When they came to her, Grischat smiled broadly, "Stay and dance with us, tonight."

"Oh, a dance!" Todd punched the air.

A dance? They were having a dance in the cargo bay?

"Oh, Mama, please!?"

"But it's so hot," Céline almost whined. "And you want to dance?"

"What better way to forget the heat," Grischat bent down closer to her, his voice in her ear, "than to dance it off?" She could hear him purring, "I hear you like to dance."

"And where did you hear that?" she stepped away from him.

He looked at Todd and winked.

Todd avoided her gaze when she looked at him.

"Please, Mama, please!?"

Later on, when she thought of this day, she thought the heat must have gone to her head, or perhaps she was just tired, or lonely for something other than the little world she had inhabited for so long. Her head was blank of any reason to say no. "Alright," she said.

The room erupted around her. Grischat picked her up by the waist, and spun her around. Then the music was on, bodies were moving with the beat, and she joined them. She danced as the sun went down and the world went dark. The music enveloped the bay, the smell of animal became stronger as the heat of the space refused to go down with the sun. Bodies moved in ways that no human being could move, and in the back of her mind, Céline came to the realization that her own body, even through years of honing with contortion, was no match in gracefulness or movement to any of these creatures that danced around her. The movement of the least graceful of these was more feral than one she could ever hope to produce, no matter how much or how well she danced. When she felt body heat too close to her, she would spin away, to enjoy the dancing on her own. Grischat ended up by her more often than not, and more than once she slipped out of his grasp with a laugh, feeling powerful and in control.

She danced with these moreaus, part of her life whether she liked it or not, until the sun came up.

# Chapter 51

"Batya," Vasili called. "The cupboard is bare."

"Old Mother Hubbard went to her cupboard to get her poor dog a bone. But when she got there, the cupboard was bare, and the poor little doggie had none," chanted Maxim.

"No bones for us," Dmitri said, rolling over to his other side.

With the heat being almost unbearable, none of them had eaten much. It was no surprise to Ilya, however, that the cabinet now held nothing. It had been an entire week since they'd gone out for a supply run. The fact that they had a week's worth of food in the den was impressive enough to the Systemist. He dragged himself up to a sitting position, his tail aflame with each movement. "Is it dark outside yet?" he asked.

"No, Batya," replied Kostya, poking his head out of the darkened den to see the living space beyond. "Not yet. In an hour or two."

The rat let out a slow, hot breath. "We'll go out when it gets dark," he drawled. Several of his sons moaned. Whether it was because of the wait or because of the task, he couldn't tell. "None of that," he muttered, closing his eyes. "Sleep a little, we will be out for a long time tonight."

It is good that we will have something productive to do, he assured himself. Keeping the puppies occupied, or at the very least not hurting each other, took up a great deal of his own personal energy. He had played small games with them, but it was difficult to maintain any of them, with the mercury trying to bust its way out of the glass.

They often played one that he taught them when they were very young, to teach limpness and immediate movement.

"I will play the guitar," he said, resting the old, salvaged thing that he'd tried to restore on his knees. He'd done a good enough job that he could play it, and it sounded like an instrument. "You must run to the sound of the music. You can go no faster," he looked at Kostya, "and you can go no slower," he looked at Vasili, "than what the music tells you."

"How does music tell you anything, Batya?" Maxim had asked.

"Oh, that's easy," Vasili had replied before Ilya could do so. "The beat of the music is how fast you go."

Ilya had looked closely at the black tipped eared boy, "Then why do you go so slow?"

Vasili looked about, his topaz eyes flashing, realizing he'd been caught in something. "Uh…"

Ilya had shaken his head and continued. "You will run with the music. When the music stops, you will fall to the ground, like a squid with no backbones."

"But we are Wild African Wolves, Batya," said Evgeny in his little, serious voice. "And we have backbones."

"We do have backbones," Ilya conceded. "But we will pretend we do not have them when we fall."

The boy had looked dubious, but accepted the explanation.

The rat had played Russian folk tunes from his childhood, upbeat quick footed things, to which Vasili ran always one exact beat behind, no matter the tune. When he stopped, the boys obediently dropped to the ground, all giggles and tension. They had to practice falling quite a bit, until Ilya said, "Like you are dead!" That, apparently, did the trick with the boys. They all dropped like stones and stayed that way. He then dragged them into a pile in the middle of the floor, putting different puppies in different positions each time. The idea was to stay 'dead', even with the weight of someone else on top of you, or with a strong rat-man dragging you across the wooden planks.

Today, however, when they'd played, the tune had been a much slower one. The running had been more like slow jogging, all six boys panting with their tongues out of their mouths, dripping saliva. When Ilya stopped playing the guitar, they'd all fallen to the floor with grateful exhalations, staying quite limp as their father dragged them to a pile, much bigger than when he'd first taught them the game. They'd done that three times, with large waits as they piled up, before Dmitri fell asleep in the pile snoring.

Ilya did not like just waiting. His dozing was filled with old memories of his brothers at arms, of former students from The Institute, of Dr. Montgomery stroking at him like a pet. But when he was awake, he was alone with his thoughts. It took too much energy to talk, to move, almost to breath. He would turn his muzzle toward the puppies and see them roll on one side, then another. They talked to each other with their tongues lolling out of their mouths, moving when they wanted something. Ilya could barely get the strength up to answer a question when asked.

His thoughts, however, were not so tired. He had to consciously keep his mind on the things at hand, sometimes concentrating on the intense heat in his tail. He had not looked upon the icon of the Queen of Heaven and the Divine Child since the voice spoke to him. He was terrified that the lovely lady on the painting would open her mouth, and that voice would come out of it, and he would forever have that scene caught in his mind's eye. He knew that couldn't happen, things like that didn't happen in real life. They happened in movies. He was not living in a movie. If he was, he would have picked a better role for himself. But it did not keep him from fearing that it would happen.

He had also avoided the mirror, which in and of itself was not a rare thing, but he went through great lengths to avoid looking at himself. It was not because of his usual surprise at seeing a rat/man hybrid standing where he thought he should be standing. It was because he was afraid that if he looked, he would see not one, but two rat/man hybrids staring at him from the reflective glass.

# Chapter 52

The streets of Chicago were kicking with the underbelly of the city at night. The scorching days kept those who called the streets their home out of sight, and out of the city's mind, as they tried to find shelter in south sides of buildings, begging the bricks for any kind of shade they could procure. When the sun finally set at nights, the fire turned into a smoldering heat, much more endurable than the burning caused by the sun when it was up in the sky.

The types of injuries that Céline found herself serving were new to her, on such a large basis. She was expecting dehydration, after all, even those people who had comfy homes were suffering from it. Chicago was not the land of air conditioning, it wasn't needed. The city had set up hydration stations in what it deemed 'strategic locations.' While these places were in the much less affluent neighborhoods of the metropolis, they still did not serve the population she felt they should. They doled out water to those who had faucets, fridges, freezers, and roofs over their heads. The homeless, who had none of those things, were edged out. They did not come out during the day, there was no relief from the intense heat. And if they did make it to a hydration station, a 16oz bottle of water was nothing in these conditions.

She and the kids took home every empty 2 liter soda bottle they could find, with or without a lids. Lids made their way home with no bottles attached to them, so that they matched up watertight caps to liters. Each child and herself, then had a large string slung about their necks, with plastic bags attached to it at close intervals, until it was almost hitting the ground. Each bag held three to four empty bottles, each string held about eight bags, so that each child carried about 32 bottles at the beginning of the night. So with approximately 160 bottles between them, they traipsed into the darkness of the Chicago city streets.

Each person she came across, Céline gave a bottle. Before she gave it, however, she had one of the kids run off and fill it at a nearby faucet.

That had worked in the beginning of the summer. After two weeks of the heat wave, Ursus came up to her, tapping her lightly on the shoulder as she looked over one of her patients.

"The bear spirit summons you, great lady," said the homeless man.

This particular homeless man was convinced she was a great Irish shamaness who controlled animal totems. Céline had never had the heart to tell him that the Irish Celts didn't have shamans or shamanesses, but rather fili, who were poets or seers. Nor did she have the heart to tell him that she wasn't Irish, but Canadian-French descent and therefore descended from the Gauls.

Céline smiled at him, then turned to her son, her eyebrows arched in question.

"There's a lock on the faucets," he said in his grizzly voice.

"A lock?" she repeated stupidly.

"All the faucets have boxes on them, so you can't get to the water," Ariste explained.

She turned to the homeless man, who stared at her confused. "Wait here one moment," she told him, holding her finger up. Following the children to the outdoor spigot, she saw they were exactly correct. A heavy, dark green, plastic box had been put on top of the entire fixture, so that one could not access it without a key. "You've gotta be kidding me," she muttered.

"I guess people are tired of other people taking their water," Khenum grumbled, shoving Naga off of his side as she leaned against him.

"We are, technically, stealing the water," Ariste said.

Céline shot her daughter a dirty look. "I can't believe they locked up the faucet." She ran her fingers through her long, honey colored hair. She took a deep breath, bending down to examine the box. She shook it slightly, it was on tight. "Khenum," she murmured, "can you break off the box without breaking the faucet?"

The ram grinned, putting both of his three fingered hands on either side of the green, plastic cube. He looked up at her, "Really?"

She nodded her head, "Really," she answered seriously.

He laughed as if she had just told him to run naked in the street, a silly, disbelieving thing. She could see him flex his fingers, the pads of his fingertips bending ever so slightly as the hard plastic cracked loudly. He pulled it apart, dropping the two halves on the asphalt.

"Fill up some of the bottles," she told them, turning from the building and heading back to her patient.

"Is all well?" asked the man.

"Indeed, sir," she answered. "The sheep spirit is taking care of it as we speak."

"You are a very powerful sorceress," he bowed his

head.

She laughed, clapping him on his bare shoulder. If he only knew how the powerful sorceress lived. "I am alright," she admitted. The kids came back with several filled bottles. She handed a two liter to the man. "You need to drink two of these a day full of water, do you understand? Keep the bottle so you can refill it." She looked at him hard. "It is important that you drink two of these and you need to be still during the day, so you don't get too hot."

The man nodded, going in on his way.

Céline couldn't tell if he would follow her directions or not. It was one of the most frustrating parts of her work.

Another injury that she wasn't expecting to be dealing with were burns. From sitting, walking, laying, or falling on the asphalt, the heat absorbed from the sun made the black blanket of roads hot enough to cause blisters. She found that people's thighs and their companion animal's feet were most susceptible.

The first time she encountered it, a pit bull, walking miserably beside a woman in a pair of torn shorts and a tank top that hung on her very skinny frame, whined with each step it took. Once she figured out what the issue was, she told the woman to stay at that same spot, a deserted back alley, blessedly warm instead of intensely hot. Giving her two bottles of water, she instructed that she and the dog drink as much as they could, until it was gone.

She hurried home, the kids following her, and began making her burn salve. She'd come across the recipe early on in her herbal research. Mixing plantain and chickweed that she had harvested from cracks in the sidewalk and empty lots, along with comfrey, which she'd grown from a cutting she'd taken from someone's backyard. Dumping it all in a jar and filling it with oil, found in a dumpster past its expiration date, she headed back to where she left the woman.

The sun was coming up, lightening and heating the world with its rays. "Stay home," she told the kids. "Don't leave the warehouse or the garden."

They nodded obediently, then she was off.

The woman was where she left her, leaning against the building with her eyes closed. The dog's tongue was already lolling out. She rubbed the woman's shoulder and smiled when she opened her eyes. "I have some medicine for you," she told her.

"Medicine?" the woman's eyes lit up. Her face immediately fell when she saw the jar of oil with weeds in it.

"This will help you to heal your burns," Céline said.

The woman looked dubious.

Céline dipped her fingers in it and smeared it on the woman's burns on the back of her thighs. "Make sure you keep them clean. This will heal it pretty quickly, and if there is dirt in it, it will seal it in. That's not good."

"You're joking," the woman replied.

Céline made herself comfortable sitting on her bottom, cross-legged. "Nope," she said. "Sometimes, if you apply it five times a day, it will heal in two or three days."

"Then why don't the doctors use it?" the woman asked, stroking her pit bull on the side.

"If the doctors told you what was in their medicine, then you could make it like I do," Céline explained. "They'd be out of business pretty quick, wouldn't they?"

The woman didn't look convinced. "I guess so."

She had to sit and talk with the woman for quite a while before the dog would let her attend to his feet. She simply dipped his paws in the oil, and then wrapped them in plastic grocery bags, tied on by the handle. "Do this when you reapply the oil to yourself," Céline explained. "If you can find cloth to use as bandages for your dog's feet, that would be better than the plastic. But if this is all you can find, just keep doing this."

The woman nodded and Céline went home, the sun high in the sky, the temperature rising, to find her children lying about on the floor, dozing, the heat of the warehouse almost intolerable.

# Chapter 53

The temperature dropped twenty degrees after the sun went down, but it was still sweltering. As the puppies stealthily roamed the back alleys of Chicago, with Ilya at their backs, they stopped frequently at spigots they found. Ilya used a whip of his tail to crack the plastic on the box, and his strong arms and sharp claws to pry it open to reveal the spigot inside. Like a chest revealing a golden treasure, the puppies laughed each time he did it and with relish, they all lapped up the cold water coming from the faucet.

They ran from their den, the distance between home and themselves growing with each moment. For their supply run, the children were hardly able to keep their energy in check. Their father had to work hard not to fuss at them, to be more careful, to be quieter. Having been cooped up for so long, and with the lowering of temperature, the freedom was heady for them. Ilya couldn't blame them. It was heady for him, too. We can hardly move in this heat, he consoled himself, and we are supposed to be stronger than humans. There can't be any human beings out here…

The dumpsters stank. Each of the seven of them

scrunched their noses instinctively as they came upon each one. They approached cautiously, as always.

Ilya had made it a game early on, once he figured out that the six boys would leap into the dumpsters with little thought of what was going on around them. Catching a homeless man on the side of the dumpster had not given the puppies any caution. "We have to be very careful," he had tried to drill into them. "Always."

Nikita had been the first to catch on, using the designated signal, a curve of their pointer finger and thumb, to alert the others of his observation. He put his hand out in the direction he thought it came from.

His brothers put their noses to the air, catching the reek and giving a thumbs up, to indicate they agreed with Nikita. Then, in formation so that there were eyes in every direction, they crept toward the smell, following their eldest brother. The rat moreau had never decided if they had a more sensitive sense of smell than he did or not. At times, it seemed that he had the better smelling receptors by far. Then other times, they would catch the scent of something he only caught a few moments later. Ilya hung back, watching them, pride swelling in his chest at the sight of the little team.

His team.

When the dumpster came into view, the boys broke into their assigned pairs, Nikita and Kostya, Dmitri and Evgeny, and Vasili and Maxim, with Ilya being alone in his position. Each pair took a direction with which to approach the dumpster, their canine bodies hunched and pressed into the shadows. Their brindle coloring hid them beautifully, only the occasional eyeshine denoting where they were to the untrained eye. Nikita indicated that Dmitri and Evgeny would be the ones to first approach their target, scouting for potential threats. There rarely were any, and when there were, they were usually rather pedestrian in nature; a homeless man or woman, a teenager who screamed at the sight of them. Every once in a while, the threat was more sinister; a person with a gun, or more likely, several people with guns. Twice now, they had come across other moreaus. Ilya's great fear, which he tried hard not to think of, was seeing a man in a dark suit emerge into the light, some new weapon at his disposal, his attention on the six puppies. But as of yet, that had not come to pass.

Gunshots sounded in the distance, followed by the faint sound of voices. Ilya had a hard time telling how far away it was, with the heat muffling his ears.

The routine remained the same for each garbage dumpster they came across, the only thing different being the pair that was sent to scout out the supply bin. Each target was secure when they approached, and thoroughly plundered when they left. As the night wore on, their arms became fuller, but their spirit of adventure did not lessen. Finally, Ilya had to announce, "One more, then we go home."

A chorus of "Awwww,"s answered him.

He didn't blame them. He didn't want to go home yet, "soon there will be no room left in our arms, and soon after that, the sun will begin to come up."

"Wouldn't want to be caught out when the sun comes up, eh Ilya Pytrovich?"

The six puppies all crouched into a fighting position, dropping their new belongings to the ground. Ilya whirled around, his mind abuzz. How had he not caught the scent of the speaker? He should have had ample time to detect him before he was close enough to speak. It took barely a moment for the rat to leap up to the top of the chain link fence that bordered the parking lot, then have the moreau on the ground, his muzzle inches away from the speaker's face. The smell of canine hit his nostrils, mixed strongly with the stench of garbage can. His scent had been hidden by the retching heat cooking away the debris of the city.

"Hold it!" The prone man underneath Ilya cried. "Back off!"

It was Toaster.

Ilya hissed and jumped off him, his gray eyes blazing with anger. "You cannot do that!"

"You wanna get killed?" Dyson came up to them and pulled Toaster to his feet. "What the hell's the matter with you?"

"I was trying to be friendly," the dog replied, rolling his shoulders.

"It is a good way to die," Ilya groused, jumping back up the chain link fence, dropping to the other side to join his puppies.

"Hello to you, too," Toaster mumbled.

Two other moreaus, a lizard of some sort and another dog, a female, with long ears. "You were about that close," the lizard, tall and pale green, put his fingers together, "to getting your face bit off." He strode toward the fence, putting his three fingered hand around one of the links. "That was fast, bro."

"I don't know why none of you people believe me," said Dyson, waltzing up to the fence.

"Because it doesn't sound believable," the other canine said, her voice high. She came to stand beside Toaster and put her hand gently on his back.

"I believe it now," Toaster muttered.

"We are in your territory?" Ilya asked, having rejoined the puppies. They all gathered around him, much like chicks to a mother hen.

The lizard nodded, but Toaster replied, "Just the edge. We like to keep an eye on things."

"You think too small, Toaster," the lizard said. He looked at Ilya again, as if sizing him up. "We've heard a lot about you from Subzero and the others, Ilya Pytrovich."

"Others?" he asked cautiously.

"People who have escaped from the Institute," Dyson said. "There are a few who remember you."

Ilya raised his eyebrows. How many moreaus have escaped?

"You haven't introduced us, Subzero," said the lizard. From his tone of voice, and from the otter's tone when he replied, it was obvious that the lizard stood above him in the hierarchy of the Grey Cats.

"Ilya Pytrovich, this is Jive," he said, motioning to the lizard. "Jive, this is the famed Ilya Pytrovich, who destroyed a legion alone."

The rat was silent for a moment, regarding the lizard warily. "If you have been told that," he said finally, "then you have been told wrong."

"You're far afield," Dyson came up to the fence that separated them. "Why so far from home?"

He looked at the puppies huddled to him, all looking shyly at the moreaus across from them. "It has been a while since we were out," he admitted. "The boys needed to run."

Jive snickered.

Ilya turned his eyes to him, his head barely moving. "Da?" he asked.

The lizard chuckled again, jumping to the top of the chain link fence, then down to the ground.

Ilya fought the urge to take a step back, to throw his hands behind him to shield the boys. I've grown anxious, he noted, though it did not lesson his fear any.

"You live by yourself, they tell me," Jive threw his head back on his long neck to the moreaus behind him.

"I live with my sons," Ilya corrected.

Jive smiled. "Seems like those with little ones tend to stick to themselves."

The Systemist wasn't sure how to take what Jive said. He had a circumspect way about him, obviously covered by bravado. At the same time, he seemed comfortable in his own skin, as if he were intimately knowledgeable about his body in a way he'd seen few moreaus be. His movements were practiced and fluid, down to the tip of his tail swaying slightly as he walked.

"You dropped your stuff," the female dog broke the silence, pointing to the bags on the ground.

He looked down at them, as if he'd forgotten they were there. "I cannot fight with my hands full," he said.

All of the others laughed, "I would say you have your hands full all the time," Jive commented. "That's more than the Medicienne."

"Oh, I am sure he's much more disciplined than she is," Dyson said. "Those puppies are his fighting team."

Hearing Dyson say those words made Ilya's chest clench. His fighting team. They were to be his special unit, where the seven of them would work as an integrated unit to do whatever it was that the Initiative set them out to do. They were to be his brothers in arms, to replace those he'd lost years ago. But they'd morphed into something different, something he was to take care of, something he loved not as an equal, but as a parent.

"They are not my fighting team," Ilya replied. He had taught them to fight so they could defend themselves, not be taken captive by anyone. He had not taught them to fight to make them a special operations unit. They were not killing machines. They were not automatons. "They are my sons."

"None of us said otherwise," Jive agreed. "We're just saying the Medicienne is a softy with her kids."

"She won't let them learn how to fight," Dyson said quickly, swinging over the fence so he was now on the same side as Jive and Ilya. "I know your boys know how to fight."

"As well as they need to," the rat said.

"You have a lot of things to carry there," the female dog pointed to the items again. "Do you want us to help you carry them to your home?"

"Better yet," Jive said, "come carry them with us to our home."

"There is plenty of room for you to stay," Dyson came forward, putting his hand on Ilya's shoulder. "For you and the kids."

Something hung the words of Grey Cats invitation, but Ilya could not decide what it was. It made him uncomfortable, tickling his stomach in a way indicated he was missing something important. He shook his head, "We are fine where we are," he assured him. "In fact, we should be getting home."

"You said one more, Batya," cried Kostya. "I haven't had a chance to find one first!"

"Net," Ilya said curtly. "We go home." He bent down to pick up the items he'd dropped, and the puppies followed suit.

"You sure you don't want us to help you carry them?" the female dog asked.

"No, thank you," Ilya replied. "We have it."

She nodded, Toaster putting his arm around her.

"The offer is always open," Dyson called.

"Yeah," Jive agreed. "You just gotta find us, and we can take you home."

He nodded again, and then led the boys around the corner, so that the other moreaus were out of sight.

"What were they talking about, Batya?" Dmitri asked.

"They want us to go home with them," Evgeny said.

"I know that," Dmitri snapped. "Why?"

"Some of them were with us in the Institute," Ilya explained. "There is safety in numbers. So they have gathered together."

"Then why don't we go to live with them?" Vasili asked.

"I don't want to leave home," Nikita said. "I like our den."

"I like it, too," Maxim chimed in.

"We are not going to live with them," Ilya had to keep hard from hissing.

"We have enough numbers to keep us safe," said Maxim. "We don't need them."

"No," Ilya replied. "We don't need them."

They walked in silence for a while, the long night and the heat beginning to get to them.

The quiet of the night was broken by a gunshot in the distance, then a scream.

The boys looked up at Ilya, who froze at the sound. It had been years since he'd heard a real scream, a live one from a living being. The scream was not a 'I have been startled' scream or a 'I lost my balance' scream. It was a real scream, a 'I am terrified' scream. The same kind he had heard so many times in Russia.

It was carried by the heat again, the muffle seemed to be gone, it clearly rang in his ears. Whether it was from his imagination or the heat had allowed the sound to slice through it, he didn't know.

He dropped his groceries again and ran toward the sound. He heard the boys copy his movement, running right behind him. He ran in as much of a straight line as he could, the sounds of struggling, another scream, muffled speaking, all getting louder as they approached. He jumped over fences, barrels, and garbage dumpsters. He came to a brick wall, twice his height, and jumped on it with ease. He paused only a moment to survey the scene below him.

A man lay on the ground, still as stone, thick red blood oozing out on the concrete from underneath him. He could see no movement of the man's chest, and the blood pooled slowly. Farther down the alley, a group of three men had backed a woman against the brick wall of a building. Another man, being held by two thugs, was struggling desperately to get to her.

"Leave her alone," he shouted, fear lacing every word he spoke.

The hairs in Ilya's ears bristled. He felt three of his sons join him on the edge of the wall, tiny ripples in the stifling air, but he did not move his eyes from the spectacle taking place below him.

The woman's shirt was ripped off, the sound of the fabric tearing seemingly louder than any of the other noises in the night. Her skin shone in the dim light, rounded parts of her body glinting like stars in the dark. Clad in only her bra and skirt, she struggled as one of them came behind her and held her fast by her torso.

When a second man approached her front, his hand raised, Ilya heard, "Batya," come from his left. He looked down to see Nikita's great blue eyes staring at him pleadingly.

If he went down there to help that woman, he would be seen.

He knew very well what would happen to the woman if he didn't. He'd seen it before, military operations that went awry, commanding officers who were far from scrupulous. He had turned and looked the other way to save his career.

He had no career now.

He leapt from the wall, landing between the two thugs who held the struggling man and the three thugs who held the woman. There was a pause in the air. The rat moreau looked past the thugs in front of him, his gray eyes meeting the dark brown orbs of the woman being held against her will. The silence that was shattered by the woman's sudden screaming.

One of them holding the woman's partner cursed, his voice a stark contrast to the high pitched echoes. He let go of the struggling man and pointed a gun at Ilya.

The world seemed to stop for a moment, slowing down until there was no movement whatsoever, not even the shadows dancing in the edges of his vision. It had been over twenty years since he had had a gun pointed at him. The barrel of the pistol became crystal clear, as did every tense movement of the perpetrator. The twitch of his finger on the trigger, the bullet spinning out of the barrel of the gun at him.

Training took over, faster than thought, as fast as the electrical impulses could travel from his brain to his muscles. He leapt into the air, a part of his mind telling him that he shouldn't be able to be so far above the ground. He landed in front of the gunman, he could see the woman's partner scrambling to back away from them. He heard the bullet hit something hard behind him, the wall perhaps? The gunman's finger twitched again, but a kick with Ilya's animalistically curved leg sent the gun flying before another bullet was fired. He landed, his tail whipping out to knock the gunman off of his feet as it bent his neck at an odd angle with a sickening crack.

The world began to move again, all of the other thugs coming at him in a rush of shouts and cursing. Without thought, Ilya knocked two guns away, one with his hand and the other with a well positioned kick. The fellow who was struck in the hand by Ilya's foot went spinning off to the side like a top. The fourth man came at him with a knife, slicing as if he were playing badminton. Ilya grabbed his forearm in a classic block, twisting it behind him until the snap told him the ligaments at his elbow were torn and he dropped the blade.

The rat expected the others to run, seeing two of their own dispatched so quickly. But to his surprise, they didn't, they both came at him with knives drawn. It confused him for a moment, that they would be so foolish as to stand against him, until he heard another gunshot.

He felt something graze his arm, his muzzle turning to bicep to see a line of red begin to swell on the parted hair of a gun graze. The familiar burn flared up and spurred him out of his surprise.

He dropped to all fours and made a rush at the group of young men who had appeared from beyond the alleyway. He heard a chorus of words in French or perhaps Creole, that he couldn't translate, but that anyone could understand. He dodged two more bullets, darting this way and that, until he was upon the group. A paw whipped out, grabbing an assailant by the hair to throw him into another, sending them both careening into the wall of a building.

His tail landed heavily on another attacker, the gun in the man's hand skittered across the asphalt, stopping in the shadows.

"Batya!" he heard one of the boys cry, "Watch out!" Turning, he saw that all six of them had come over the wall, and Nikita was on top of a thug who had a knife aimed at Ilya's ribs. The boy expertly swung around, his feet tearing the muscle of the man's shoulders, before the boy landed in front of him, growling and kicking him in the gut. The knifeman went flying across the alley.

Ilya was not sure how many humans there were, but by their yelling and colors, he was sure now they were Bonecrushers. The Haitian gang must have been trolling in a large group, and the contingent that he and his sons had come across was akin to a scouting party. All he knew was that he and the boys were outnumbered, but he doubted they were over their heads. The boys were fighting admirably, just as he had taught them, trained them, in years of isolation underneath a business building. While the original group of thugs had not fled, their reinforcements saw that losing fight.

Someone yelled something, again in Creole or French, and Ilya caught the word, "werewolves." The entire group of men turned to flee the way they'd come.

But Maxim and Vasili dropped down to block their way.

Again the world paused, slowing down until it barely moved. Upon landing, the boys relaxed, just as he had been trained, looking as if they were about to hang out with their brothers. Then Ilya saw Maxim raise his lips instinctively in a growl, bearing his long canines. Vasili turned his head slightly, a raised lip causing one long tooth to shine in the dark.

The world began to move again, as the group converged on the two boys. Ilya ran toward them, watching as one man went down, two, blood splaying where one of them had cut an artery with either their teeth or claws.

Then a howl of pain pierced the air.

Ilya stopped breathing. In his mind, he knew that was the worst thing he could do, ever, would be to stop breathing. Breath was the core of life, it was the core of death, it was the core of Systema. His heart thumped in this chest, so that he was sure if he looked down he would be able to see the fur undulate over it. His feet couldn't move fast enough, couldn't get purchase to propel him forward at the rate he wanted to go. He wanted there to be no elapse in time, that he could be from one place to another, But that is not how the world works, he could hear himself explain to his sons. He took air in through his long nose, out through his mouth, in again, out again, and then reached the two boys.

All emotion left him but calm. His body relaxed, his mind went black, he could feel the soul of those around him push against his own, so that just as when he was human, he could fight as one of the most elite martial artists in the world. He noted that stepped in warm blood. One man was torn down. A curved knife came for him, but the assailant did not even get within an arm's distance of the rat. Two men down. His elbow cracked into the nose of someone close enough to get near to him. Three men down.

Then he was at his son, Vasili snarling like a mad thing at anyone who came near. A human lay mutilated at his feet. And next to the human, in a still heap, lay Maxim.

# Chapter 54

Céline knew the only things saving her garden this summer were the buildings that surrounded her plot. She normally complained about them, how they covered her garden in shade at the most inopportune times. Gardening was not an easy feat for her, she had planted, moved, and replanted dozens and dozens of plants all over the former parking lot in an attempt to make things live. She had many of the perennials established, but many of her annuals, usually vegetables, had not yet revealed where their perfect planting spot was. And this summer, she would not find out as the heat tried to cook everything.

The shade that was normally so annoying was, indeed, the saving grace this year. Because the buildings blocked the sun except for the hottest parts of the day, her plants didn't bake into crispy bits of leaves barely good enough for the compost pile.

Coming out in the dark before even the predawn, Céline toted water in two five gallon buckets, one in each hand, around the garden to water the plants before the heat of the day made the water scalding. The garden was a mixed bagged of vegetation, with herbs next to vegetables, flowers underneath shrubbery, ground cover webbing its way in between each of them and the worn paths of concrete chunks. She made it a point to maximize her growing space, if she could harvest an herb or edible plant from somewhere in the city, then she did not waste space growing it in her own garden.

Carefully tipping over the bucket, she watered the roots of the juniper bush, the unmarked gravestone of little Aquila. In her mind's eye, he was no longer a female, and no longer a mismatch of parts, but a handsome, white feathered fellow, proud and strong, like an eagle. Maybe that is how his spirit looks, she had thought more than once.

"Good morning, young man," she said very quietly to the bush. "I hope your night wasn't too hot. Your brothers and sisters aren't up yet, but they will be shortly."

She always listened for a reply from him, but even when she meditated by the juniper, her mind blank, she never received one.

She took several buckets full of water for the other plants, soaking the ground about them as the distant sky began to turn gray.

"Who's making all that noise?" Ariste called from the kitchen window. The cat moreau stuck her head out of it, blearily looking down at her mother.

"What noise?" she asked.

"Someone's calling for you," she heard Ursus say.

She listened, tilting her head to the side while looking at her daughter, but could hear nothing.

Ariste's face turned from groggy agitation to alarm. "Mama, someone's hurt!" She jumped from the kitchen to the rope that led down to the garden.

"Medicienne!" she finally heard in the distance. "Come quick!"

# Chapter 55

The heat of the oppressive Chicago summer permeated even to the underground. The subway, the service tunnels, the sewers, were all fetid, hot places, the air so thick it was difficult to breathe even for those who were not its normal denizens. For Elias Montgomery, the smell of rats was overwhelming. Usually the combination of musk and grapes was a comfort, but in the past weeks, even that was becoming oppressive. Both he and Evangeline wanted to touch each other for social bonding, but neither one of them could stand to be touched by such heat that the other person produced. It was the same for all the rats. There was fighting, battles to the death, and the voices in Montgomery's head were scattered thoughts of dying animals or the adrenaline filled battle cry of a victor. In the background of that, there was the muffled sound of a Russian voice which he could never quite reach. The heat seemed to affect his very thoughts, making his mind fuzzy and scattered.

He wasn't sure how he ended up above ground. He was roaming the sewers with his entourage of rodents, the service tunnels, and then he was in the open air, where it should have been fresh and brisk. However, despite it being open and in the dead of night, the air was just as oppressive up here, seeming to push on his body, pressing him against the sides of buildings, which he would have stuck to anyway in an effort to fend off the gaping expansiveness of the world. The heat was even worse. At least the ground kept some of the fire from the sun's rays at bay. But the smell was easier to handle, in that while there were more individual smells, none of them were as overwhelming as the smell of sewage or of his fellow rats as they were underground.

One of the smells that caught his attention was food—Italian food. Lasagna? Spaghetti? Perhaps a stuffed pasta shell of some kind? He recalled, long ago, that he liked Italian food, the pungent tomato sauce made his cheeks clench slightly in anticipation. He followed the scent, as if it were a physical thing, tickling his nose and leading him onward.

With a grumbling stomach, he stopped at the back of a restaurant, his body pressed against the dark, green dumpster. The smell was coming from the container, and it took a great deal of his concentration to listen for signs of life about him. The restaurant was closed for the evening, the smell of human beings was faint and residual. He could smell cats, dogs, what might have been a reptile of some kind, and of course the vermin that were close to the dumpster already. The mice, roaches, raccoons, opossums, and of course, rats. He lifted the lid, it made no sound at all, but the smell of the food almost made him drop it. A wave of his own rats coursed through the opening, Evangeline among them. He was jostled, causing his grip on the lid to slip, sending the metal sheet onto his hunched shoulders.

He let out something akin to a shout and a squeak, his body half in half out of the dumpster, his nine tails thrashing behind him as he tried to wiggle in. He finally did, the lid closing him in the fetid darkness, the sounds of masticating and scuffling all about him.

The smell was strong, mixed, and his fuzzed brain had trouble sorting it all out. However, the smell of dog and reptile got closer. The animals in the bin smelled it too, some of them began making threatening growls and chirps.

"They can't get in here," he said out loud. "They don't have hands."

As if to prove him wrong, the lid of the dumpster opened, letting light from a street lamp in. The smell of dog, and man, washed into the space, and the head of a canine peered over the edge. "I told you he was in here," he said.

The sound of a "humph," along with the smell of reptile, answered it.

"Come on, little man," the dog moreau reached into the dumpster with a huge, muscled arm. His head, now that Montgomery could see it better, was that of a doberman pinscher. That was one of the standard canines that The Institute used in their moreaus. Montgomery had no way of knowing who the individual behind him was, there were way too many of them to distinguish. The hand caught him by the scruff of the neck, and suddenly fear gripped the grotesque caricature of a rat moreau. The Institute had found him!

He turned his head on his long neck, trying to bite into the large arm that held him, but he couldn't reach. He was lifted out of the dumpster with a heave and thrown to the concrete ground. He scrambled to all fours, bearing his teeth, long and yellowed, and hissing loudly.

"Come on," a reptile came into view, something not quite an anything in particular, except lizard and man. He, too, was heavily built, and like a pair of thugs, they stood in front of Montgomery. "Come peacefully and we won't hurt you."

Montgomery hissed again, backing away, the fur on his neck rising. "He's not going to," the doberman said. "Bag him."

"You bag him," the reptile replied.

The doberman let out a yelp, suddenly, high pitched and doglike. "What the?" He looked down, and kicked, sending little, white Evangeline flying across the concrete.

Montgomery turned to run, scrambling away, but the doberman was suddenly in front of him, as if appearing out of nowhere. "Don't think so," he said.

A hard blow hit Montgomery in the back of the head, and then the world went black.

He came to, he didn't know how much later, in a dark room…a real room, with a bed and a dresser and paintings on the wall. The door opened, and a tall, well-built man in a business suit entered, the light from behind him obscuring his features. The doberman and the reptile were flanking him, like looming bodyguards. "Ah," he said in a slight Asian accent. "You have finally awoken."

The Institute had kept him alive. Why? To experiment on him? Find out what went wrong. "Why have you not killed me?" Montgomery asked.

"Kill you?" the man said, shaking his head. His hair waved as he did so. "No," he assured the rat-like moreau. "I want you to help me. You cannot do that if you are dead."

# Chapter 56

Ilya ran with the boy in his arms, sensing the other five puppies behind him. Kostya, his youngest and fastest, was right at his heels. He could hear Vasili behind him, weeping as he ran. Ilya followed his nose, instinctively going wherever the smell of sea otter led him. "Dyson!" he called, as the scent became stronger. "Dyson!" Please, he prayed, please let him be here. I cannot fix this. Please.

The sea otter appeared behind a corner, followed by the three other moreaus. He took one look at the bloody bundle in Ilya's arms, and a look of panic crossed his face. "What happened?" he asked, as the two came together, Dyson put his arm out and grabbed Ilya's shoulder.

"You said you had a doctor," the rat all but cried. He felt as if someone had reached inside of his gut and torn his stomach out through his throat.

Dyson turned to one of the men behind him, "Go get the Medicienne."

"But Subzero," he said, "Grischat—"

"You want the kid to die?" Subzero leaned down and glared at Toaster.

The dog stared at him, eyes wide.

"Go!" the sea otter ordered. He then turned back to Ilya, "Come on," he pulled on the rat's shoulder, to indicate he was to come with them.

As he followed his former subordinate, he fought to keep his mind in the here and now. It kept careening into the past, back into Russia, into his war days, to seeing people flee with their little ones in their arms, crying and bloodied. He said a prayer for each one he passed, as did every one of his teammates. They were soldiers, doing their jobs, they were not killing for the joy of it. These thugs, these people, these humans, they were human beings, were killing because they wanted to. Because they got joy out of it. If his son died, he would hunt every single one of them down and dissect them like lab experiments, he promised himself.

Thunder resounded in the distance.

"Comment?" What is it? he heard an accented voice say, as they rounded the corner.

He tensed, was it the Haitian gang that had done this to Maxim. They spoke French in Haiti, didn't they? He sensed that no one else around him tensed up, they continued their running, until they came to a stop at the loading section of a great big open warehouse.

A gray cat , with a white patch around one eye and one white paw, stood shirtless, an appraising look on his face. His hazel eyes scanned the group, landing on each of Ilya's children, and then on Ilya himself. The rat tensed reflexively, and was surprised. It had been a long while since he'd reacted due to animal instinct to the species of a moreau.  The cat seemed to have the same reaction, for he swished his tail, brought his ears forward, and it was a long minute before he spoke. "Bring him inside," it was his voice that had the Haitian accent. "La Petite Medicienne is on her way."

He didn't have time for someone to be on their way. He could feel the wet soaking into his fur, soaking into the fur of his little boy, who lay limp in his arms. When the cat stopped walking, Ilya sank down to the ground, cradling the puppy in his lap. The last thing he had said to Maxim was…what was it? He couldn't even remember now. He felt the other five puppies press against him, all about his body, seeking the comfort of touch as their brother bled to death in their father's arms.

"Where is he?" he heard a woman's voice call. He turned to see a…a human! A human woman was running toward him, followed by four older children, a cat, a bear, a sheep, and a snake. He clutched Maxim closer to his chest. Instinct tried to grip him and shake him senseless, the cat and snake sent his heart racing. The bear and the sheep were inconsequential. It was a human who had done this to him. Why would he let a human touch him now?

She crouched down, and dark green eyes stared into him, concern written all over them. He clung to Maxim as the woman reached out to touch him, almost recoiling. Her face was filled with compassion, her golden eyebrows drawing together. "You have to let him go so I can see him," she said gently.

He stared at her, like an animal, fear and panic holding him in a strong embrace, so that even breathing seemed to have little effect on his consciousness.

"I can help him," the woman said again, flipping her braid over her shoulder so it hung down her back. She smelled of honey and olive oil, herbs and flowers. Her hand levitated above Maxim's head, pressed against Ilya's breast. "But you have to let me see him."

The rat slowly peeled the boy from him, the cold air hitting his blood wet fur. The puppy lay lifeless, like a stuffed toy. His thoughts ran in his mind, around his breathing, around the counting of his breath, in circles, daring him to catch one of them. But if he reached out to one, then they all converged on him, in a mad dash, that his brain buzzed.

He heard the woman take in a deep breath, and then

she began to rummage through her bag. "Are these the only wounds he has?" she motioned to the bloody slashes on his torso.

"Da," Ilya said, his voice cracking. "I think so." He brought the boy back to his chest again, instinctively, beyond his control.

She reached out and touched his hand, her skin almost white against his bright pink fingers. "You can hold him," she reassured him. "But I need to be able to get to his cuts, can you turn him around?"

It took a moment for the request to make its way through Ilya's foggy brain. She was touching him. Another person, besides one of his sons, was touching him. A human hand was touching him. How long had it been since a human hand had touched him in such a manner? Since any hand had touched him in such a manner, gentle and considerate, in an attempt to be kind? He turned the boy over gently, so he was holding him still, but his front was facing away from him. He put his hand on the puppy's head, his three fingers stroking Maxim's ear. His eyes grasped at the woman in front of him, as if reaching for an anchor for the whirring of thoughts in his brain. She smiled at him again, nodding encouragingly, and relief washed through him. With it, tears sprang to his eyes, and he felt the fur near his muzzle wet with them.

The woman smiled at him, a sweet smile, meant to reassure the person to whom it was given. Her eyes traveled to his hand on Maxim's head, and then down to the boy's torso, where his skin was splayed apart and the black, red, and white fur was matted with red. "These were done with a knife?" she asked, holding her hand out behind her.

The cat, a girl who had not long ago entered puberty, handed her a razor blade.

In his mind, Ilya knew it was to shave the fur from around Max's wounds, but his body wanted to reach out and grab the woman's wrist, twist it, break it, and make her drop the blade. He wanted to seize the boy to him, turn around, and run. The smell of his blood made him flick his tongue out of his mouth in an instinctive movement to lick it, to get it to stop. Queen of Heaven, he prayed the familiar prayer, have compassion and rescue us.

The woman scraped the first stab with the razor, and then took a bottle of some sort of herbal wash, and poured it on the injury. The boy stirred slightly, and she smiled again, her eyes thoughtful. "What's his name?" she asked, not taking her eyes from the slash on which she was working.

"Maxim," Ilya managed to get out.

"Maxim," she repeated, attempting to copy his accent. She did a decent job, but the end of her word came out too nasally. "Maxim?" She held her hand out behind her again, and the cat put a threaded needle in it. "Can you hear me?"

"Da," the boy answered, his voice weak and gravelly.

"You have been cut very badly. I know that it hurts, but I need to try and stay as still as you can, alright?"

Maxim let out a groan, and Ilya was not sure if it was an agreement or not.

Ilya watched in fascination, calming with each breath, as the woman worked on patching the boy up, telling him what she was doing with each move she made. "You may feel a pull on your skin," she said. "I am shaving the fur away so I can get a better look at it, OK?" Her hand was steady, Ilya saw, her demeanor calm. "This is an antiseptic wash, it will help to keep it from getting infected," she explained as she poured some more of the liquid from the bottle over a wound, and then wiped the wash and the blood away with a cloth. As the cloth became too bloodied, the cat would hand her a clean one. "This cut isn't jagged, but it's wide and deep." She furrowed her brow, "And curved." She clicked her tongue, putting her face close to Maxim's body to get a better look. "I think I am going to have to put in two sets of stitches." She looked up at Ilya apologetically.

The rat nodded, blinking away more tears.

"You're doing so well, Maxim," she crooned, pulling the thread through his muscle.

And he was doing well. Ilya felt a surge of pride, just another emotion to blend in with the fear and the desire to run away, at his little son's bravery. The boy occasionally let out a groan of pain, but he stayed still, his eyes squeezed shut, his lips set in a pained grimace. "Relax your body," he whispered in Russian. "Breath out the pain." The boy began to huff, almost a pant, as he'd been taught, and then relaxed his body. As the woman pulled on the stitch, he began his panted breathing again, through his teeth.

"This is horse hair," she said, holding up the needle, as she tied the thread off in a knot. "It isn't fancy," she looked up at the rat, "but it was used for thousands of years before the synthetic stuff came about."

Ilya nodded his head again, his brain clearing some with the doctor talking to him. "We used it in Russia in the field," he told her. "They still use it in some civilian hospitals to suture up people." She looked up at him quizzically, only for a moment, and then was back at her task of Maxim. "There are many horses in Russia," he said. "But sometimes, there are little supplies."

She smiled again, and he noticed it seemed to be a pattern for her; a look of great concentration, and then a reassuring smile, then back to an intense regard for her work. "The set of stitches in your body will dissolve with time," she said to the boy.

Now that he had gotten his mind to think on something else, Ilya was able to hold onto a thought for longer than a fleeting moment. The woman in front of him looked vaguely familiar, but he couldn't place where he had seen her before.

She wore her long, dark golden hair in a braid that lay across her back. Wisps of platinum blond escaped and framed her head like a white halo. Her skin was pale, and when she looked up at him, he saw she had green eyes, like a dark jade. On her temples were round scars that looked like burn marks. When she looked up occasionally and smiled at him, her smile was warm and genuine. He felt a quick tightening in his chest that he had to breathe away, followed by a relaxation that he was surprised to find with the rest of his body so tense.

The moreaus that were with her, children, like his, only older, had each taken up positions about her, in a practiced and easy way. The cat was obviously the nurse, fetching and holding things out to the doctor as she asked for them. The snake, also a girl he noted, had come over to Vasily, who was still crying, and put her arm about his shoulder. He could smell her strongly, the musk and cinnamon of a predator, and the contrast with the warm gesture she gave his son, so close to his body, put him ill at ease. The bear and the sheep, both boys, had come over to his other little ones, the ones that were pressed behind him, and whispered softly to them.

"She's really good at this."

"He'll be OK, you'll see."

"What's your name?"

They were trying to make his sons feel better. Someone else, besides him, was trying to comfort his puppies.

She had finished several sets of stitches, and he could see the bleeding had slowed considerably. Maxim opened his eyes, and Ilya caught them in his own. The rat felt a rush of relief, the very next breath taking the tension out of his body and relaxing him considerably. Once he did, he felt his son relax in his arms, despite the needle piercing his flesh. The woman must have felt the boy relax, also, because she asked, "Does it not hurt as much anymore?"

"No," Maxim answered. "It's numb."

"I'm almost done," her voice was soft and motherly. And then she was, her instruments were put in a bowl of the antiseptic wash, and she was washing her hands with soap. She looked Ilya in the eyes, and smiled that reassuring smile, though she hesitated before speaking. "He should be just fine," she said. "Make sure to keep him hydrated, and eat as much iron rich foods as you can get in him." She then turned her attention to Max. "You hear that? Drink lots and eat lots of spinach."

"Spinach?" Maxim asked, his eyes going wide.

"What?" the woman backed away, her own eyes disbelieving. "You don't like spinach?"

The cat giggled.

Maxim looked at her, and then at the woman again. "No," he said quietly.

She shook her head, a sad look on her face. "You will be forced to eat fish, then," she said with a sigh. "Do you know how to fish?"

The boy's face turned to one of dejection. "No," he admitted. "I've never been by the water."

She looked up at Ilya, and her smile was teasing. Ilya was surprised at himself that he still knew what a teasing smile was. "Do you know how to fish?"

"Da," he answered, holding Maxim close to him. "I do."

"Then you will have to take your little ones to the water," she told him, her eyes twinkling, "and teach them how to fish for their brother's dinner."

# Chapter 57

Céline put her attention on her gear, getting it cleaned up and put away, so that the rat moreau could spend as private a moment as was possible with his hurt son.

She was very impressed with how calm the two of them had been, both the father and the boy. She wasn't sure if she would not have broken down into hysterics if one of her children was lying in her arms bleeding the way he was. The rat had seemed sublimely calm, almost removed, except for the gripping of his hands and arms at the little body in his lap and the wet fur underneath his eyes. The boy had been braver than she would have expected someone his age to be. He seemed about seven or eight, and he had remained calm, and still while she stitched. He had done a type of Lamaze breathing occasionally, and she wondered if that was an instinctual reflex or if Maxim had learned it from somewhere.

Upon hearing what the Grey Cat sent to her warehouse had to say, she'd rushed to the Cargo Bay faster than she had ever gone before, for any injury. "There is a little boy," the pretty pigeon moreau said, "he's been stabbed."

"One of you stabbed a little boy?" she demanded.

She fully expected her to get defensive, to exclaim it was an accident, Grischat wouldn't allow for such an atrocity, even in his necessarily ruthless rule.

"No, a human did," she replied.

There was no more conversation as they ran, the pigeon moreau flying ahead of them to announce their arrival.

Why would the Grey Cats care that a boy had been stabbed? She was quite sure that the group of moreaus had left young people to die of grievous injuries before, without remorse. What made this one different?

Subzero was waiting for her when she arrived, his body, long and curved on his short, stocky legs, tense with unexpended energy. "One of the puppies has been hurt," he said, as if she should know what he was talking about.

"Puppies?" she muttered, her brows furrowing to cause a wrinkle at the bridge of her nose.

He did not answer her, just led her toward the bay entrances to present her to a rat moreau surrounded by a group of dog children.

The rat had looked so calm, almost stoic, as he held the limp boy in his arms. Kneeling down, as if resigned that the child was dying, he looked at him with a steady gaze until she had caught his attention. He'd raised his head slowly, and his stoic look had turned to one of shock.

She was under no illusion what he was surprised about. She was a human being, in a sea of moreaus. Humans had probably only tried to capture or kill him. Poor thing.

But only for a moment. It was serene once again in a heartbeat. It was unreal. How could he look in such a way in such a situation? Had he lost other little ones, that this did not affect him? He watched her intently as she knelt across from and began to tend to his son.

His son.

This man had sons.

Children, who were his.

Were they by birth and changed in the moreau process? Or were they changed and then he took care of them, as she did with her little ones? How had he obtained them? Where had he been living? Why hadn't she ever heard of him?

She had so many questions, questions that slowly faded from her mind as she concentrated on Maxim, sewing the lacerations that dotted the boy's body. They were not easy to sew up, the knife that had stabbed him multiple times had been curved, so that the cuts were deep in one place and shallow in another. In several places, she had to put in two sets of stitches, something she never liked doing. The stitches in the muscle below the epidermis were out of her view. Though she had never had it happen, she was always terrified of an infection, and having to cut her patient open again to deal with it. Vivisection was never pleasant, for her or the recipient.

The boy, on his part, had behaved admirably. It was a sign of masculinity, within the Grey Cats, for those injured not to complain when being stitched up. She heard through the grapevine that complaining afterward was perfectly acceptable. Maxim had acted just as the gang members had, not a single complaint coming from him, so that Céline had thought he was unconscious. She'd been genuinely surprised when he wasn't.

Now, she could hear her children speaking to the rat's puppies, and she felt a flush of pride bloom through her. This is the first time they have come across anyone close to their own age, she smiled smugly, and they are being so kind.

Kindness matters, she had tried to teach them that all of their lives. She was surprised, she wasn't sure why, that they had actually listened.

"Thank you," said the rat in front of her, nodding his head politely. "I will take Maxim home now."

His words snapped her out of her reverie. She heard Grischat laugh. He's still here, at my side? "You can't take him home," she said firmly.

The rat raised his eyebrows, giving her a clear view of his gray eyes. "Thank you," he repeated. "I will take Maxim home now." He stood up, as if she hadn't spoken.

"He isn't in any shape to go anywhere," she continued, scrambling up after him. "He's lost a lot of blood. He needs to be looked after."

"I shall look after him," he brought the boy close to his chest, cradling him like an infant.

~The boy can't go~, said the voice that was her voice but not her voice.

"What if something else happens to him?"

Ilya drew himself up, his demeanor still very calm. "I shall look after him."

"What if you can't look after him?" she asked.

Céline noticed that her children and his had parted ways, his gathering behind him, and hers moving to the side. Grischat, she saw from the corner of her eye, made no move at all, only stood still, smirking.

The rat paused, stock still as if he was a statue. "I have looked after him so far," he replied, turning from her.

The boy can't go.

Céline's brows came together hard at the bridge of her nose, causing a deep line. "You can't just take him away," she replied, her voice becoming forced. "He has a huge risk for infection! He has open wounds that need to be cared for. He has to be thoroughly cleaned!" Panic began to grip her, and she wanted to grab at the little thing in his arms, pulling him out of them and into her own, then steal him away. She reached for the rat and having nothing else to grab onto, hooked her hand in the waist of his pants as he retreated.

He whirled about, causing her to jerk forward as her

hand was pulled before she was able to let go of him. He let out a revving, hiss, his tail cracking like a whip behind him. His ears lay flat on his head, and he bared his teeth.

Only a moment later, his puppies were at his back, all of their eyeteeth clearly shown through their curled lips. She felt her own children behind her, heard Ariste hiss, higher pitched and smoother than the one Ilya let out. Khenum physically pressed himself against his mother, she felt the air moving out of his chest in a silent huff. Grischat was at her side, slightly in front of her, his claw extended in his hands, Cottontail Coney and Jive in her peripheral vision.

Her eyes registered the movement before her brain could. Her brain registered it before her mouth could say anything. No, no, no, this isn't what I meant, she heard herself say in her head. All she could do was see everyone moving, the air crackling around them, but she couldn't seem to get her body to move fast enough to keep up.

"Ilya Pytrovich," Subzero was at the rat's side, his hand on his shoulder. The strain in the sea otter's voice was so strong that Céline could feel it carried on the tension in the air. Next to him was a group of other moreaus, all different animals, tense and ready to strike. "Teacher, she is trying to help your son."

Teacher? Had Céline heard him right?

The rat moreau relaxed, his ears drooping to the sides of his head, his eyes hooding slightly. He slumped his shoulders, and his tail slowly returned to the floor behind him.

"Batya?" one of the boys asked, his canine face a mask of confusion.

Ilya Pytrovich looked down at the dog moreau and let out a deep breath. "He cannot stay here by himself," he said to the boy who had spoken.

"There's room for all of you here," Subzero said quickly, looking up to Grischat.

The cat, his lip still curled, growled slightly.

The sea otter flinched.

The boy cannot go.

"There is plenty of room for all of you here," Céline said quickly, putting her hand on Grischat's arm. The fur was silky, a stark contrast to hostility about them.

Subzero nodded quickly, his small triangular head bobbing on his long, thick neck.

Grischat snuffed. "Mais, oui," he admitted, his shoulder's relaxing. "There is plenty of room." He waved his white paw about him vaguely, turning to Céline. "You will be staying, then, Ma Petite Medicienne," he said. "To care for the puppy."

She blinked at him, surprised. "Here?" she asked.

"Oui," he replied. "You cannot have your patient, who is so intent on keeping near you, here when you are not, non?"

~The boy cannot go~, said the voice again.

She regarded him, feeling trapped now, instead of panicked. "I suppose not," she agreed.

Grischat smiled smugly. "Get rooms ready for all of our guests," he instructed no one in particular, with a wave of his white paw. Then he turned his hazel eyes on Céline. "Welcome home."

Dear Reader,

I hope you enjoyed the first book of The Therian Initiative series, Man of Light and Shadows. Book two, Lady of Lost Souls will be out soon to continue Ilya and Céline's story.

If you would like to stay abreast of my latest stories, of which I always have something coming out, please consider subscribing to my newsletter. I'll never spam you. You'll get first dibs on all my work, and discounts on my books when they first come out.

I have a favor to ask of you. Please return to the platform where you bought this book (amazon, Barnes & Nobel, Smashwords) and leave an honest review. Tell me and others what you thought of the story. Reviews are an author's bread and butter, it is how I get seen in the slew of stories that are out there and all the help I get by you, my loyal readers, is greatly appreciated. And since reviews don't transfer from platform to platform, if you could copy and paste your review onto the reader site of your choice (Goodreads, bookbub, etc.) I would also greatly appreciate that.

If you would like to contact me, there are a myriad of ways to do so on most social media outlets and my website Missives from a Hummingbird at www.katherinelewite.com. I will answer all correspondence I get, I just can't guarantee that it will be answered in a timely manner. Hummingbirds are known for their flightiness, after all.

Yours flightfully,

Katherine LE White

# About the Author

Katherine L. E. White is an award-winning poet, essayist, and international bestselling fiction writer, who has had the privilege of growing up all over the world. A rare beauty with green eyes and crazy titian curls, she goes about having grand (mis)adventures with her family and many friends, and then tries hard not to write about them. She often champions the causes of those on the fringes of society in her writing, while pretending to be an urban farmer in real life. Pretending being the operative word. If others were to rely on her skills to eat, they would most assuredly starve. She lives in Southern Appalachia with her husband, two children, and several animals, all of whom, thankfully, are better urban farmers than she is. If you'd like to know more about her, visit her website at http://www.katherinelewhite.com/

Made in the USA
Columbia, SC
03 May 2022

59864833R00193